SEA GLASS CASTLE

Sea Glass Castle

T. I. LOWE

Tyndale House Publishers, Inc.
Carol Stream, Illinois

Visit Tyndale online at tyndale.com.

Visit T. I. Lowe at tilowe.com.

TYNDALE and Tyndale's quill logo are registered trademarks of Tyndale House Publishers.

Sea Glass Castle

Designed by Faceout Studio, Jeff Miller

Edited by Kathryn S. Olson

Published in association with the literary agency of Browne & Miller Literary Associates, LLC, 52 Village Place, Hinsdale, IL 60521

Sea Glass Castle is a work of fiction. Where real people, events, establishments, organizations, or locales appear, they are used fictitiously. All other elements of the novel are drawn from the author's imagination.

For information about special discounts for bulk purchases, please contact Tyndale House Publishers at csresponse@tyndale.com, or call 1-800-323-9400.

ISBN 978-1-4964-4050-1

Printed in the United States of America

26	25	24	23	22	21	20
7	6	5	4	3	2	1

To my daughter, Lydia Lu.

Dare to declare your own destiny.

We are pressed on every side by troubles,
but we are not crushed. We are perplexed,
but not driven to despair. We are hunted
down, but never abandoned by God. We get
knocked down, but we are not destroyed.

2 CORINTHIANS 4:8-9

1

Darkness was a gift that hid most anything Sophia Prescott wanted to keep at bay—the ruins of her marriage, the still-fading scars, and the inner debris of her self-worth, which had been scattered about so severely that she was pretty sure there was no hope of mending it. The shadows graciously did their part to shroud life, even if it was for only a brief period on Mondays. Every Sunday her parents kept her two-year-old after church, overnight, and until nightfall on Monday. During this time of seclusion, Sophia kept to the shadows and let herself fall apart before having to pull herself back into a presentable form for her son. Collin deserved her whole. Not broken.

But Mondays she broke.

Hunkered down underneath a thick quilt, Sophia pried her eyes open when the soft click of the door closing caught her sluggish attention. Knowing what was coming, she braced herself for the fight, fisting the blanket in both hands and squeezing her eyes shut.

A few forceful tugs and struggling grunts came from the other side of the blanket before the darkness was snatched out of her grasp. Blazing light poured in through the windows as the little sprite fluttered around the room to open even more curtains.

"Stop it, Opal!" Sophia screeched. "Too bright!" She buried her head beneath the pillow, hoping to escape the light and whatever her busybody friend was up to.

"Nonsense. It's a beautiful summer day. One that begs for you to be outside enjoying it. Come on. Let's go be one with nature." Opal jostled the bed.

Sophia lost her grip on the pillow, opening her eyes just in time to see it fly across the room. "I live on a golf course. Nothing I want to go be *one* with," she grumbled, sitting up to fix her best friend with her best glare.

Opal's sparkling green eyes never dulled of their merriment. At the moment, they appeared to be holding a measure of amusement too. "There's beautiful landscaping on this golf course. Don't let my dad hear you sassing about his place."

"I'm paying him rent for this condo, so I can sass about it all I want." Sophia rubbed her eyes, wishing when she reopened them, the darkness would be back. But she knew Opal Gilbert Cole too well. There was no other option but to go along with her. "What do you want?"

"I want lots of things." Opal grinned, twisting her golden-red curls into a messy bun, the blonde tips flickering every which way. "But I'll settle for you helping me solve a mystery today."

"It's Monday. Shouldn't you be working?" Sophia watched as Opal began rummaging through her armoire. It was a plain white piece of furniture that went along with the coastal theme of the condo. She was pretty surprised when moving in to find the place without Opal's signature written all over it, but since it was a rental property, Opal's family wanted to leave it more generic. The town called her the furniture fairy, and she deserved that title and then some given the way she could work magic into old pieces and turn them into something new.

Opal was known to use that magic on people as well, so Sophia was wary about the attention she was receiving all of a sudden. She stared at the bathroom door and contemplated locking herself inside to avoid whatever was about to go down.

"Bless This Mess isn't open to the public on Mondays. You know that. And there aren't any urgent furniture orders to work on." Opal tossed a pair of burgundy tights and a gray- and orange-striped T-shirt dress onto the bed, two things Sophia had never paired together. It wouldn't be happening today, either. "Besides, I have other pressing business."

"What are you talking about?" Sophia crossed her arms when Opal pointed to the pile of clothes. "I'm already dressed for the day."

Opal's eyes narrowed and coasted along the plain black shirt and yoga pants Sophia was wearing. "Black has never looked good on you. It even washes out those teal eyes." Opal tsked, like she had any room to judge wardrobe choices.

With a condescending look, Sophia flicked a hand toward Opal's psychedelic halter top, which made her dizzy just looking at it, and her bright-blue Bermuda shorts. "Are you kidding me right now?"

Opal pranced around in a circle, pausing to shimmy her backside. "At least I don't look like the living dead. I'm groovy, baby!" She gave it her best Austin Powers impression. The Sand Queens had watched the late-nineties movie repeatedly back in the day.

That almost pulled a smile to Sophia's pinched lips. *Almost.* "Opal, stop talking in loops and spit out whatever harebrained idea you have for the day already." She fell back on the bed and huffed. "Or better yet, don't and say we did. Be sure to lock the door behind you."

"No, seriously." Opal reached over and began yanking on Sophia's arm until she gave in and sat up on the edge of the bed. "Someone moved in next door and I'm a little weirded out about it. I need you to come over and tell me what your instinct says."

"My instinct stinks anymore," Sophia muttered, dropping her gaze to her hands, resting in her lap. For the first time in years her nails were bare of acrylic and polish. And for the first time in years she had no desire to do anything about it.

"Only thing stinking is your breath. Phew!" Opal wrinkled her nose and nodded her head toward the bathroom. "Do me a favor and go fix that."

It took another long stretch of time before Sophia was persuaded to go wash the funk out of her mouth and to run a brush through her tangled hair, and she refused to change her clothes. If Opal was dragging her out of the condo, it would be in the black shroud of gloom. After sliding on a pair of giant sunglasses and an equally giant sun hat, Sophia dragged her feet all the way to Opal's van and wondered how she avoided tripping over her bottom lip in the process.

•   •   •

"I'm so tickled the Sand Queens are back together!" Opal scooted around the table on her back deck and grabbed a glass of lemonade. The summer day was warm and sunny, with a breeze carrying laughter from beachgoers and squawking from seagulls.

"Me too," Josie agreed as she tucked a wayward wave of white-blonde hair behind her ear. "Two months is too long to go between meetings. I'm glad I talked August into giving me the afternoon off from the camp."

"Your husband knows how important we are to you,

so of course he'd give you some time off," Opal said in that reassuring tone, the one that was trying to relay a hidden meaning.

Sophia caught the meaning but chose to ignore it. Yes, it was she who had stood up the other two, but tough. That was life. And for the past several months—closer to a few *years*—life had served her a platter brimming with unfairness.

"Sophia, aren't you glad to be spending time with us today?" Josie asked in that small voice that never really suited her.

Sophia looked at Josie's long, paint-stained fingers where they rested on her forearm. "Nothing against the two of you, but I'd rather spend my Monday alone. . . . I have a lot on my mind." Yes, the warmth of the sun and the softness of the breeze felt good on her skin, but that was neither here nor there.

"Oh, I bet. Are you considering signing Collin up for the preschool program at the church this fall? I heard Momma talking with you about it after Sunday school yesterday." Opal took a sip of her drink and gave Sophia an innocent look that was really her meddling expression.

Sophia let go of a long sigh and decided not to call her out on it. Instead, she gave the excuse "He has to be potty trained before they will accept him."

"That's easy enough." Opal shrugged. "YouTube some tutorials and go get him one of those tiny toilets."

"I'd rather he decide when he's ready. So far there's no interest." Sophia tucked her left thumb underneath her ring finger and couldn't contain the cringe at finding it bare. It was a habit she had formed right after Ty slid the flashy engagement ring onto her finger. Touching the back of the ring had always offered comfort and a reminder of promises. She was still struggling to grasp that the wedding ring—and the promises—no longer belonged to her.

"I'm sure you want to help Collin along. The preschool would be a great opportunity for him to interact with children his age. And it would allow you to get a job." Josie smiled but seemed uncertain. She wasn't nearly as good at meddling as Opal.

Sophia narrowed her eyes at both women, wondering what their game was. "I have alimony and child support and a nice severance package. I don't need a job."

Ty's PR team had been quick to get most of his dirt swept under the rug, and the lawyers even quicker to finalize the divorce. Sophia had only been required to sign nondisclosures about the abuse allegations that prevented her from ever speaking about it publicly, and that was fine by her. She agreed after they added a clause that Ty had to undergo anger management counseling and could have only supervised visits with Collin.

"That's hogwash. Never has your strong backbone stood for someone else taking care of you and—"

Before Opal could carry on her rant, Josie piped in. "But a job would be a great reason to get out of the house and be around adults. Plus, you're too talented not to be out there doing something with yourself."

Sophia had recently endured not only the demise of her marriage, but also the demise of her career. When Southeastern Public Relations had to choose between a replaceable consultant and their star athlete, the decision to let Sophia go was more than easy.

"Really? Southeastern seemed to think I'm nothing more than a grunt worker who somehow deserved to be beaten up by her famous husband for catching him in bed with another woman." Sophia growled and slammed her glass down, sending a fountain of pale-yellow liquid sloshing onto the table. That didn't release enough of her pent-up anger, so she added stomping her feet against the sandy deck and another growl.

Sophia's intuition had always been spot-on. She was an ace at using that skill for the betterment of others and keeping the firm's clients out of hot water. Herself, not so much. It didn't do her a darn bit of good when it came to the bronze-haired Adonis with his lustrous skin tone and that aw-shucks smile. Ty Prescott's stunning facade had fooled her right along with the masses. Months had passed since Ty had completely removed his mask while taking a part of her soul with it, yet she was still dealing with the wreckage. She was so mad at herself for allowing it to happen in the first place. The worst part was that she'd failed not only herself but also her son.

"Then why are you allowing their opinion such power if you don't believe it to be true?" Opal asked, knowing exactly what button to push. "You sure have been acting like you believe it."

For months, Sophia had allowed circumstances to dictate her self-worth. The only days she had any hope of turning things around were the days she could make her baby smile, and that wasn't nearly as often as it needed to be. A saying her grandmother shared once flickered through her thoughts as she pounded her fists against the arms of her Adirondack chair. *"Never underestimate the power of a good ole hissy fit."*

The haze of despondency cleared momentarily as Sophia had herself one glorified conniption. "I'm not a nobody! I have just as much talent as that giant schmuck running around a dumb field with a ball! I want to slap that smirk off his lips! I want to show him he didn't break me!"

Opal nodded exuberantly. "This is good!"

"What?" Sophia snapped back, hot tears cascading

down her flushed face. She caught Josie echoing her question on a much more subdued whisper.

"You're alive!" Opal fist-pumped and jumped up and down. "She's alive! Hallelujah!" She turned back to Sophia and shook her by the shoulders. "For a hot minute I thought you'd turned into a robot." Opal giggled, followed by Josie snickering, and that had Sophia snorting. And it escalated to an outlandish round of laughter.

And that was Opal for you. Always twisting and turning a touchy situation until she could figure out how to defuse the tension. It was one of the reasons Sophia loved her so much—and also the reason she wanted to pinch Opal's little button nose half the time.

"Y'all, I'm sorry . . . I'm just having a hard time getting my act together." Sophia shook her head. "I never thought I'd let a man manipulate me or lay a hand on me out of anger."

Josie moved over and knelt in front of Sophia's chair. "I sure wish you had confided in us about what was really going on."

"I was embarrassed. Still am." Sophia watched Opal join Josie in front of the chair, their wall of support causing a heaviness to press against her chest. Clearing her throat, she whispered, "It didn't happen that many times, but it was enough to leave a lasting effect. Made me doubt my strength and character. I hate being weak."

"One time is way too many times." Opal squeezed Sophia's knee. "But who says you're weak?"

The question had Sophia coming up short, so she only responded with a halfhearted shrug.

"You are the owner of your self-esteem. Don't let circumstance dictate it. Show Ty and everyone else you're still that crazy-smart, fiercely driven woman who lets no one and nothing get the best of her."

Josie bobbed her head in agreement. "Opal's right. You've achieved everything you've ever set your mind to. You are the former reigning Miss Sunset Cove, you were the captain of the cheerleading squad, valedictorian of your graduating class, you formed Beach Preserve Coalition for your senior project when the rest of us only took the time to write a research paper—"

"Oh! I love that charity." Opal's face lit with admiration, mirroring Josie's. "Girl, you got the entire town *and* my daddy, the senator, on board with keeping our beach a litter-free, healthy environment."

They were doing what the Sand Queens did best: lifting one another up when life tried beating them down by redirecting the focus to all of the good and positives.

Sophia's tears of anger transformed into tears of appreciation as she leaned forward and hugged both wonderful friends God had blessed her with for as long as she could remember. Even though she was a year ahead of them in age and school grade, their bond had always been ironclad.

After the three women hugged it out and resettled in their own chairs, Sophia finally asked, "What was all that talk about a mystery neighbor?"

"There's no mys—"

"I think a vampire moved in last night." Opal was quick to cut Josie off, but Sophia dismissed it when she processed what the silly woman had just spouted off.

"A vampire?" She wiped the last of the tears from her cheeks and rolled her eyes at Opal's absurd words.

"Yes. Possibly two of them." Opal leaned toward Sophia and Josie in a conspiring fashion and glanced around. She nodded her head to the cookie-cutter, saltbox-style beach house to the right of Opal's. Instead of the orange-sherbet paint job, it was whitewashed with dusty-blue shutters.

"A moving truck showed up late last night. I saw two men slinking around in the dark, and they kept at it until sunrise. Then all went eerily quiet over there."

Sophia pulled her sunglasses down the bridge of her nose and looked for any sign of life. A nice set of outdoor furniture had been placed on the back deck and a beach bike was propped against the side of the house, but nothing looked amiss. She slid the shades back into place and was about to look away when the curtain at the kitchen window fluttered, revealing a hint of a shadowed figure. Sitting up taller and angling her head to the side, she whispered, "Someone's in the kitchen." She heard Opal gasp and Josie snort.

All three leaned over the railing, like that would actually get them close enough to see more clearly. Sophia knew they looked like a bunch of nosy rubberneckers, but she kept leaning until a loud boom ricocheted from the neighboring house. Three sets of feet cleared the deck as squealing burst from each of the women.

"What was that?" Sophia whisper-yelled, ducking down behind the deck railing and clutching her pounding chest.

"See!" Opal crouched beside her. "I told you something's not right with him."

"How do you even know it's a *him*?" Sophia narrowed her eyes and glanced over to find Josie settling back into her chair, obviously the only sane one out of the bunch. She stood and followed suit.

"I already told you. It's two guys and I saw them hauling in things last night. One of which was a long box." Opal stretched her arms as wide as they would go while her eyes bugged out. "I'm pretty sure it may have been a coffin."

Josie snorted again. "Get up from there, silly, and knock it off."

Opal stood and dusted the sand off her brightly colored shorts. "I'm serious. That house has been sitting there vacant since Mrs. Clark vanished last year—" Her eyes rounded again. "Oooh! The neighbor did it!"

"With the candlestick in the dining room!" Josie interjected with a thick coating of sarcasm.

"I have the weirdest friends," Sophia muttered, propping her cheek on the palm of her hand and slouching against the side of the chair.

Josie disregarded the jab and said to Opal, "You know Mrs. Clark went to live with her sister in Florida."

"So they say . . ." Opal's words trailed off as she jabbed a finger toward the house. "She could have been holed up in the basement all this time."

"Your husband oversaw the renovations to the house just last month. To be sure, Linc would have noticed an old lady tied up somewhere." Josie rolled her eyes and picked up a cookie from the plate. She gave it a cautious sniff. "You didn't bake these, did you, Opal?"

"You know Linc doesn't let me near the oven. Momma made them." Opal drummed her fingertips against the table while eyeing next door. Suddenly she jolted in such a spastic manner that it caught Sophia's waning attention. "The curtain moved again!"

Sophia blinked slowly at her friend before moving her sights over to next door. All she could see were shadows moving past the windows. They appeared to be drifting about in no particular direction. Much the same way she was doing as of late.

"I think we need to go over there and check things out."

"We're doing no such thing," Josie ordered while swiping two more cookies and handing one to Sophia. "Seriously, Opal, that's enough. You keep on and I'm calling Linc to come get ahold of you."

Sophia sniffed the cookie out of habit since it came from Opal, finding only the delicious aromas of vanilla and chocolate chips. She took a bite and chewed absently, realizing her sluggish attention was missing something. From Opal's outlandish behavior over the new neighbor and Josie's snorting responses to it all, clearly she wasn't catching on to whatever was happening. But she didn't care enough to try figuring it out.

2

The smell of fresh paint mixed with a lemony scent the cleaning crew had left in their wake had been welcoming the prior evening. But after pulling an all-nighter and sorting through moving boxes until the sun showed up, Weston Sawyer was over it. Squinting his tired eyes at his watch and finding it past noon, the only scent he wanted assailing his senses was coffee. Stat.

"Looks like the neighborhood watch is already on to you," Seth mumbled as he peered out the kitchen window of Wes's new home.

Wes rummaged through the third box marked *kitchen*, hoping to unearth the coffeemaker. If his search came up empty once more, he was heading out the door to find some form of caffeine. "Why's that?"

"There are three women sitting on the deck next door watching us. Been there for a while now."

"Aha!" Wes held up the coffeemaker's carafe as if it were a grand prize. At the moment, it certainly was, to him. He yanked the machine part out next and walked it over to the counter to put it to work. He glanced out the window as he filled the pot with water and spotted his audience. A blonde sat chowing down on cookies while another woman in a giant sun hat looked to be melting into her chair from slumping down so much. He couldn't help but chuckle at the wild one with her hands flailing

13

around. "The redhead is my new neighbor, Opal Cole. Her husband remodeled the house and the doctor's office for me." Wes surveyed the space and was quite impressed with the clean lines of the kitchen. The white marble countertops with subtle veining weren't like anything he'd ever had in a home. Taking in the espresso wood floors and the crisp gray walls, he concluded nothing was, for that matter. *Lincoln Cole nailed it.*

"Oh." Seth kept looking out the window. "She dropped those cookies off earlier, right?"

"Yes. She promised she didn't bake them. Whatever that means." Wes scooped the ground coffee into the filter and inhaled deeply of the robust scent. "They'll go good with some coffee. I hope between the sugar and the caffeine, we can muster enough energy to set up a few rooms before I have to take you to the airport." He glanced at his brother out of the corner of his eye. It was like looking in the mirror, but his brother's image reflected an untarnished spirit that Wes's never would. "Sure wish you could stay longer than just one day."

Seth turned away from the window and grabbed up another box. "I drove that stinking moving van all the way here and helped you unload it for a better part of the night. I call my brotherly duties done." Seth's teasing smirk vanished as he stumbled and dropped the box, sending an explosive clanging ringing out.

"Man, if you messed up my pots . . ." Wes moved over to work the tape off the lid so he could inspect them.

Seth let out an obnoxious snort. "You're so particular over everything, old man. They're just pots and pans."

"There's nothing wrong with wanting to take care of my belongings." Wes's words choked off as soon as he realized what he'd said. He'd failed at taking care of what belonged to him when it had mattered the most. Without inspecting the contents of the box, he straightened and walked back to the coffeemaker. His eyes fixed on the ribbon of rich-brown liquid filling the pot as he gripped the back of his neck with both hands.

"I hope you give this fresh start a real chance, Wes." Seth moved behind him and clamped him on the shoulder. "You know it's time. You deserve to be happy again."

Finalizing the sale of the house that held too many broken dreams and walking away from the successful practice he'd helped to build from the ground up in Alabama was supposed to be the ending of a long, difficult chapter.

Signing the paperwork to purchase the beach house and small medical practice in Sunset Cove was supposed to be the beginning of a new, calmer chapter.

Thus far, Wes found himself trapped in the tragic-twist part of the story. He wasn't sure he'd ever figure out how to give a new chapter any real hope.

Seth squeezed his shoulder. "You hear me, man?"

Wes dropped his hands away from his neck and worked on filling two mugs with coffee. "I already had happiness once." He lifted one of the mugs and breathed in the scent before taking a sip, as the what-ifs began a worn-out mantra. "I'm not here looking for that. I just want some peace and quiet."

Seth reached over and took the other mug. "It's been well over three years—"

"Yet it feels like just yesterday." Shaking his head, Wes moved over to the spacious breakfast nook surrounded by bay windows and plopped down in a chair that faced the ocean. The table set, with a custom-built bench seat along the back and chairs on the other three sides, was stark white and chunky. Clean-cut, yet comfortable. It was new, just like all of the furniture pieces. His old furniture, along with the rest of the material belongings from his last chapter, was left behind in storage.

Too bad he couldn't do the same thing with his memories.

•   •   •

He read the nameplate on the office door for probably the hundredth time. *Weston Sawyer, MD.* It was his name, yet he was unconvinced it should be gracing the new door. He opened it and motioned for the older gentleman with white Einstein hair and a woolly mustache to enter.

"Are you sure you're ready to step down from this?" Wes had spent a majority of the first three days at Carolina Pediatrics fielding questions on why Doc Nelson wasn't there. Most folks wanted to know if it was possible for Wes to call him up for a second opinion. "Seems the town isn't ready."

Doc settled in the chair in front of Wes's desk and folded his hands over his belly that was becoming slightly paunchy. "Kid, I've got one foot in the grave and the other on a slippery banana peel. I ain't ready to slide on in just yet. Got some fishing to get in first, and staying here won't give me the time to do it."

Wes sat in his chair, being mindful not to slouch. Doc had called him *kid* from day one, but at age thirty-seven nothing about him felt youthful anymore. "But—"

"You know where to find me if you need me. From what I've heard from Agnes, you're doing just fine. No complaints so far, so that's a good sign."

"Well, if you're not here to kick me out, to what do I owe this honor?" Wes steepled his fingers and tried not to hold his breath, knowing something was up.

"Agnes and I have talked it over, and well . . . we've decided it's time for her to retire, too." Doc nodded again, encouraging the fluff of hair to flicker about in his enthusiasm.

Wes sat up straighter. "But you said she'd be here to help with the transition." He shook his head in disbelief as he rubbed his jaw. "I don't have time to see after patients *and* run the office. Especially with having to deal with your outdated paper filing system. Your wife promised to stay on."

Doc reached over and patted Wes's arm. "Calm down, kid. Agnes is already searching for a new office manager. And she's not cutting out on you until she trains whoever takes the position."

Wes let out a long exhale as he stood, even though he really didn't feel any better about it. "Okay. Got any more surprises you care to drop on me before I open the doors for the day?" He removed his suit jacket and replaced it with his white lab coat. After wrapping the stethoscope around his neck and straightening his tie, he moved over to the door and waited for Doc's reply.

"Nah." Doc smoothed his mustache, looking thoughtful. "But I'll get back to you as soon as I do." He slowly stood, his knees popping out a tune. "Kid, don't worry about the mule; just load the wagon."

"I'll do my best, but you know how I am." Wes chuckled quietly and accepted the fatherly hug the old man offered before exiting the office. Doc liked to call him out on his obsessive need to keep to a precise plan. Life had proven to him in the cruelest way that most things were out of his control, so he did his best to keep a firm thumb on anything he *could* control. Looking around the freshly painted blue hallway and then to the man beside him, he was beginning to doubt he had any control in his current situation.

"Do better than your best." Doc waved over his

shoulder and headed toward his wife's office down the hall.

The first time Wes met Dr. Wallace Nelson was at a conference eleven years earlier. The spunky old man was the keynote speaker. As soon as he took his place behind the podium and began speaking in his rich, Southern vernacular, everyone in the place seemed enamored of him. Fact of the matter, the man knew his stuff when it came to pediatric health. He had just enough mix of old-school with cutting-edge science that it got the job done when it came to a sick patient in need of healing. Wes knew he was blessed to call the brilliant man his mentor, even though Doc always liked to bestow the quirkiest colloquialisms on him. Recalling some of the wise nonsense Doc had shared with him through the years, Wes gave in to a private chuckle and moved to the front of the office to get the day going.

The gamut of earaches, sinus infections, and wellness visits were like a calm breeze compared to his grueling days at Regional Pediatric Hematology/Oncology. That was a medical field that required a significant portion of a doctor's soul, and after his personal life crumbled, Wes didn't have any soul left to pour into it. The plan was to walk away from his medical career and allow the darkness of his loss to do its worst. He stayed buried in that desolate place for the better part of three years, until a phone call early last year from Doc left him with no choice but to honor a promise made long ago.

Wes pushed back the lingering thoughts he wished would stay in Alabama and focused on the next chart, which indicated the patient was suffering from a rash. Just as he turned to head to the exam room, the front door burst open, producing a frenzied mess of a woman with a toddler clinging to her.

The new open-area layout allowed the visitors in the waiting room a clear view of the reception area, and it also made It easy for Wes to watch as the distraught woman rushed toward him without pausing to check in. Several comments followed behind her from the adults in the waiting room.

"Hey!"

"You have to wait your turn!"

"My daughter is next!"

As she jogged past him, wearing a giant straw hat and designer sunglasses, something in the back of his mind registered her as familiar, but he dismissed the notion and hurried to catch up with her. "Ma'am, you need to check in at the front and—"

"It's an emergency!" the petite woman yelled over her shoulder as she let herself into a vacant exam room, holding the little boy for dear life.

Wes entered the sea turtle room, where several of the green creatures swam along the back wall in the hand-painted ocean mural. He walked over and ran his hand over the child's brown curls, hoping to coax him to look up. "What's wrong, little man?" The only response he received was a tiny sob as the child clung closer to his mother, burying his face in the crook of her neck.

"He has a severe stomachache. Poor thing was rolling around on the floor in pain," the mother answered, her voice remaining pitched high in panic.

"Has he seen in this office before?"

The mother nodded, setting the large brim of the hat to bouncing up and down. A tangle of dark hair was haphazardly tucked underneath. "His name is Collin Prescott."

Wes stuck his head out the door and beckoned the nurse to retrieve the child's file. After washing his hands, he walked back over to the exam table. "Could you please set him down so I can have a look?"

The frantic woman did as he said, but she didn't move out of his way. "He's been like this since this morning. I thought . . . I thought it would pass, but it's only gotten worse. Perhaps I should have gone straight to the emergency room instead of here. . . ." She kept rambling while Wes tried dodging around her.

"Ma'am, if you could step aside." Wes was using his most soothing voice, but it wasn't having the desired effect. He had an inclination that the toddler was more upset over his mother's reaction than the actual bellyache. If she'd move out of his way, he'd be able to prove his theory. Wes gently nudged her aside so he had some access to the boy. Refraining from huffing his frustration, he began the examination by practically reaching over the petite woman's head and shoulder.

Once the nurse brought in the file and he'd concluded the exam with a round of questions, he was confident the diagnosis was constipation. Clearly the mother didn't agree. Her face began tingeing a vibrant pink, at least what he could see of it. "Mrs. Prescott, the lighting is dim enough in here that you can safely remove the sunglasses."

She sucked her teeth. "It's Sophia. And I'd rather leave them on, thank you very much. But there's more to this than what you think. My son needs more tests. What about an X-ray or MRI?"

Wes tried explaining it to her again. "He has no fever and—"

"But he's been clutching his left side!"

He held up a hand. "And that's a very good sign, considering his appendix is on the right side."

"Doc Nelson wouldn't be treating us like this!" she

screeched while tugging at the neckline of her black T-shirt as if it were choking her.

It's exactly what Wes felt like doing to her at the moment.

Clenching his fists and shoving them into the pockets of his lab coat, Wes barely held on to his bedside manners. "Mrs. Prescott, I've treated you in a professional—"

"I demand an X-ray!" She stomped her foot, sending the toddler into another round of sobs.

If she cuts me off one more time . . . "You know what? You're right. Let's do an X-ray." Shaking his head, Wes led them to the room in the back, knowing exactly what the film would prove.

Once he'd captured two images, he ushered the mother and child to the waiting area. "I'll call you back in a bit with the results."

He left her there and went to apologize to the rash patient who'd been in the coral reef exam room for the better part of the last hour. *There goes my plan for staying on schedule . . .*

As he finished up with three other patients, trying to settle down the agitated mothers who had been impatiently waiting, Wes studied the films of Collin's abdomen and found exactly what he knew would be there. He left his office and turned on the X-ray light box at the back of the reception area. It needed to be relocated now that the waiting area had a clear view of it. Somehow they'd overlooked that in the remodel.

"Mrs. Prescott?" he called and waved her over.

She held the boy close and hurried toward him. "Please call me Sophia. What did you find?" Maybe she'd run out of steam while waiting, but she was no longer screeching. Wes was surprised her natural voice was quite husky for such a small woman.

Wes pointed to the bowels. "Do you see the thick white areas here?"

The woman slid the giant sunglasses down the bridge of her nose and peered at the film. She gasped and sent the shades back up. "Yes! See? I told you!"

"Ma'am, that white area is fecal matter. Your son is constipated." Wes tried to say it low enough just for the mother to hear, but from the snickers coming from the waiting area, he'd failed.

"What?" Her face turned bright red, indicating she had heard him right.

"Collin needs to poop." He handed over a list of recommended enema brands and several pamphlets on proper nutrition. "Might I suggest you work on a healthier diet for this little guy? Lots of water, high fiber, and stay away from processed foods. That will help to prevent this from happening again."

"But . . ." She seemed to snap out of her embarrassment and head right back into indignation. "Are you calling me a bad mother?"

"Ma'am, you need to lower your voice. I won't allow you to make a scene."

"So I'm supposed to stand here while you tell me I'm a bad mother?" She jabbed a finger toward him, halting just before stabbing him in the chest. "You have another think coming, sir."

Wes couldn't suppress the sigh any longer. "What is a typical meal for Collin?" When she didn't answer right away, he plowed on. "Tell me what he had at mealtimes yesterday."

"A donut, a Happy Meal, and . . . another Happy Meal." Sophia cast her face to the ground. Good, he'd hoped she'd humble herself.

"So no fruits and vegetables. Just plain garbage."

Maybe he should have kept the last part to himself, but the woman had worn down his patience until there was hardly any left. Besides, she was the one to blame for her son's condition in the first place.

"He's been through a lot lately. . . . I just . . ." She sniffed, but it didn't soften Wes, not one bit.

"That's no excuse. And to be honest, it's irresponsible to teach your child that when life gets difficult, it's okay to neglect his health in this manner." He began to walk away, knowing he'd already said more than enough, but the urge to throw one last jab over his shoulder won out. "It would probably be a great time to try out potty training, because it will be more than a diaperful once the medicine is administered." He held the X-ray slide up to drive home his point.

The child was almost three and the mother had admitted during the exam she wasn't even trying to potty train him yet. Wes shook his head and tried to tamp down his building anger. It was imperative for him to keep his personal feelings out of the office, but he was already failing in just the first week.

"How dare you talk to me like that! You can consider this the last time you see my son! We won't be back!"

Good riddance, he thought but remained silent and slipped into his office to get away from the ruined day. All because some self-righteous priss thought she could storm into his office like she owned the place.

And all because he would have given anything to have a son to feed properly and to potty train. And to love.

3

Several strings of Edison-style lights swayed in the ocean breeze overhead at dusk as the gathering swelled in numbers on Opal and Lincoln Cole's back deck. Sophia listened to the lighthearted chatter that was sprinkled with sweet laughter. Standing on the fringes of such joy, she felt utterly alone.

"There you are!" Opal sashayed over, looking like a fifties pinup with her hair rolled and a saucy dress.

"Wow, Opal. That dress is so cute," Sophia commented as she smoothed her palm down the side of her floral maxi dress, feeling anything but.

Opal danced a little circle, sending the hem of her navy swing dress dotted with bright-red cherries flaring out. "Thanks. Linc says I'm totally rockabilly tonight." She handed Sophia a glass of summer punch. The very same recipe they'd sipped at most every summer party since she could remember. Pineapple juice mixed with pink lemonade concentrate—frozen, then mixed with ginger ale and served slushy style.

"Honey, your husband walks around in threadbare tees, holey jeans, and barefoot most of the time. How does he even know anything about rockabilly fashion?" Sophia took a sip of the sweet and tangy slushy.

"Wouldn't you like to know?" Lincoln said, all brooding smugness, as he joined them. He reached over and tugged the end of Sophia's hair. "Glad to see you found a brush."

Sophia barely contained an eye roll. "Glad you did the same and have that mess out of your eyes for a change." No man should have such pretty hair, especially a giant Neanderthal such as Lincoln Cole, Sophia thought.

"Don't be jealous," Lincoln teased as if he could read her thoughts and made a show of smoothing back his dark hair. It was shoulder-length and hung in glossy waves.

"Don't be a dork." She went ahead and rolled her eyes. For some reason, Lincoln had taken it upon himself to become her surrogate big brother. Teasing her every chance he got on one hand, yet fiercely protective of her on the other. She still couldn't get over him getting into a pretty heated shoving match with Ty when she showed up covered in bruises that last time. Lincoln liked to aggravate her to no end but wouldn't allow anyone else to do so. No matter how annoying he was, she sure did like having him in her corner. He was definitely a good one, and she couldn't thank the good Lord enough for sending him to Opal. Those two together were an invincible team.

"She even managed wearing something besides funeral attire." This smart remark came from the other man who loved to get under her skin.

Sophia spun around and glared at August, who was grinning ear to ear as he swiped her half-empty glass of punch and finished it off. "Hey!" She reached over and pinched him good and hard.

August flinched out of her reach. "Dang it, Sophia! What have we told you about keeping your claws to your-self?" August tsked and had the audacity to hand her the empty cup.

She was about to go another round or two with the town's famed artist, but someone walked by and caught not only her attention but that of the others standing around her.

"Wes! You made it!" Opal shouted over the music and chatter to get his attention.

Dr. Weston Sawyer was one smartly dressed man in a light-blue dress shirt and perfectly pressed khakis, and Sophia couldn't help but stare as he sauntered over in a confident stride to join the group. Polished and poised, he tipped his head to each lady while holding a careful smile on his face, catching on Sophia for a punctuated moment. Apparently he didn't recognize her or care to look any longer, so he moved his attention back to Opal.

"Thank you for inviting me. Sorry I didn't have time Monday morning to get acquainted, but the cookies were delicious."

Two things struck Sophia at once. First, the man spoke in such a smooth tone she wanted to snuggle up beside it. And second, she was disgusted with herself for even thinking it. Clearly the loneliness of her newfound single life was to blame. But then a third thing struck after actually taking in the words he said. She narrowed her eyes at Opal, but her friend was dutifully ignoring her.

"You had to unpack. There's nothing to apologize for. I'm just glad you enjoyed the cookies." Opal smiled, full of warmth.

"Where did you swipe the cookies, Opal? Surely they were stolen goods if they were edible," August commented as he draped an arm over Josie's shoulder as she joined the group.

Sophia smiled at Josie but couldn't keep her eyes from wandering back to the man who accused her of being a bad mother. Her lips sloped into a frown at that thought as she studied him, hoping to find a flaw to revel in. His hair was a mix of blond and brown, as if the locks couldn't make their minds up on what color to be. A striking set of hazel eyes seemed to be in the same indecisive predicament. Of course his youthful face held no stubble and each of those wavy locks of caramel hair were perfectly placed. Not even a bump on the bridge of his straight nose or any sign of crow's-feet around his eyes. Nope, not one physical flaw could be found. She'd just have to stick with knowing his attitude held enough flaws to trump his handsomeness.

Wes glanced at her again, no recognition evident, before sliding his attention to August. He reached out a hand. "It's nice to finally meet you." Wes shook August's hand and Josie's hand next. "The two of you did a great job on the exam room murals. The children really like them."

Josie blushed as predicted and August kissed her pink cheek as always. Truly, they were one of those adorable couples that sent some in awe while painting others green with envy. Sophia understood this because she'd been on both sides of those feelings.

She noticed Opal slipping away and followed. "I should pinch you too."

"Why on earth would you want to do that?" Opal asked while waving at a few guests.

"You knew who Weston Sawyer was the entire time we sat on this deck playing your silly 'I Spy the Vampire' game."

Opal swatted the accusation away and moved over to the refreshment table set up on the farther side of the deck. "That was us just having some fun. No sense in getting your panties in a twist over it."

"No, that's you thinking you're so slick, Mrs. Meddler."

Opal refilled Sophia's glass with punch, then hers, before taking a sip. "I have no idea what you're referring to."

"You were hoping Wes would come over while I was here the other day. Why?"

Opal looked around, maybe searching for an answer that would save her hide. "Well, I ran into Agnes Nelson at Growler's, and the poor thing is in such a pickle."

"Ugh. Please, Opal. I don't have the patience for your loopy talk. Just say it straight." Sophia's eyes darted to the pretentious man where he stood with August and Lincoln. Impeccably groomed, he appeared too graceful and proper to be hanging out with those two scruffy country boys. She moved her gaze to the two ruggedly handsome men—one with long hair and a thick beard, the other tattooed and wearing a five-o'clock shadow like a boss—thinking how Weston Sawyer couldn't be more opposite of them.

I wonder what all that neat put-togetherness is hiding.

"My, you're snippy today," Opal sassed, snapping Sophia out of her staring, while cajoling her elbow to guide the glass of punch to her lips. "You need a few more servings of this sugar." When Sophia had taken a long slurp of the punch, she continued. "Agnes wants to retire with Doc so they can spend some quality time together, but she can't do that until she finds a replacement. Poor thing."

"Yeah. Poor thing . . . ," Sophia parroted, not caring for the path the conversation was headed. She was about to walk away from it, but Opal locked their arms together before she could manage a step.

"I think the office manager position would be a good fit for you."

Sophia scoffed. "Hardly. That would fit about as good as a pair of shoes two sizes too small. Agonizing and awkward."

"Come on, Sophia. I think it's just what you need."

"No." Sophia scanned the group of guests, but her gaze halted on August, who was pointing at her while both Weston and Lincoln looked her way. "What is that idiot doing?" she asked just as Weston gave her a cursory sweep. His head tipped to the side as recognition flashed in his hazel eyes.

Before she could untangle her arm from Opal's grasp, Weston was standing before her. The sweet punch turned sour on her tongue from the shrewd look he was giving her.

"I'm sorry I didn't recognize you without the giant sun hat and shades, Mrs. Prescott." Wes slid his hands into his pant pockets as he rocked back on his heels.

"It's Ms. Prescott, if you must know, but Sophia is just fine." She set the glass down, having had her fill of it as well as the party. She caught a glimpse of Opal scurrying away but decided to deal with her later.

"I hope you've been giving your son some fruits and vegetables. How is he?"

Accusation followed by concern. It made Sophia want to smack him instead of answering, but she somehow pulled out her manners and wore them with the grace her mother had instilled in her. "Much better. Thank you for asking."

"Regular bowel movements? Any more stomach pain?"

"He's fine." She kept to a short answer, not wanting to get riled up, and waved an arm around. "It's a party. You shouldn't be in doctor mode."

Wes sniffed and glanced over her shoulder. "It's the only mode I can function in properly." He lowered his chin and walked away.

"Well, that conversation was enthralling." Sophia rolled her eyes and decided she'd had enough socializing for one day. She glanced around and found her meddling group of friends watching on. Jabbing a finger in their direction along with a measured scowl, Sophia let them know she'd deal with them later, before stomping off the deck.

As the jovial melody of the party droned on behind

her, Sophia walked around to the front of the beach house. A long sigh caught her attention from next door, where Weston Sawyer sat on the porch steps studying his hands.

"I'm not a bad mother, Dr. Sawyer," Sophia blurted.

"I thought you didn't want doctor mode." He sighed again. "Just call me Wes."

Sophia could think of a few other things to call him but decided to keep them to herself. She drew closer to his porch, not wanting anyone else to catch their exchange. "You embarrassed me in your office. I don't take too kindly to that."

"And I didn't appreciate you disrespecting me in my office in front of other patients." Wes kept his face cast toward the sandy steps before him, but his hazel eyes rose to look at her. "Let's be clear on the fact that your negligent behavior was the cause of your son's issue in the first place." Apparently he couldn't resist adding the snide remark, but his voice was just above a whisper. It made Sophia wonder if he knew how to raise his pompous voice any higher, or was he too dignified for such?

"Do you have children, Dr. Sawyer?" As soon as she asked, a subtle flinch tightened his shoulders. If she wasn't paying attention, she would have missed it.

"No."

"Then you have no right to judge those of us who do, trying to raise our children the best we know how. Your job is to diagnose and treat patients. You'd be mindful to remember that in this town."

Sophia was finished speaking her piece, so she left the doctor and headed home to hopefully hide in the dark for a while before having to pick up Collin from her parents. Sure, she was well aware that she was failing her son, but she didn't need some snob such as Dr. Weston Sawyer to point it out.

•   •   •

No matter how difficult life could become, a trip to
Driftwood Diner always made things more bearable.
Well, that was typically the case, but this morning a fiery
sprite was working on ruining it. Sophia offered Collin
a bite of her biscuit as she listened to Opal lay into her.

"You had no business telling that new momma to go
to the next town's pediatric office. There's nothing wrong
with the office here in Sunset Cove and you know it."
Opal huffed while settling into the seat opposite Sophia.

It had been several days since the deck party, and during that time, Sophia had refused all calls and visits from
the Sand Queens and their pesky husbands. She wouldn't
be strong-armed into any job—or any other decision, for
that matter.

"Why are you creeping on my Facebook page?"
Sophia glared at her friend while taking a sip of coffee.

"It's the only way I know what's going on with you,
since you won't answer your phone or door. You changed
the locks at the condo, didn't you?" It was Opal's turn to
glare.

"There's no reason for you to have a key to my place
anyway. And that momma was asking for pediatric office
recommendations, so I simply offered one." Sophia lifted
a bored shoulder and wiped syrup off Collin's cheeks.

"Ofal, wan' fome?" Collin mushed a chunk of pancake
onto his fork, using both hands to secure it there, and
lifted it toward her. Opal, good sport that she was, happily
took the bite.

"Yum!" she garbled out, making a silly face in the process that sent the little guy into a fit of giggles. She looked
back to Sophia and grew serious. "I heard you speaking
to Wes on his porch."

Sophia briefly closed her eyes. "Of course you did. Nosy much?"

"You don't know enough about him to speak the way you did." Opal took a sip of water. "He's a widower."

"That doesn't give him the right to be all snide about my parenting practices." Even though she tried to come off as reproachful, her stomach tightened uncomfortably. He looked too young to have such a title as *widower* attached to him. She tucked her thumb along the back of her ring finger before she could stop herself.

"Maybe, but then you go asking him if he has a child." Opal tsked, sounding rather miffed.

"So?"

Opal leaned closer and lowered her voice to a whisper. "Wes not only lost his wife, but he also lost an unborn child. She was eight months pregnant when she died in a car wreck."

Sophia gasped but then settled back down. "How do you know so much about him?"

"I spent a good bit of time with Doc Nelson during the remodel of the doctor's office. He's known Wes for years." Opal reached down and picked up the sippy cup Collin had accidentally sent to the floor. She righted herself and placed the cup on his high chair. "Doc said it happened almost four years ago. Wes walked away from his practice in Alabama and pretty much became a hermit. . . . Sounds like someone else I know." Opal raised an eyebrow and leveled a meaningful look at Sophia.

Sophia combed her fingers through Collin's brown curls, having no clue how she'd be able to breathe if she ever lost him. Sure, the demise of her marriage and career was tragic, but she couldn't imagine living through a loss such as Dr. Sawyer's. Shame sent a lump to lodge in her throat over how she'd spoken to him.

"That's not for public knowledge, so it stays just between us," Opal said, tapping the table to make sure Sophia understood.

Sophia nodded her head and waved to get the waitress's attention without responding to her friend. Really, what was there to say to all that? Nothing was what. "Can I get the check, please?"

The young waitress smiled warmly. "Mr. Jasper said it's on him today."

Sophia scoffed. "Your boss says it's on him every day."

"You know how he is. Best thing to do is just go with it." She waved off Sophia's protests and hurried on to another table. Josie's dad had been a second daddy to each Sand Queen and had fed them more times than one could count.

"I'm heading into work. What does the rest of the day look like for the two of you?" Opal asked, swiping the last of Sophia's biscuit.

"I need to go grocery shopping." Sophia packed Collin's sippy cup into the diaper bag and settled him on her hip. The list tucked in the pocket of her baggy pants was filled with fresh everything to start at least one new step of cooking at home and laying off eating out so much. She'd taken the snooty doctor's advice and had cut the Happy Meals down to only once a week.

"It's a beautiful day. You two should head to my house afterward and spend the afternoon on the beach."

"*Pease*, Mommy." Collin twirled his sticky fingers in her hair.

"We'll see, baby," she offered, her go-to answer for not really giving an answer.

"*Pease*, Sophia, bring my bubby to the beach. We can sweet-talk Linc into grilling us something for supper, too." Opal winked at Sophia before giving the toddler an exaggerated kiss and pulling another loud giggle from him. Opal specialized in that and Sophia would be willing to keep the meddling woman around for no other reason. Collin didn't smile or laugh nearly as much as a child his age should.

Sophia's mind was in repeat mode, worrying about Collin's happiness all the way to the grocery store, and kept skipping back to it as she strapped Collin into the shopping-cart seat. She made silly faces while picking out fruit, danced around a display of chips, and tickled Collin's side as they moved around the store. He'd respond but the happiness never lingered, not even making it from one aisle to the next.

As she turned into the cereal aisle, normally the one strip of shopping fun for the toddler, she really began to worry when he didn't immediately start begging for the brightly colored boxes of pure sugar. She bent down and rested her chin on the cart handle, bringing her eye to eye with him. Studying his puffy blue eyes, the lingering effects of a long, restless night, Sophia searched for some hidden sign that he was okay. Collin curiously watched her as he crammed a finger up his nose.

Snickering, she yanked it out and asked, "What do you want, baby? You get to pick." She tried not to think about the disapproving lecture the starchy doctor would give her for allowing Collin the cereal of his choosing.

"Daddy. I wan' Daddy." His little eyes lit up with hope.

"I know, baby. Daddy's working . . . but soon, okay?"

Collin didn't seem agreeable with her answer, his eyes glassing over as his pouty lips curved into a trembling frown. Both were warning signs of a tantrum working loose.

Sophia straightened and did the only thing a desperate mother in her situation could come up with—she clutched the cart handle firmly with both hands and took off like a streak of lightning down the cereal aisle at a breakneck speed while making race car sounds. It took a couple of turns on the grocery aisle track before the little guy let loose his own sound effects. Those pouty lips vibrated as he revved his motor, and it was pure music to her ears.

A stock boy reprimanded her when she sideswiped a tower of toilet paper, leaving an avalanche of rolls in her wake, but she had no regrets. By the time they reached the yogurt section, she was right winded, but her baby was smiling with no traces of tears in sight. Collin even picked out a healthy choice of yogurt, unbeknownst to him, but still. He was participating. For a few brief moments in the dairy aisle, Sophia felt like a normal momma doing something normal with her toddler. The haze of hurt waned, allowing her to breathe a little easier.

As Sophia began pushing the cart toward the front of the store, a small herd of children passed by while skipping around their mother's cart. She noticed Collin looking on with a faint smile on his face.

She'd kept Collin tucked underneath her wing for close to three years, but watching him watch those children with longing, it made her realize that maybe doing so hadn't been in his best interest. *Wasn't it normal not to want your baby to grow up too fast?* she wondered. It seemed like a motherly way of thinking, but now she was realizing her intentions might have been on the selfish side.

Maybe it's time to consider preschool, she thought as she unloaded the groceries at the cash register. She'd almost talked herself into hurrying back to the diaper aisle to grab a pack of training Pull-Ups when the little card machine made an obnoxious sound she'd never had directed to her. Squinting at the small screen, she realized it was alerting her that the debit card had been declined.

The cashier shrugged her shoulders as she tapped several keys on her register. "Try swiping it again. Sometimes the card reader has a glitch."

Sophia did as instructed, but the little machine sent out that menacing alert tone again. "Let me try another card." She put the debit card back and fished out a credit card. She swiped it and grabbed up the pen to sign off on the transaction, but the alert sounded again. "This makes no sense. Is your machine broken?"

"I can try it on my register." The cashier held her hand out for the card, and Sophia handed it over quickly.

Looking around, Sophia was thankful no one was waiting in line behind her. Sure, she'd witnessed shoppers turn bright red with humiliation a time or two when their cards had been declined, but it was something she'd never experienced personally until now. "There's no reason for my cards not to work. Surely the store system is to blame."

"It's still not working." The cashier made a sympathetic face and handed the card back.

Sophia clucked her tongue, pulling on a lofty attitude even though her palms were sweating and her heart racing. "This is ridiculous. Can you get a manager?"

Several long, humiliating minutes later, after the manager tried both cards on two other registers and Sophia made a call to the bank, she sat behind the wheel of her fancy SUV in the parking lot and stared out the windshield in disbelief. There was always an abundance of money waiting to meet her needs and wants at the swipe of a card. Until now. Stunned, all she could do was sit there and tap her thumb underneath her bare ring finger.

When Collin began whining, she pulled herself together enough to drive. With no groceries to put away and no clear ideas on how to remedy that problem, she drove around aimlessly for a while until finding herself parking beside Opal and Lincoln's beach house. A glance in the rearview mirror confirmed the little guy was sacked out, so she put the SUV in park but didn't shut it off.

With shaky hands, she managed to pull up Ty's number on her cell phone and hit the Call button.

"The number you have dialed is no longer in service . . ."

Sniffing back the tears, she tried it three more times before giving up.

"What have you done, Ty?" Sophia whispered while staring at the phone in disbelief.

Frozen accounts. IRS tax levy. Federal investigation. With those unfamiliar words the bank president had shared on the phone whirling through the tangles of her muddled mind, Sophia leaned her forehead against the steering wheel and tried to cry as quietly as possible.

4

So far, Sunset Cove was living up to its small coastal town charm. It was quiet and most folks kept to themselves. Most folks, that was, with the exception of a small group of old ladies. Wes had nicknamed them the beauty-shop hens. About a half dozen in total, with bouffant hair and too many questions. They'd been showing up randomly at his door to share covered dishes, baked goods, and servings of gossip ever since he arrived in town. It was easy to brush off the clucking the first week, but then they started dropping tidbits that included him to a certain degree along with one other person. Namely, Sophia Grace Prescott was attached to near about every conversation.

Huffing in frustration, Wes picked up his pace into a sprint while dodging beachgoers. It was Wednesday, and Doc had always closed at noon on Wednesdays. It was church night and most people seemed not to have colds and such on that particular day, according to the older doctor. Wes kept the original schedule, but he didn't like the idle time it left on his hands, so he moved his morning run to noon on Wednesdays to help combat it. Too bad he couldn't outrun his thoughts this particular day.

"Sophia Grace is the ex-wife of that celebrity NFL player Ty Prescott."

"Sophia was an uppity PR consultant in North Carolina until they fired her."

"It was all over the news about their split."

"He cheated."

"A nasty divorce."

"She was photographed with numerous bruises and a busted lip earlier this year."

Every shared snippet from the beauty-shop hens had been delivered with either a clucking of their tongues or a "bless her heart" tagged to the end. He'd not turned on a TV in years and never had time or tolerance for social media, so Wes had no idea who Ty Prescott was. Nor did he really care. And he certainly didn't care who Sophia Prescott was either, until the rumor mill shared with him about her smear campaign on social media earlier this week. The hens claimed she was telling everyone he was a bad doctor and encouraging parents to take their children to the pediatric office over in the next town.

Wes had agreed to come to Sunset Cove when Doc assured him peace and quiet would be his neighbors, but the mouthy brunette was making that unattainable. If he couldn't figure out a way to keep those hens at bay and Sophia's mouth shut, he was ready to pack up and make a run for it. Problem was, he had nowhere to go.

His Apple Watch alerted him that he'd reached another mile, so he looped around to head back to the beach house. Once the house was in sight, he slowed his pace to a leisurely jog to cool down, progressing to a walk as he rounded the side of his house. Mopping the sweat from his brow with the back of his forearm, Wes came to a halt at the sight of a giant SUV haphazardly parked— half in the Coles' driveway and half in his. Through the dark-tinted window he could make out a woman rest- ing her head on the steering wheel. Moving closer, he caught a glimpse of a small child sleeping in his car seat in the back.

Wes had a pretty good idea of who the woman was, and he had a pretty good idea it was in his best interest to walk away. She'd not seen him, so no harm, no foul. But his mind didn't relay the message to his hand fast enough, and before he realized it, he was gently tapping his knuckles against the driver's window.

Sophia jumped, her head jerking up to look at him, but quickly turned away and dug around in her bag until producing those giant sunglasses. She slid on what he was beginning to realize was her shield before opening her window.

"Hello, Sophia," he greeted quietly, not wanting to disturb Collin or startle her again.

"Hi," she rasped, sounding more than a little addled.

Wes considered her and the situation, at a loss on what to do. Tears were rolling down her cheeks as her bottom lip trembled. Clearly she was upset about something. Too upset to be driving around, as evidenced by the mushed palm plant underneath her rear tire. *But what to do?* He glanced toward his house, not wanting to invite them in. Every fiber of his being screamed to run, to stay out of the woman's business, but he remained rooted beside her car door.

"Has Collin been sleeping long?"

"No . . ." She sniffled.

"He'd be more comfortable lying down, instead of in that cramped seat." Wes regarded his house once again and then glanced at Collin. The little guy's head lobbed to the side at what seemed to be an uncomfortable angle. "Why don't you bring him inside to finish out his nap?"

"Opal . . . ," Sophia began, sounding disoriented but sober.

Wes scanned the neighbor's driveway even though he already knew it was empty. "There's no one home."

"Oh . . ." Sophia's shoulders managed to slump further as she dropped her chin.

"Maybe Opal will be home soon. You're welcome to come inside and wait for her." He opened Sophia's door, hoping to encourage her to exit.

"Okay." She slid out and slowly shuffled to the back to gather the diaper bag and then the toddler. Without saying anything, she headed up his porch and waited by the door.

Wes reached around the steering wheel to turn off the SUV and then closed the two doors Sophia had left ajar before following. He ushered her inside and led her to the first-floor guest room.

"I'll let you get him settled," he whispered before taking the stairs two at a time up to his room. He swapped the sweaty tee for a fresh one and washed his face and hands. Knowing he couldn't hide in his room from whatever was going on, he went back downstairs and found Sophia sitting at the breakfast nook table.

The giant sunglasses still covered most of her face, and Wes noticed she was dressed in a shroud of baggy black. He recalled how radiant she had been at the party in that elegant floral print dress with her hair brushed in long dark waves. No doubt, the woman was a knockout, and he could just bet she was a pro at lighting up a room by flashing those vivid blue eyes. Too bad something had dimmed her. Slumped at his table, she looked so defeated that he had a feeling those abuse rumors might have actually been derived from the truth. A pang of empathy clenched his abdomen.

Clearing his throat to announce his return, Wes walked over to the fridge and retrieved a pitcher filled with water and sliced lemons. "Would you care for a glass?" He held up the pitcher.

"Okay," Sophia answered without turning away from gazing out the bay windows. It was a tranquil view of the ocean with the sun casting a glitter on top of the water. He'd hoped she was finding some solace in it.

Wes placed a glass on the table in front of Sophia before sitting across from her. They sipped their water in silence until his glass was empty and hers halfway. His eyes slid to the clock above the mantel to check the time. Forty minutes had passed and yet she remained in her zombie state.

Sighing, he whispered, "Do you need to talk about it?"

"No," she whispered back.

As a kite sailed by the windows, he searched for something to say, but he'd always favored silence over idle chit-chat, so his lips remained clamped shut.

As he listened to the muffled hum of the ocean, Wes noticed her running her thumb along the underside of her ring finger. It was the same absentminded habit he was trying to break himself. Just last year he'd finally removed his wedding ring. The silver band once held such profound sentiment. Perhaps their story lines were different, but apparently some key points were similar.

"This entire place looks brand-new," Sophia said out of the blue, breaking the silence and jolting Wes out of his spiraling thoughts.

"It's what I asked Lincoln to do." Wes scanned the room. The outdated wood-panel walls had been replaced with smooth Sheetrock painted a tasteful gray and topped off with sophisticated crown molding. The floors had been stripped of the honey-hue stain and darkened considerably. "I requested contemporary comfort, and I think he delivered."

"He did. I like it," she whispered, her sultry voice so incongruous with her petite body.

Wes was an average height, just under six feet, but she made him feel like a giant. One would expect a woman as tiny as Sophia to have a soft, girlish voice. And so the throaty cadence of her tone caught him off guard each time she spoke.

Staring at his glass, he murmured, "Thank you."

"What did you name it?"

Wes glanced in her direction, only to meet his reflection in the giant sunglasses. He noticed his hair was going in every direction from the run and then his hasty shirt change, but he tamped down the urge to straighten it. Instead, he focused on her pouty lips. Maybe that wasn't a good idea either, but he kept staring at them anyway. "Pardon?"

"The beach house." She motioned around the space.

"Oh yeah. I didn't even know that was a thing until I moved here. I kept the original name."

"Sea Glass Castle," Sophia answered.

"Yes." He looked toward the mantel and pointed. "You see the sea glass filling that vase?"

"They're beautiful," Sophia commented.

"Lincoln Cole and his crew collected each one from all over the house while they were renovating it, so it felt right to leave the original name."

"That's sentimental. I've always wanted a beach house to name. Guess that'll never happen now . . ." Sophia trailed off and ended their conversation on a weird vibe.

Awkward didn't even come close to describing their situation, and Wes couldn't quite wrap his mind around why he had allowed a practical stranger into his home. A raucous round of flatulence sounded from the guest room, reminding him of the reason. *For the safety of the child.*

Sophia bit her lip and stood from the table. "Little man

is awake." She hurried to the room and was back within minutes with the groggy toddler.

"Hello, Collin." Wes gave the boy a wave.

"Hey, poo-poo man." He rubbed his eyes and looked around. "I fursy."

Wes arched an eyebrow, making Sophia bite her lip again. This time it didn't quite conceal the hint of a smile. "Would you like some water?"

Sophia placed Collin on his feet and began rummaging around in the diaper bag. "Let me get his cup." *Finally* the sunglasses seemed to be getting in her way, so she took them off and tossed them into the bag.

As Wes watched her, Collin waddled over and climbed into his lap. It caught him off guard at first, making his shoulders stiffen and his stomach flip, but then he relaxed and privately relished the way the little guy was trusting him. Collin squirmed and grunted and elbowed him until settling sideways and resting his head on Wes's chest. His hand smoothed the boy's hair as he breathed in the scent of maple syrup and baby lotion. He glanced up and noticed Sophia holding the sippy cup while watching him carefully, so he dropped his hand.

Sophia cleared her throat. "I'm going to get him some water if that's all right."

"Sure. Do you mind refilling my glass as well?" Wes reached over and held his glass up. Sophia obliged, but he noticed the pitcher didn't look steady in her grasp. "Here. Let me." He took the pitcher and maneuvered filling all three cups without jostling Collin.

No one seemed to be in the mood to share any words, so they sipped their water in silence. The only sounds were the waves rolling in just outside and Collin's slurps each time he took a pull from his cup.

Collin managed a grown man–size burp, earning a reprimand from his mother. The little guy garbled out, "'Scuse me." Follow by "I hungwy. You feed me, poo-poo man?" He was so sincere even when calling Wes such a silly name that he immediately nodded and began mentally inventorying the contents of his fridge.

"We need to head home."

Sophia was suggesting they leave, the exact thing he needed her to do, but his mouth did something it never did. It spoke up. "I have a shrimp and pasta salad. I don't recall any seafood allergies in his chart."

"No allergies, but I'm not sure he'll eat that." Sophia made a face and tucked a thick lock of brown hair behind her ear. The color reminded Wes of his espresso floors.

"Only one way to find out." Wes stood and tried setting the boy down, but Collin clung to him like Velcro, so he settled him on his hip and walked over to the fridge.

Once the salad was on the table with plates and forks, Wes led them in prayer. As he took his first bite, he realized this was the first shared meal in the house. His throat thickened at the thought, but he managed to swallow it down and take another bite.

"This kid is a vegetable-eating machine." He glanced down, and as if on cue, the little guy spit out a chunk of celery before scrunching his face. That was okay, though, because Collin had picked out the cherry tomatoes from both his plate and Wes's, so he considered that progress.

Sophia pushed the food around her plate without eating any of it. She looked at her son and pulled on a halfhearted smile.

"Poo, I wan' more of dees." Collin held up a squished tomato.

"We both know it's your fault he's calling me that inappropriate name." Wes pointed his fork at Sophia before using it to spear several tomatoes and placing them on Collin's plate. "You need to rectify that."

Her bright-blue eyes flashed with a little life. "Perhaps the name suits you."

"It's in poor taste and, as already stated, inappropriate. You shouldn't be encouraging your child to call people names." It was supposed to be in tease, but it somehow turned into a doctor lecture. Not what he was going for at all. And by the looks of Sophia, not the right time either.

She jolted from her chair and picked up Collin just as he fisted a handful of tomatoes. "I'm not a bad mother, Dr. Sawyer." She had the diaper bag slung over her shoulder and was out the door before he came to terms with his folly.

Hurrying outside, Wes countered, "And I'm not a bad doctor."

She ignored him, loaded up, and was gone in a flash, leaving only a mangled plant in her wake.

Wes sat on the steps, staring down the road long after the dust she'd kicked up settled. Eventually the frustrating mood dissipated and a faint smile lifted his lips. At least by the time she left, Sophia seemed much more alive than when he'd found her earlier. The shadowy defeated version was something he just couldn't handle, but that tiny woman all riled up and feisty was a different story.

Considering his good deed done for the day, Wes moved back inside but lingered by the door and peered around. It was truly a beautiful house, but for the past hour or so there had been a breath of life added to it that transformed it into more of a home. Now that Sophia and Collin were gone, the quietness had a heavier quality to it than before.

His eyes caught on the two overstuffed cream sofas

with gray and pale-green pinstripes. Neither piece of furniture had ever held a guest—not even Wes—and only emphasized the loneliness trapped within the gray walls.

Shaking off the desolate notion that was his reality, Wes moved over to the table to clear away the dishes. He then made his way into the guest room to straighten it. As he shook out the blanket, a toy car toppled to the floor.

It had taken well over a year into his heartache before Wes learned how to outrun his grief, but something as unassuming as a toy car could still derail those assiduous efforts and cast him right back into it so deeply he felt for sure he'd die of suffocation. Three years suddenly coiled back and sent him to his knees.

Clutching the toy to his burning chest, Wes gasped for air. Air he didn't deserve. Air that should have been filling his wife and his own son with life. Air that he begged God to take from him so he wasn't left behind without them.

5

Mahogany . . . endless mahogany. Sophia perused the bookcases, the clunky desk chairs and side tables, until focusing on the desk sitting before her. Everything was in the same glossy shade of mahogany.

"Ms. Prescott," Mr. Billingsley greeted as he hurried into the office, bearing a thick folder and a grim expression. "I'm sorry we couldn't meet with you any sooner, but Mr. Prescott's attorney hasn't been very cooperative."

Sophia stood, straightened the navy tailored jacket that matched her trousers, and accepted the portly man's hand. She shook it firmly enough to convey confidence, just as her dad had shown her long ago before she was to meet the governor after winning first place in the middle school governor's essay contest. That was a nervous yet exciting day for her. Too bad her current day was just filled with nervousness. Nothing exciting was to come of it if Mr. Billingsley's demeanor was any indication.

"I understand," Sophia said, even though she didn't. She didn't understood anything. She didn't understand why she was caught up in the middle of Ty's financial fiasco since they were divorced. And she definitely didn't understand why Weston Sawyer had been hospitable on that wretched day last week when she'd made this discovery. But in the days since then, she had willed her thoughts to stay focused on making an IOU list for the

groceries and other necessities that her parents had provided, rather than trying to figure out Weston's kindness
and quietly showing up in the midst of an awful moment
to help her. It was just lunch and a place to rest, but it had
been so much more.

"As of now, we've managed to free up your severance
from Southeastern, and I advise you to keep a portion
in cash on your person and open a new account for the
remainder of it." Her attorney made a grunting sound as
he sat behind the desk and began flipping through the
file, bringing her attention back to him and the absurd
situation. "As for alimony and child support, I'm sorry to
tell you there's no clear indicator when you'll have access
to those funds. It all depends on how the other attorneys
proceed."

"That's better than nothing, I suppose." Sophia gave
him her most proper smile and head nod as she signed
off on the thick stack of documents he slid to her side of
the desk.

"I've included in your folder recommendations for
an accountant. It's imperative that you do everything
by the book, because the IRS will definitely be keeping
an eye on you for an indefinite length of time. We have
proof that you filed individual tax returns for the last two
years, so you shouldn't be implicated in your husband's
misconduct."

Once Mr. Billingsley went over the documents and
provided her copies, he walked her to the back exit.

"Thank you again for agreeing to meet so early." She
hitched her purse onto her shoulder after fishing out her
keys.

"I understand your need for discretion in this situation. You have my card. Don't hesitate to call if any more
reporters show up."

"I will. Thank you again." Her careful smile detoured into a frown as she stepped outside and into the thick blanket of fog that looked as heavy as her thoughts. A cursory glance around found no reporters or photographers lurking, so she hurried over and loaded up into the SUV. Thankfully, it had been purchased outright with cash.

At least it won't disappear into thin air like my marriage, my career, my money, and my dignity . . .

Sophia rotated her neck, hoping to get rid of some of the pressure, and cranked the SUV. Before she could back out, the Bless This Mess van blocked her in.

"Err! Not today, Opal," she mumbled and refrained from beating her head against the steering wheel.

Opal wrenched the passenger door open. "Hey, chick!"

Sophia stared at her blankly, not feeling up for pleasantries. "Are you following me?"

"No, silly. I knew you had an appointment." Opal leaned inside.

"Well, I did and now it's done, so—"

"I have an appointment too. I need you and Jo to go with me. She's already in the van, so hurry up." Opal snapped her fingers.

The only appointment Sophia wanted to be a part of included her bed with the curtains drawn tight. It was Monday, after all. Yet it looked like she wouldn't be getting her wish. "I can follow you."

"No, no, no. Just hop in with us. That'll give us some Sand Queens time."

Sophia heaved a frustrated sigh, knowing her friend wasn't going to back down. "As long as you have me back here within an hour."

"We should be able to make that happen." Opal closed the passenger door and skipped back to her van.

Sophia gathered her purse and looked heavenward. "Please, Lord, give me strength."

Ten minutes later, Sophia decided God wasn't in the strength-giving mood.

"No." Sophia said the one word with enough terseness that the subject should have been closed, but Opal patiently stood by the open van door and tried coaxing her out.

"But this is all good things. Promise." She tugged Sophia's arm.

Sophia yanked her arm free and remained seated. "Opal Cole, you're up to something."

"Just come inside." Opal gestured toward the side entrance to Carolina Pediatrics.

"But Weston Sawyer will be in there." Just saying his name made a wave of humiliation ripple over Sophia's already-sensitive nerves.

"Of course. He *is* the doctor." Opal laced her fingers with Sophia's and finally got her out of the van and to the building entrance.

Agnes Nelson let them in and then locked the door behind them. That was when Sophia realized the place wasn't even open yet. Before she could voice her concerns, Agnes said, "If it isn't the lovely Sand Queens." The older lady gave each one a hug and then led them to her office. "Lincoln and August are already inside. Go ahead in and I'll be right back."

Sophia caught Josie's eye and mouthed, "What's going on?"

Josie shrugged, looking just as confused as she felt. "Maybe there's another remodel job and they need our help. It's the only thing I can come up with."

"Maybe," Sophia repeated as they walked inside.

"Yo, ladies," August welcomed on a yawn. He looked

right comfy behind Agnes's desk with his feet propped on the corner and his hands laced behind his head.

Lincoln looked too big for the guest chair in front of the desk. He reached out and pulled Opal onto his lap. She giggled as he wrapped his arms around her.

Sophia would probably have offered an *aww* over the romantic gesture if she were in a better mood. Instead, she stayed tight-lipped and stood by the wall.

Wes stepped inside with a file tucked underneath his arm and a friendly smile gracing his face. In a tailored charcoal suit and navy tie, the man was what her aunt Matilda would call a *GQ* cover model. He caught Sophia staring. His lips briefly kicked up on one side before he moved his attention to Lincoln and Opal. "Shall I?" he spoke in that smooth baritone.

"Please." Lincoln beamed, and that was saying something for the normally brooding man.

"It's truly an honor that you've appointed me to be Baby Cole's pediatrician. I look forward to meeting him or her early next year." Wes slid those warm hazel eyes around the room, watching his words sink in.

Sophia gasped, Josie burst into tears, and Opal giggled.

August knocked a tissue box off the desk as his feet hit the floor with a heavy thud. He let out a rumbly whoop before jumping clear over the desk to slap Lincoln on the shoulder and kiss Opal's cheek.

Sophia rolled her eyes, thinking August Bradford was just too cute for his own good.

"We're two months along," Opal supplied as Lincoln caressed her flat tummy.

Wes shook Lincoln's hand and then Opal's before leaving the group of friends to celebrate.

As the shock wore off, pure joy replaced it, sending

happy tears flooding Sophia's eyes. "This is awesome! Best news ever! I'm finally going to be an aunt!" She wrapped her arms around Josie, and the two of them squealed like schoolgirls, jumping up and down. After they concluded their happy dance, the women offered congratulatory hugs to Opal and Lincoln.

The celebration stretched out as the couple shared the due date and other details. They'd told their family the prior weekend at a cookout but wanted to share the news with the three friends in a private manner.

Sophia was already planning the baby shower when Agnes stepped inside the office and cleared her throat. "Sophia, may I have a word with you?"

"Umm . . ." Sophia cut Opal a look, knowing the redhead would sneak in some meddling somehow. "Yes, ma'am."

Everyone exited, but not before bestowing a gamut of silent messages. Josie gave her a sympathetic smile and halfhearted shrug, Opal gave her a spirited wink and thumbs-up, and Lincoln gave her a pointed look that said she better do whatever it was that she was about to be asked to do and not screw it up. August simply offered her a supportive fist bump. Sophia bumped her tiny fist to his paint-stained one while glaring at the other three, who seemed to be in on Opal's meddling.

Once the door was closed, Agnes took the seat beside Sophia and cut to the chase. "Honey, I need to retire. And from what Opal has shared with me in confidence, you need a job." She held her hand up to halt the words about to spew from Sophia. "Now hear me out. This job comes with reasonable hours, benefits, and an impressive salary. It's exactly what a single mom such as yourself needs. I can't leave Wes without properly filling my position. Not just any ole body will do. I need *you*."

Sophia knew there was no choice but to get a job now that Ty up and ruined things. The severance package would maybe keep her afloat two more months at best. But as she glanced around Agnes's quaint office, she just wasn't sure this was the best choice for her.

"Wes . . . and I . . . we don't get along." Her thumb swept underneath her ring finger as she contemplated the offer.

Agnes chuckled. "Honey, do you think Doc and I have always gotten along while working these past forty years together?" She leaned closer and whispered, "I even got into a little tiff just last week with Wes. He thought his way was better than mine, but we had ourselves a come-to-Jesus meeting and he was seeing it my way by the end of it." The older lady winked with a good bit of spunk.

Sophia remained serious. "I really do need a job."

"Then it's settled." Agnes glanced at her watch. "We have time to speak with him before the doors open."

Fifteen minutes later, Sophia and Agnes sat opposite Wes in his office. His fingers steepled in front of him, he listened in silence until the office manager concluded her spiel on why Sophia's PR background and MBA made her more than qualified for the position.

Wes looked from Agnes to Sophia and then back to Agnes. "No."

Both women were jolted.

Sophia's face heated at record speed as the sting of his rejection hit her eyes and nose.

"Why on earth are you saying no?" Agnes clucked her tongue, looking like she was ready to grab him by the ear and place his nose in the corner until he gave the correct answer.

Sniffing back the tears, Sophia wondered just how

many more blows she could take before giving up completely. She wanted to beg him to give her a break, to overlook the mess of a woman she'd been lately. To assure Wes that the woman he'd met wasn't her, but she could barely breathe, let alone speak. Another clue she wasn't her normal self.

"Ms. Prescott caused a scene and disrespected me in front of several patients. She's also gone on social media to discredit me as a doctor. From what I've gathered, she has a substantial following, and you know as well as I do, Agnes, we've received more than a handful of phone calls about it. I've never been questioned more about my credibility as a doctor in my entire career as I have since arriving here."

Sophia cringed, wondering how he even knew about the social media incident and how it had gotten so blown out of proportion. "I only endorsed another pediatrician when a new mother on Facebook asked for recommendations. Your name was never mentioned." Mortified, she watched as he responded by shaking his head.

"I just don't believe Carolina Pediatrics is the right place for you, Ms. Prescott. Best of luck finding employment elsewhere." Wes gave Sophia a curt nod before moving his attention to his computer screen, effectively dismissing her.

Agnes sucked her teeth and cast him a withering look. "I have a good mind to walk out on your prickly behind. Wait until Doc gets wind of this." She waggled a finger at him as she led Sophia out of the office.

Humiliation and indignation followed Sophia out like one of those thunderclouds that follow crestfallen cartoon characters. She loaded up in the back of Opal's van and glared out the window.

"When do you start?" Opal asked as she drove out of the parking lot.

"I don't."

Josie turned in the passenger seat and gaped at her in disbelief. "Why not?"

"Because Dr. Stuck-Up refused to hire me."

"That's absolutely ridiculous. What was his reason?" Opal asked, flipping the turn signal on.

"When I brought Collin in that first week, he claims I caused a scene, and he somehow got wind of the twisted version of that Facebook post." Sophia groaned and swiped her hands down her face. "Sounds like the town gossips have added a good bit to it, and so I really don't blame him for not wanting to work with me."

"I warned you," Opal mumbled, sending Sophia a pointed look in the rearview mirror.

Silence took over as Opal drove on, but Sophia could tell the redhead's mind was already at work. She confirmed it after another mile down the road when a knowing smile lit her face. "That's an easy fix. All you have to do is share a fluffy post on how great Carolina Pediatrics is and how you trust Dr. Sawyer to care for your son. Let the gossipers blow that up and you'll be sitting pretty in Agnes's office by the end of the week. No way can that turn into a negative."

Sophia considered the suggestion, and it really wasn't a bad idea. "I can probably do that," she mumbled, already working on a hook for the post.

"Sophia, my truck is at the diner. Can you give me a ride over there?" Josie asked as Opal pulled back up at the attorney's office.

"Sure." The sun was quickly burning off the fog and upping the brightness factor by a million. Sophia squinted and rummaged around her bag for her keys and a pair of sunglasses.

"I have a few projects to work on, so I better head over to the store. I'll catch you gals later," Opal said, that ever-present smile somehow making her more radiant than normal.

They exchanged another round of heartfelt congratulations and hugs with Opal before parting ways.

As Sophia headed toward Driftwood Diner, she stole a quick peek at Josie before looking back to the road. "So, umm . . . our Opal is going to be a mommy. *Wow.*"

Josie snickered. "I can hardly believe it."

"I know, right?" Sophia shook her head and grinned. "I just worry what she'll try dressing the poor baby in."

Josie laughed. "We'll have to keep her in check with the wardrobe choices."

Sophia rolled to a stop at a red light. She glanced at Josie as her curiosity got the better of her. "You and August aren't ready to start a family?"

"Eventually, sure, but right now the camp and art projects are our babies. The camp has become so popular that August and Carter are working on adding a spring and fall session next year." Josie reached over and squeezed Sophia's arm. "I know what you're getting at, and it's sweet of you. We're not even trying yet. And I am over the moon for Opal."

Sophia drove on and smiled. Josie didn't have a jealous bone in her body, but that didn't stop Sophia from wanting to be certain her friend was okay about it. "I can't wait to spoil her baby like she does Collin. Payback time."

The plan was to drop Josie off and make her getaway, but Josie roped Sophia into having breakfast with her. Even though an appetite had been something lost to her, along with everything else in the past year, she managed picking around a plate of grits and eggs until Josie finished hers and had to leave.

The ride back to the condo was quiet with her mind whirling around Opal's great news and Wes's rejection. She managed to make it to her room and close the curtains before her phone began to ring. An unfamiliar number flashed across the screen.

"Hello?" she answered tentatively while slipping her feet out of the sensible heels.

"Babe." The one word was all it took to cause her heart to skip a beat and her stomach to flutter.

She sat on the edge of the bed and clutched her stomach with her free hand, hating that he still had such a profound effect on her. "Ty?"

"Yeah, babe." The deep timbre of his voice wove through the phone. "This is my new number. Be sure to save it, okay?"

Swallowing, she managed a frail "Okay."

"Look, you already heard about the sh—er, crap that just went down. Only thing you need to know right now is that the mess is my idiot manager's and the accountant's fault. Not mine. But I'm working on getting it all sorted." There was some shuffling in the background, sounding like he was busy doing something, as always. "So sit tight and in the meantime let your parents take care of you and Collin."

That was supposed to be your job, as promised in your vows, she thought as her eyes began to sting.

"I'll pay them back."

Clearing her throat, she whispered, "Ty, I'm no longer your responsibility."

"That doesn't change the fact that I want you to be . . . I've been attending the anger management classes and counseling sessions. All for you." He sighed heavily into the phone and muttered a few choice words. "Babe, I love you. Nothing's changed that either."

When Ty loved her, she couldn't ask for a better husband. He practically worshiped her. But when he allowed his demons free, he was the worst.

Sophia needed to redirect her thoughts before his bogus sweetness reeled her in. The loneliness was unbearable, so it would be too easy to give in to it. She pictured her baby boy with the sadness in his eyes. "Collin misses you."

Ty sighed again. "I miss you both. I'll get out there soon. Promise."

"Okay," she muttered, knowing it was probably another empty promise.

Voices echoed in the background. "I'll be there in a minute," Ty called out. "Look, babe, I have to head to practice. Give little man a hug for me."

As the phone disconnected, the tears freed right along with a guttural sob. Each time she heard from Ty, it was like taking a knife to her heart all over again. Even though she wouldn't say it to him, she still loved her ex-husband and had no clue as to how to stop.

Ty was no longer allowed to physically hurt her, but Sophia still ached all over as if the last beating were still fresh on her bruised body. With trembling hands, she managed to shrug out of her jacket and pants before climbing into bed. Cocooned under the blanket, the world darkened and took with it the thread of strength she was holding on to. Ty was supposed to be her strength, her partner. There to lean on and provide comfort. Yet she was cowering in a bed that wasn't their marriage bed, still trying to recover from the pain he'd carelessly inflicted. Alone and scared with nothing but ruined promises.

Sophia blinked back tears as the night of the team

party during the last year of their marriage invaded her thoughts. . . .

Sophia felt like an outsider, invited only out of obligation. She took special care to dress in her trophy-wife uniform of formfitting cocktail dress and mile-high stilettos with enough flashy diamonds to blind someone, even going as far as having her hair and makeup professionally done. She should have fit in quite well with the glamorous evening, but as she navigated the thick crowd celebrating in a rather raucous manner, she could hardly suppress the urge to strip the shoes from her feet and make a run for it. Life had grown too loud, and her heart was homesick for the quieter life back home in Sunset Cove, South Carolina.

"Darling, you look gorgeous tonight. Simply *fabulous*. The indigo blue really is your color," Ty's mother complimented, scrutinizing Sophia head to toe. "It really sets off the teal in your eyes."

"Thank you, Helen. It's the team color." Sophia tugged at the hem of the slinky dress, feeling anything but fabulous. She scanned the crowd and caught a glimpse of a tall blonde leading an obviously cooperative Ty out of the room. "Excuse me."

Mrs. Prescott tried to distract Sophia, but she'd looked the other way for far too long. She managed to get away from the clingy woman and scooted through the crowd. Hands shaking, she pushed through the door and on down the hall. Giggles and groans floated her way from a side corridor. Her heart begged her to turn back and leave well enough alone, but Sophia knew it was time to face her husband's infidelity head-on.

Swallowing the lump in her throat, Sophia took a deep breath and demanded, "Get your lips off my husband."

The blonde jumped and then tumbled sideways, but Ty caught her as he shot Sophia a warning look. "Mind your own business, Sophia."

"I'm pretty sure this *is* my business." Her voice came out much calmer than she felt as she watched the woman hang her head and try to scurry past her. "It's a little too late to be ashamed of fooling around with a married man now, honey." Sophia's tart comment had the woman setting off in a sprint, nearly tumbling a few times in her heels.

"It was just a friendly kiss . . ." Ty's innocent facade held in place until the blonde was good and gone before it slipped to reveal the darker version lurking just below his surface. The gold flecks in his brown eyes grew into a raging fire as his nostrils flared. "It's my night, and you're ruining it with this bitter-wife act." Ty gritted the words through clenched teeth as his massive hand reached out and gripped Sophia's upper arm, his fingers pinching into her flesh.

"You're hurting me, Ty. . . . You said . . . you said you wouldn't again." She blinked back the tears, refusing to give him the satisfaction.

He dropped his hand as if her skin singed him, and he stalked out of the hall and away with the last sliver of dignity Sophia had been carefully hanging on to.

6

Quietness pressed down around him as Wes stared at the mountain of paperwork on his desk Wednesday afternoon. Sure, it was Agnes's job, but he was on her bad side at the moment. He chose to keep his comments to himself and simply told her he'd happily take care of it. She cackled all the way out the door, obviously thinking he couldn't handle it.

Yanking his tie off and unfastening the top button of his dress shirt, Wes slipped on his reading glasses and hunkered down in his chair. He rolled up his sleeves, determined to do what needed to be done.

"I'll show Agnes who's boss." Pep-talking himself for the task at hand, Wes picked up the top file and got down to business.

A few hours later, the mountain had dwindled into a manageable hill and Wes's eyes were blurring. He set the pen down, pulled off his readers, and massaged his temples. His stomach let out a mean growl, an irritating reminder that he'd skipped lunch and would be skipping supper also if he wanted to prove a point to his stubborn office manager.

After a litany of growls vibrated through him, Wes decided to go plunder Agnes's snack drawer. She'd shown it to him on the first day and said he could help himself.

That offer had probably been retracted as of Monday, but he was going to help himself anyway. As he stood to stretch his sore back, the door flew open and banged against the wall with such exuberant force his entire body jolted.

"Have you gone pure fool?" Doc bellowed, his white tufts vibrating with rage.

"I don't believe so, sir." Wes had seen that wild-eyed look before, so he readied himself for the lecture that was about to commence.

"You ain't supposed to look a gift horse in the mouth." Doc trudged over and shooed Wes out of the way so he could take his chair.

"I haven't seen a horse since arriving in Sunset Cove." Wes walked around to the other side of the desk but remained standing.

"Don't get smart with me, kid." Doc picked up the top sheet of the open file and tsked at it before releasing it to float back into the pile. He crossed his arms and let out a harrumph. "That young lady would be an asset to this office, yet you turned her away faster than you would a door-to-door salesman."

"I don't think Ms. Prescott is suited—"

"That dog won't hunt, kid." Doc leveled a look at him. "My wife says I ain't allowed back into my own bed until I talk some sense into you." He pointed toward the files in disgust. "But I'm thinking you're a lost cause."

Wes mirrored Doc, crossing his arms and scowling. "I'm not making excuses. And this wouldn't even be an issue if you'd switched over to computerized record keeping ages ago, like the rest of the world."

"If you'd hire that perfectly capable woman, she'd square away these files into some fancy computerized hogwash for you in a heartbeat."

"Ms. Prescott's disrespecting me and publicly questioning my credibility are both valid reasons not to hire her."

"You've gone and went off with your pistol half-cocked again. How many times have I told you not to be so foolish?"

"But—"

"Kid, I've heard what happened here in the office." Doc leaned back in the chair and grew solemn. "Sophia has had her world fall down on her in the past year. Now I know that's neither here nor there, but she came in here a distraught mother needing her child's physician to give her some reassurance her baby was okay. She didn't need snide judgments cast on her over her parenting skills. She needed you to do your job and nothing more."

When Wes didn't comment, Doc pressed on.

"I know you don't do the social media stuff. I don't either, but I had enough wits about me to ask my daughter to pull up Sophia's page so I could see the post myself. All the woman did was suggest the pediatric office on the other side of the waterway. Good doctors over there, if you want my opinion."

When it was all laid out like that, Wes felt right foolish for getting so upset over it. "You know I came here because I promised . . . but I've never wanted to break a promise so bad in all my life." He shoved his hands into his pockets and walked over to the window, noticing for the first time that a heavy rain was coming down. He peered over his shoulder and met Doc's dark eyes. "In return, you promised I'd be left alone. You swore I'd have peace and quiet."

"Wes, son . . ." Doc slowly shook his head. "You gotta get on with living, and sometimes that can be a bit unruly."

"So I'm supposed to hire her and let in unwanted unruliness?"

"Won't be like that as long as you don't allow it."

"I haven't had any control over matters since arriving." Wes released a pithy snort and leaned against the windowsill. "Can I get a refund?"

"You don't want that," Doc commented as Wes's stomach let loose another growl. "But I can buy you supper and then you can sit with me during Bible study tonight, being as I'm in the doghouse with my wife because of you."

It sounded more like Wes was doing Doc the favor, but he was too hungry to protest. He walked over and gathered the stack of files and his briefcase, determined to finish the paperwork before Agnes arrived the next morning. *Maybe even tie it sweetly with a bow . . .*

The men gorged themselves on flounder sandwiches and hush puppies at Sunset Seafood House before heading over to Sunset Cove First Baptist. They entered the cozy sanctuary and were met up with friendly greetings and chatter.

"Come on, let's sit over here." Doc led the way to the left side of the aisle.

With a quick glance around, Wes found Agnes sitting with none other than Sophia Prescott on the right side. Clearly the battle lines had been drawn.

After opening prayer, a short lady, who was about as round as she was tall, led a dozen toddlers to the stage. "Good evenin'. The Mission Friends would like to share a song with y'all before class."

A head full of unruly brown curls caught Wes's attention, sending a smile to his face. Collin spotted him at the same time and began waving.

"Hey, poo!" Collin shouted, interrupting the teacher's little spiel about the class.

Laughter skipped through the congregation, sending the tips of Wes's ears up in flames. *At least he shortened it to only one poo . . .* Collin continued to wave and seemed to have no intention of stopping until Wes acknowledged him, so Wes offered a small wave.

"Now that the greetings are out of the way, we are going to sing 'This Little Light of Mine.' The children have . . ." The teacher yammered on, but Wes tuned her out when he looked over and found a red-faced brunette staring him down.

"Sorry," Sophia mouthed.

Wes shrugged it off and moved his attention back to the group of toddlers just as one in particular scooted down the steps on his bottom. Once Collin reached the last step, he beat a path straight to Wes.

"Collin," the teacher called out to the little boy.

"He my fwiend!" Collin hollered back. He pushed past Doc and climbed into Wes's lap. "My fwiend!"

"Hey, buddy," Wes whispered. "I was hoping to hear you sing."

"You sing wiff me." It was not a request but a command. He scooted back down and began tugging Wes's hand.

Really, the kid gave him no choice, so Wes rose to his feet and allowed Collin to pull him down to the front. He sat on the edge of the stage, well aware that every set of eyes in the sanctuary was fastened on him.

"Good thing I know this song," Wes commented with a self-deprecating smile. A murmur of chuckles followed it. The first two pews seemed to be reserved for the group of old ladies. Their ringleader, Bertie Matthews, caught Wes's attention as she handed out peppermint disks to those around her. Smirking, as she always appeared to be doing, she winked at him over the top of her glasses as if they were in on a secret together.

As the pianist began playing, Wes pretended not to see the wink and chanced a quick glance at Sophia. Still blushing with her eyes rounded, she mouthed again, "Sorry."

Collin stood proudly beside Wes, garbling the verses of the song as only a toddler could do while Wes quietly sang along. He was a good sport about it and even participated in the hand motions, which was basically waggling his index finger back and forth. He assumed it represented a candle.

After the song concluded and the teacher led the children out to go to their class, a boldness with maybe a dash of spite had Wes moving over to the right side of the sanctuary. As he passed by Bertie, the little lady held out a peppermint for him. He thanked her before popping it into his mouth and continued making his way to a certain pew.

"Hello, ladies," Wes greeted quietly as he wedged himself between Agnes and Sophia.

"I'm surprised to see you tonight. Figured you'd still be working," Agnes whispered as the pastor went over a few announcements.

Wes stretched an arm along the back of the pew behind her. "That paperwork will be complete and waiting on your desk in the morning, ma'am." He leaned a little closer just to annoy her. "You're welcome."

Agnes clucked her tongue and scooted away from him. For a seventy-three-year-old, she sure was spunky.

"I'd like to share with you about a special gift from God," the pastor said. "One that we as Christians should take advantage of and guard with our hearts. It's the gift of hope." He flipped through his Bible. "Romans 12:12 says, 'Be joyful in hope, patient in affliction, faithful in prayer.' After reading this, I had to read it again." The elderly man paced the stage, looking around at the congregation. "In the same verse of hope, affliction is mentioned. It's a reminder that, yes, affliction will come, but no, we are not defeated. We have a hope in our Savior. Don't let anything steal the joy in that."

The pews were aligned at an angle, which put Sophia in Wes's periphery for the entire service. While he listened to the pastor offer words of encouragement about over-coming affliction and finding joy in hope, he watched Sophia quietly weep. As tears slid down her hollowed cheeks, he wanted to reach over, protectively tuck her into his side and give her some form of comfort, but it was not his place to offer any of that. Instead, he clasped his hands together in his lap to prevent himself from reach-ing out to her.

"Let us pray," the pastor said, sending all heads to bow and eyes to close.

Wes sensed her movement to his left, and when the pastor said *amen*, he opened his eyes and found the spot beside him empty. *It's probably for the best. You have no business trying to comfort anyone.*

"I *hope* this means you're reconsidering your hasty decision on Monday," Agnes said, drawing Wes's atten-tion away from the empty spot.

"I'm glad you have hope, Agnes. It's a good thing." He hitched a thumb in his mentor's direction. "And I *hope* you allow Doc back into his bed tonight."

7

Festivals along the Grand Strand always attracted a considerable crowd. Tourists as well as locals were drawn to the quaintness provided by regional foods, entertainment, contests, games and prizes, and craft vendors. The Fish and Grits Festival in Sunset Cove was no exception. On this balmy summer evening, the beach and boardwalk were lined with vendors and surrounded by onlookers.

Opal hooked her arm around Sophia's and maneuvered them over to a popcorn stand. "I just love those big ole copper kettles they cook it up in. You reckon I can talk Linc into buying me one?"

Sophia snickered. "Honey, if you asked that big lug to buy you the moon, he'd be on the phone with NASA to figure out how to make it happen."

Opal giggled. "Ooh, look at all the choices."

The vendor offered the spirited redhead a sample of each flavor—salty sweet, white cheddar, cocoa, jalapeño, and caramel. He offered Sophia samples as well, but she politely declined.

The appealing scent of burnt sugar and popcorn perfumed the air but gave her no desire to eat. Her stomach had remained in knots since the incident at the grocery store. Ty's phone call and Wes's refusal to hire her had only made it worse.

"Okay, I need a bag of the white cheddar and the caramel . . . No, wait. Is there any way you could mix all the flavors into one bag?"

Sophia turned her attention back to Opal and wrinkled her nose. "All mixed together?"

"Sure. Sounds yummy, doesn't it?" Opal smiled at the vendor, looking hopeful.

"Sorry, but she's pregnant," Sophia interjected, although Opal's weird taste buds came naturally and had nothing to do with hormone changes.

It softened the man to the idea, and within minutes he was handing over a mix of the popcorn. Opal dug in the pocket of her long floppy skirt, produced a five-dollar bill, and paid before they moved on to a row of jewelry artisans.

Sophia scanned the crowd and got at least her fifth glimpse of Wes that day. Earlier, he'd been trapped at the Chamber of Commerce tent, giving out balloons. Later in the day, he'd been handing out wellness pamphlets and pens at the pediatric health booth. After that, she'd seen him helping children with coloring pages at the church tent. Collin was with her then, and it was all she could do to pull the little guy away from Wes. And each time she spotted Wes, the man was surrounded by different groups of women.

"Oh, my goodness. What has Agnes roped poor Wes into doing this evening?" Opal giggled and pointed over to where Sophia's attention was already snagged. They watched Wes dish fried flounder and grits onto Styrofoam plates at the fire and rescue squad's booth.

"What do you mean about Agnes?" Sophia questioned, watching as he handed over another plate. He wore a rescue-squad ball cap now and should have worn one earlier by the looks of his sunburnt cheeks and nose. It matched the dark-navy tee they must have given him. Snickering, she recalled the various tees he'd worn throughout the day with his perfectly pressed khaki shorts and Sperry boat shoes.

"Ever since he refused to hire you on Monday, she's divvied out a world of pain and aggravation on the poor guy. He's been doing her paperwork and anything else she decides he needs to do to teach him a lesson. Said he tried getting smart with her over the paperwork and so now she's poured her wrath out on him full force. She's the one who signed him up to work so many events today."

"That woman is a piece of work. . . . How do you know all this anyway? Have you been hanging out with those women from the Knitting Club? I warned you about those gossipers." Sophia was watching Wes fill another plate as he lifted his head and caught her. The glare he pierced her with certainly didn't look like he was changing his mind about hiring her. She turned away and pulled Opal out of his line of sight.

"No, silly. I heard it straight from the horse's mouth. Agnes and I are like this." Opal held up two fingers and touched them together.

"Since when?" Sophia looked at her dubiously.

"Since way back." Opal flicked her wrist. "If you ask me, she's doing it so he'll see how much easier life would be if he'd go ahead and allow her to retire in peace." She shoveled in a handful of popcorn and chewed thoughtfully before adding, "She keeps this up and he'll be at your door on his hands and knees *begging* you to work for him."

Sophia couldn't stop herself from glancing over her shoulder. Wes was swamped. Plate after plate he filled and handed out. She turned back around. "You go ahead and head over to Josie and August's tent. I'll meet you there later."

"Where are you going?" Opal asked before Sophia made much headway through the crowd.

"I feel responsible for Agnes treating Wes this way. The least I can do is help him serve plates."

"That's a great idea. I'll catch up with you later." There was laughter in Opal's voice, but Sophia paid it no mind. She was on a mission and needed to focus on it.

Apparently the Facebook posts Sophia had created this week weren't enough to change his mind about her. She'd put several together, giving Carolina Pediatrics high accolades. Even went as far as putting together a pro-file post to welcome Dr. Weston Sawyer to Sunset Cove. She'd included a small yet impressive bio and a picture she copied from a medical journal he'd been featured in. The picture was four years old, but the man appeared just as clean-cut handsome as he did now.

Taking a fortifying breath of the salty air, Sophia made a beeline to the fire chief. "Hey, Billy. Can I give you guys a hand?"

Billy handed over the money-collecting duties to another firemen and gave Sophia his full attention. "Sure thing, sweetheart. You won't ever hear us turning down help from a beautiful lady." He winked and pointed to where a small portable sink was stationed near the rear of the tent.

She quickly washed her hands and eased her way into the service line right beside Wes. She took over placing golden-brown fillets of fish on top of the dollop of grits he dished onto the plates. He continued working without acknowledging her, but each time their elbows touched, she caught sight of the muscle in his jaw flexing.

As the supper rush dwindled, Wes pulled his apron off and spoke for the first time in the last hour. "Billy, looks like you men can handle it from here." He shook the chief's hand and then returned to Sophia and whispered, "We need to have a talk. Now."

Her stomach did a somersault as if she were being called into the principal's office for something she hadn't done. Just like the time Opal thought it would be cute to rearrange their youth group's room, yet Sophia was blamed for it.

"Umm . . . I thought I'd stay and help a little longer." She picked up another plate, but he yanked it out of her hand and ignored her attempt at begging off.

Wes laced his fingers with hers, stalked off past the sand dunes, and didn't slow until they were far enough down the beach for the music and lights of the festival to fade. He let go of her hand and pivoted around to face her.

"What do I have to do to get you to leave me the heck alone?" Wes tossed his hands in the air.

"I've not bothered you." Sophia took a step back. She had learned the hard way not to stay within reach of an angry man.

"No?" Wes yanked the hat off just to shove it down on his head again before glaring at her from underneath the brim. He would have looked boyish and downright cute had it not been for the severity of that scowl. "This past week has been a nightmare!"

"I had nothing to do with how Agnes treated you this week."

"No, but you did enough with those ridiculous media posts. Please, for the love of all good things, do not put anything else up about me." His brows furrowed as he loomed over her.

"But it was nothing but positive accolades about you." The wind whipped her hair around, so she pushed it out of her face and decided to put a little more space between them.

"That 'bio' read like a singles ad for a dating website. You do have a way with words, Ms. Prescott. The only thing it garnered was a plethora of single moms worrying me slap crazy. My recycle bin at work is filled with phone numbers." Wes paced a tight circle and pinched the bridge of his sunburnt nose. Flinching, he dropped his hand and stopped short. "I'm a professional. And you've made a mockery of me and my practice."

Sophia sucked in a disjointed breath and placed a palm over her heart. "That wasn't my intention. You have to believe I was only trying to right my wrongs." She burst into tears. "All I do is try my best, but all I do is fail!" A sob rushed out as she plopped down in the sand.

"Why don't you take down your posts and just leave me alone and we can forget this entire mess." He moved to stand in front of her, but she looked no further up than his tanned knees.

Sophia tried to dry it up but only produced another hiccuping round of sobs. "I need a job is why."

Wes snorted like what she said was absurd. "Why? Because you're bored?"

Sophia snorted back but wished she hadn't. Using the back of her hand to wipe underneath her nose, she muttered, "No. I need a job because I'm broke and have a child to support all on my own."

Wes grew still and planted his hands on his lean hips. "But what about your ex—?"

"But nothing." She knew where that was headed. "Do you not watch the news? Or read your Yahoo! headlines?"

"I don't believe in TV."

"Of course you don't, Dr. Perfect. If you did, you'd know my ex is being investigated for tax fraud. Our accounts have been frozen." She sniffed and wiped her nose again. "So boredom is the least of my problems. I have an MBA and a stellar résumé, but I'm basically flat broke."

Wes let out a long sigh as he sat beside her. "Seems we have a few problems that need sorting."

"Ya think?" Sophia fixed her watery gaze on the moonlit waves. Such a gorgeous night for such a miserable conversation.

Wes drew his knees up and folded his arms around them. "Let's think this through."

They remained silent, watching the waves roll in, until she said, "I'm sorry. I have no idea how to fix the mess with the women hounding you, but . . . you could turn it into a good thing and maybe find a woman to share your free time with." Out of the corner of her eye, she noticed him shaking his head.

"I'm still in love with my wife. The fact that she's dead doesn't change how I feel about her. I have no desire to give someone else my heart when it still belongs to Claire."

Ty's handsome face with his aw-shucks grin flashed before Sophia's eyes, causing her chest to tighten. "I can understand that, to an extent. The part about not wanting to give your heart to another." She scooped up a handful of sand and let it funnel through her fingers. "Seems the divorce papers didn't inform my heart. I know I'm not supposed to love my ex. Well, I still love the man I fell in love with. Certainly not the man he turned out to be."

The final breaking point shoved its way to the front of her thoughts, a blaring reminder of how wrong she'd been about Ty. Sophia had flown out to California, where Ty was working on a sports apparel ad, to try rekindling their relationship. It seemed like a perfect idea at the time. Looking back now, Sophia knew she never should have gotten on that plane to go surprise him. She never should have walked through that hotel suite to confront the betrayal she heard coming from the bedroom. She never should have gotten back on that plane with more bruises than she could cover up. She never should have hoped the fissures of their broken marriage would some-how mend themselves.

Another spell of silence blanketed them as the litany of *never should have*s kept hounding her. Sophia watched the lights of a ship off in the distance, wondering what it would feel like to be on it, sailing away from all her problems.

Finally, when she was sick of dwelling on her own issues, she redirected her attention to the silent man sitting beside her who seemed just as lost in the world as she felt. "Wes, I'm really sorry about your wife and child. Opal said—"

"I don't want your platitudes. I've already heard enough of them to make a living writing sympathy cards," he snapped, cutting off any sympathy she was ready to impart.

"Sorry," she snapped back before muttering under her breath, "Jerk."

They both grew quiet again, the only gesture they seemed comfortable sharing with each other.

The music halted as an announcement echoed through the speakers at the festival. "Last call for the Ferris wheel."

Sophia had ridden the Ferris wheel a minimum of four times with Collin earlier in the day. Even though the thrill of the ride was long gone, she'd rather be on it at the moment instead of sitting in the sand with her haughty company.

"Perhaps we can make a deal of some sort." Wes dropped his arms and angled to face her. "I'll agree to hire you under one—no, two conditions."

"What are the conditions?" Sophia asked hesitantly.

Wes gave her a brief once-over. "You have to date me, for one. And you also have to promise you'll start eating."

She replayed what he'd just said in her head, trying to rearrange the words until it made some sense, but it kept on sounding preposterous. "Come again?"

"Not really date me, just fake date. It would get those women to leave me alone."

"I just don't—"

"It's your fault all those women are chasing after me in the first place. I think it's your responsibility to put a stop to it." Wes tapped the side of her leg. "What better way than to take me off the market?"

Sophia looked at him hard, trying to find tease in his expression, but only found seriousness wrapped in titanium. "I don't want to date anyone!"

"That's my point. Neither do I . . . but we can work this in both our favor. You're a beautiful single woman, so surely this will help you keep unwanted attention from other men away."

Sophia shook her head, totally taken aback by the strange conversation. Truth be told, she had a few men hanging around her since moving back, but she had no desire to jump into dating anytime soon. Thinking it over, she asked, "What is fake dating?"

"I'm not sure. Never done this before." Wes rubbed his jaw and scanned the beach as if it would reveal an answer. "We'll have to make it up as we go along. I'm guessing we should go out to dinner or something once a week and sit together at church so we can be seen in public together."

"That doesn't sound too bad. But what about Collin?"

"What about him?"

"He's already attached to you for some reason." That had completely baffled her, considering she felt totally opposite. "I don't want to confuse him. He's already gone through enough. If . . . if he gets used to having you around, then once we end this fake dating, I fear he'll be brokenhearted."

"We'll have to be careful." Wes sighed heavily. "Honestly, I'm starting to get attached to him too. I've joined the church and we live in the same community, so I don't see why we can't remain buddies no matter what." He released a dry laugh. "Plus, I've already been roped into singing with him again next week."

The singing incident was the cutest thing ever, but she refused to own up to how she felt about Wes doing that for her son. Sophia also wouldn't let that blind her to what was important at the moment. "If you promise not to hurt my baby—because if you do, rabid women chasing after you will be the least of your worries—then we can give this a try. For a while."

"Promise. August and Lincoln already warned me at the deck party to never get on your bad side. They said you like to pinch." He gave her a pointed look. "But you'll have to eat."

"How do you know anything about my eating habits?"

"Agnes. The woman has made me live, eat, and breathe all things Sophia Grace Prescott this week. She mentioned you've stopped eating, but I already knew that just by looking at you. How long has this been going on?"

Sophia tried conjuring up a believable laugh, but it creaked like a rusty gate. "Well, highly publicized scandals have been proven to be the most effective diet program out there. Especially when you mix in adultery and domestic abuse. It's all the rage right now." She looked over, thinking she'd find a smirk on his face, but he remained fixed in seriousness.

Wes placed his warm hand on her chilled arm, and his

thumb began drawing a comforting circle on her wrist. "Sophia—"

She dropped her gaze to the sand as tears began to well up again. "I . . . My stomach hurts all the time ever since . . . Eating isn't appealing."

"Describe the pain," Wes said, easily slipping into doctor mode.

She moved her free hand to her chest and pressed her palm there. "It's an ache that sits right here." Her hand moved to rest on her concave belly. "And it escalates here."

Sympathy crossed his face as Wes slowly nodded. "I'm an expert on that type of pain. And I know a few remedies. We'll work on it."

"Wes, I don't want your pity any more than you want mine."

He pushed out another sigh and followed it with a slower nod. "We'll also work on not pitying each other, okay?"

Sophia agreed, even though she didn't have much confidence in finding a way to alleviate the pain, short of a rewind button to take her back to when her marriage was glorious, her career successful, and her baby boy happy.

8

Weston Sawyer had always prided himself on making sound decisions with levelheaded logic, but he was beginning to think Sunset Cove was dumbing him down somehow. Was it too many carbs? Fried seafood? Was the salt water slipping into his drinking water?

No, he wasn't that dumb. He knew the blame was on Sophia Prescott. The agreement on the beach about working together and the dating scheme had seemed like a win-win, but once he arrived home, the prospect of spending a large amount of time with her hit him like a ton of bricks. He hadn't taken that into consideration. The feisty brunette was annoying at best, and he had come to crave his solitude.

Perhaps Doc had a point about him always going off with his pistol half-cocked, because he certainly hadn't thought this proposal all the way through. Now, on the way to work, his mind wouldn't settle on a solution for his idiocy. The only idea that was even reasonable was figuring out how to have her work part-time. Sure, he would have to handle some of the paperwork himself, but Agnes already had him doing a chunk of it now.

"What have I done?" Wes mumbled as he pulled into the parking lot and found Sophia's silver SUV in his spot. The one extravagant request he had when agreeing to take over the practice was that a reserved spot would be appointed in the back lot, so his BMW sports coupe would be safely tucked away from any dangers of dents and dings.

Agnes had clucked her tongue at his request and called it frivolous until Doc warned her off. Afterward, she went out of her way to make it happen, going as far as having signs made to let people know the lot was private. Another sign with his name on it was posted in front of his parking space.

Evidently Doc had filled her in on why the car was so precious to him. Claire had presented it to him the day he and his team of researchers had a breakthrough in an experimental treatment. Hours upon hours of work had gone into it. His team worked assiduously to keep their patients alive, so it was a day to celebrate when a four-year-old's scan came back clean after the last-resort treatment had been completed.

It was the last gift she was ever to give him.

A horn beeped behind him. Wes blinked back to the less appealing present, noticing he'd stopped in the middle of the driveway. The nurse was waiting to pull in. He offered a rueful wave and drove over to the offending SUV, parking directly behind it to block her in and make a point.

Wes let himself in through the side door and prepared a speech to inform Miss Priss about how things were going to work around *his* office. He just knew the two women were meeting early to share a good ole laugh at his expense. He'd set the both of them straight.

Voices floated down the hallway from Agnes's office. ". . . appreciate what you were trying to do for me, but that was no way to treat Dr. Sawyer."

His stride slowed. Sophia was in there taking up for him. He pressed a palm to the wall to help steady his

composure. He'd been alone in this battle of life for the
past three and a half years, maneuvering it with the sole
purpose to just survive. His family begged to be on his
team and to be there through the rougher patches of grief,
but Wes refused. The place he dwelled after losing Claire
and Luke was desolate, something he didn't want anyone
he loved to experience. The woman on the other side of
the wall was experienced in bleakness, but he wasn't sure
about wanting her on his team.

"I didn't mean anything by it, sugar. I just thought the
stubborn man could use some hard love to get him to see
the error of his ways."

"I think Wes has lived enough hard to last a lifetime.
I know your heart was in the right place, but we've used
enough vinegar with the poor guy. How about using some
honey?"

Agnes cackled. "Now you sound like Doc!"

Appreciative yet baffled, Wes pushed off the wall and
knocked on Agnes's partially open door before popping
his head in. "Good morning, ladies," he greeted quietly,
glancing at Agnes behind her desk and then at Sophia,
who had a chair pulled up beside the older lady's. "Sophia,
may I have a word with you in my office?"

"Okay." She seemed unsure but stood and followed
him.

Wes gestured toward the small table tucked in the
corner of the room. "Have a seat." He dropped his briefcase by the desk and then carried a small cooler bag over
and handed it to her.

Sophia peeked inside. "What's this?" She looked up at
Wes with her dainty eyebrows pinched together.

Wes settled in the seat opposite her. "It's breakfast."

Hesitantly, she pulled a blue bottle out and read the
label out loud. "PediaSure Grow & Gain?"

"It tastes better than the adult version," Wes said, but she made no move to drink it. He took another bottle out of the bag, removed the cap, and took a generous sip. "Days when I don't have an appetite but know I need fuel, I'll drink the adult version of these."

A small smile played around her lips. "You're doctoring me."

"I don't know any other way, so you'll have to humor me." He pointed to her bottle and was relieved when she drank it. "You look nice today," he commented, surprising them both.

Sophia straightened the collar of her suit jacket and murmured, "Thank you. I was going for business casual. Is this appropriate attire?"

Wes gave the gray pantsuit she'd paired with a coral blouse an admiring perusal. It was tailored and stylish, yet slightly too big on her frail frame, but they were going to work on that. "Agnes wears tracksuits most days, so don't fret over fashion." He leaned closer and whispered, "I much prefer your style over hers. It's classic and very much appropriate . . . but don't tell her I said that."

Sophia smiled, a blush warming her face. "Okay. I won't say a word."

"Good. Now, I'd like to discuss your schedule before giving you back to Agnes . . ."

Ten minutes later, Sophia's face was still flushed but for much different reasons. She stood by the door with the knob in her grip. "I refuse."

"I'm the boss, or have you already forgotten?" He straightened his tie and rotated his jaw, but it did nothing to alleviate some of the tension.

"I'm not a superhero. No way can I do all the responsibilities of an office manager only three days a week. I'm working five, and that's that!"

"Well, our first date is Thursday night. You better be ready by six, and I don't want to hear any lip about it." He jabbed a finger at the fuming spitfire. *There, I told her.*

"Fine!" Sophia slammed the door behind her, making his wall calendar lose its grip on the hook and fall to the floor.

Control. All he needed was some control.

Yanking his suit jacket off and trading it for his lab coat, he resigned himself to the fact that it wasn't happening in this case. Surely he could formulate a way they could fake date without actually seeing each other . . .

Wes scoffed at his own stupidity and hurried to the front to start the day.

● ● ●

The week slid by virtually pain-free. Much to Wes's relief, Agnes and Sophia mostly stayed out of sight. The only time they spent together was first thing in the morning when Wes called Sophia into his office and presented her a cooler bag with the addition of a protein bar or fresh fruit to go along with the PediaSure. Surprisingly she would return the bag each day empty and tell him she could feed herself, but it didn't deter him from packing it. That was a challenge he found quite rewarding, but the one facing him at the moment was making it hard for him to swallow.

Standing outside Sophia's condo, he pulled in a deep breath that was seasoned with fresh-cut grass and some type of flower. Taking a few more in and out, he raised his knuckles to knock, but the door flew open before he managed to follow through.

"Oh, good! You're on time." Sophia shut the door and hurried past him. "Let's get this over with."

He watched her retreating figure wrapped in a long

flowy dress that was similar to the one she'd worn at the party a couple of weeks ago. But this one had so many blue tones it reminded him of a tropical waterfall. With his eyes riveted to the ribbons of blue swishing around from her clipped pace, Wes followed. *Please be in a good mood.*

Wes rushed to open Sophia's door, tucked her inside, and then rounded the front of the car to get in. He glanced over as he started the car. She sat woodenly, staring straight ahead. If the woman didn't loosen up, no one was going to buy their dating act.

Bravely he reached over and tucked a thick lock of hair behind her ear but quickly moved his hand back to his side of the car. "You look lovely, Sophia."

Sophia shot him a jaded look he wasn't expecting to receive. "You don't have to woo me. A deal is a deal."

"I'm not trying to woo you. I was just simply stating the truth."

She twirled her fingers in an onward motion, acting as though he hadn't spoken. "I need to be home within two hours to tuck Collin into bed."

Keeping his comments to himself, Wes drove them over to Sunset Seafood House. It was one of the most popular restaurants in Sunset Cove, which meant plenty of eyes to catch their date. Sophia had voiced her concerns that morning about not being comfortable with lying, but he promised they would do no such thing. All they would do was make public appearances together and allow the townspeople to form their own misguided opinions.

After they were seated and their orders taken, Wes tried to come up with something to say. Small talk was not his forte, but he'd witnessed the feisty brunette manage it with a graceful ease all week at the office. *Sure wish she'd take the lead now . . .*

He shifted in his seat and adjusted his tie as he watched Sophia rearrange the salt and pepper shakers. When she seemed content with their placement, she did the same with the bottles of cocktail sauce and tartar sauce.

"How are you settling into the position this week?" Wes asked when she finally stopped fiddling with the condiments.

"Fine." Sophia looked to her left and offered a small wave.

Wes glanced over and found a young mother with four familiar children, recalling her slipping him her number on Tuesday. He nodded in greeting, then turned back to Sophia. He sure hoped after these public appearances with her the surfeit of unwanted advances would come to an end.

Taking a deep breath, he chose to do something he hardly ever did anymore. After practicing the delivery a few times in his head, he leaned closer and whispered, "Doc says that lady over there keeps giving the milk out for free, so none of the men want to buy the cow."

Sophia's eyes widened and her mouth popped open, and Wes felt a little smug about catching her off guard. He had a pretty good idea that wasn't easily done. She tilted her head back and laughed with not only her mouth but her entire body. It was rich and alluring and Wes could have sworn the exquisite sound alone caused the room to tilt.

"Oh. My. Word. I can't believe something like that just came out of your proper mouth," Sophia said around another chuckle. She dabbed the corners of her eyes with her napkin and caught him staring. "What?"

Left off-kilter by her warm reaction, Wes mumbled, "Sophia Grace, you should spend all of your time doing nothing but laughing." He shook his head and leaned closer at the same time she did. "That beautiful sound could be bottled up and sold as a cure for any ailment."

Both shocked by his admission, they quickly sat back and looked anywhere but at each other. *Great, Wes. Way to ruin loosening up a tightly wound woman.* He'd rambled off one of Doc's silly sayings for nothing.

During the remainder of their first fake date, Wes ate his seared scallops and watched Sophia poke at hers without eating much. They made polite conversation, mostly centering around Collin, and by the time they returned to the condo, Wes found himself asking for something he had no business asking for.

At Sophia's door, Wes placed a hand on her shoulder before she got away. "May I please say good night to Collin?"

Sophia's brow furrowed and her eyes swept around as if she were searching for an escape. "Uh, okay." She led him inside. The place was cozy, but it didn't look like a style she would have chosen. It was homey; she seemed to lean more toward modern, if her tailored suits and fancy SUV were any indication.

A woman with the same Italian features as Sophia came hurrying down the hall. "Oh, honey, you're already back so soon?"

"Yes, ma'am. Momma, this is Dr. Sawyer." Sophia flicked her wrist and swatted toward him like an afterthought.

Wes offered his hand. "Weston, but please call me Wes. It's nice to meet you."

"Luciana, but please call me Lucy." She winked a blue eye that was a few shades darker than her daughter's tropical hue.

"Is Collin already asleep?" Sophia asked with more optimism than Wes cared for.

"No, we just finished up his bath and now he's playing in his room," Lucy answered while looking between Wes and Sophia.

"May I?" Wes motioned down the hall.

"Uh, sure. First door on the left." Sophia gave him a small smile.

Wes headed that way and peeked inside the room to find Collin looking in the closet. Closing it with a sigh of frustration, the little boy turned and eyed the other side of the room. His tiny frame was clothed in race car pajamas and the shirt had ridden up to show off his cute belly button. Without noticing Wes standing by the door, Collin yanked the hem down and moved over to his toddler bed, which was dressed in a football-theme cover set. Dropping to his hands and knees, he crawled around the edge, peering underneath.

"What are you looking for, buddy?" Wes asked, taking cautious steps inside the room to avoid the toy cars and brightly colored building blocks that were scattered everywhere.

Collin turned and sat down with a sturdy grunt, sounding like an old man. He leaned back against the side of his bed and looked up at Wes with the saddest eyes. "My daddy's footbaw. I lose it. I lose my daddy too. Him gone-gone."

Wes could hardly swallow. *Yeah. And I lost my son.* He sat beside the little guy and focused on the bookshelf across from them.

Collin rested his head against Wes's arm. "I wan' my daddy."

I want my son.

They sat in silence for a while with Wes combing his fingers through Collin's slightly damp curls. The smell of baby shampoo was painfully sweet.

"Do you want me to read you a book?" Wes asked, wishing to take Collin's pain away for at least a short spell. He knew there was no permanent fix for missing someone, though.

Collin sighed. "I wanna pay caws wiff you."

Wes ruffled his hair one last time and chuckled quietly at how somber the child sounded with his request. "Okay. We can play cars for a little while."

As they revved motors and crawled around the floor, Wes had to diligently suppress the anguish clawing at the back of his throat. He should have been granted the gift of doing this with his own son. Instead, his baby boy was in a casket with his momma.

After Collin grew bored with the cars, he selected a book off the shelf and handed it to Wes. "Pease?"

Unable to tell the toddler no, he settled back on the floor by the bed and read Collin the story of Jonah and the whale. By the time he'd gotten to the end, where Jonah finally understood that everyone was worth God's compassion, the sweet smell of baby shampoo was trumped by another odor.

"Poo, I poo-pooed." Collin looked up and scrunched his tiny nose.

"Buddy, if you're old enough to tell me what you did, then you're old enough to be doing that business in the toilet."

"I wan' it off me. You change my heinie?" Collin stared at him with all seriousness.

"No sir." Wes stood and hollered for Sophia.

Not even a minute later they were in the midst of a standoff.

"You're the one who found it. The rule is that you're the one to clean it." Wes saw the amusement twinkling through the starbursts of her vivid blue eyes.

"In all fairness, I've never been informed of this rule." Wes held the little guy by his armpits as far away from him as possible while trying to persuade Sophia into taking him. Each step he took forward, she matched it with one step back. "I admit I found an odor. I'll spray the air with something. Here." He pushed the squirming child closer with both Sophia and her mother laughing at him.

"I wan' it off, Poo. Pease!" Collin whined between them where he was dangling, cracking the adults up.

After Sophia teased Wes several more rounds, she took the stinky toddler off his hands. Wes bid them good night. Even though the odor was a foul one, at least the night ended on a sweeter note than he'd expected.

•   •   •

The office was relatively quiet the following week, and Wes was still struggling to get used to the more lax schedule. Back in the world of hematology and oncology, a quiet day was nonexistent. A day didn't pass without some adrenaline-infused crisis or cutting-edge discovery.

As Wes flipped through a file on his desk, his eyes slowly drooped. Blinking a few times, he tried to refocus on the page only to have it slip through his fingers as his head nodded once again.

Just as his eyes drifted shut, a knock on the door startled him awake. Clearing his throat, he called out, "Come in."

His nurse appeared with another old-school paper file in her hand. "We have a small emergency." Krista gave him a sympathetic look as she handed over the thick file.

Wes didn't care how small; he was just eager to have a challenge of any sort on his hands. He glanced quickly at the top sheet, noting the number nine on the age line, before rushing into the only occupied exam room. Thinking he was still a little groggy from boredom, Wes squinted at the patient with a fishing hook through her thumb.

Said patient was dressed in a floral shirt, camouflage overalls, and hot-pink ballet flats. She wore a trucker hat backward, and it seemed to be losing the battle of helping hold the long white hair out of the way. Confused yet slightly amused, he glanced again at the file. This time he noticed a zero following the nine.

Giving up on it making any sense, Wes set the file down and edged closer to the woman. "Uh . . . good morning, Miss Dalma."

"Not really," Dalma grumbled as she held up her hand.

Wes plucked a pair of gloves from the box and put them on, still baffled as to why she was here, in a pediatric office. This little lady was always with the other hens who continuously popped up with baked goods and gossip, but she was less clucky and only added an off-the-wall anecdote every now and then.

"Did someone bring you here?" Wes asked as he inspected the hook. It was a simple bait hook with a tiny barb, and it had only penetrated the epidermis, so he was fairly confident that it would be easy to remove.

"Oh yes. August Bradford is in the waiting room. Such a sweet boy."

"Were you two out fishing?"

"No. Not this time. I was looking through my jewelry box for a ring I wanted to give him for Josie, but this hook got me." She hitched a thin shoulder up, looking as baffled by that declaration as Wes. "Darnedest thing."

Wes gave her an apologetic smile before saying, "I believe August brought you to the wrong office."

"No, honey. Doc has been treating me for years. And it's much more fun here than the other office filled with a bunch of old geezers, wheezing and whining about their arthritis and bunions."

Wes took a good look at Dalma, finding only lucidity in her cloudy-blue eyes. Biting his cheek to hold in the chuckle, he tore the gloves off. "Can you sit tight for a second?" When she nodded, he moved toward the door. "I'm going to get Nurse Krista to numb your thumb. Then I'll be back to remove the hook."

"*Numb* and *thumb* rhyme. See? Much more fun. They don't say anything fun or silly at that old geezer place." Dalma grinned, swinging her legs, looking the opposite of old.

Wes returned her grin. This was the most silly fun he'd had since the pooping date incident last week. After giving Krista instructions, he had to go share the silliness of the situation with Sophia. He genuinely enjoyed having someone to share moments like these with for the first time in a long time, and she was always eager to listen.

He gave the slightly open door a quick knock before slipping inside.

"Yes?" Sophia asked, finishing up whatever she was typing before looking up. She was smartly dressed in another pantsuit, black with a teal blouse. Her dark hair was pulled neatly into a low bun. No doubt about it, the woman was stunning.

Between the weird episode with Dalma and now openly checking Sophia out, Wes was beginning to think he was still sleeping. Blinking out of the daze, he tried to recall why he'd even gone into her office in the first place. *Ninety-year-old patient!* "I'm currently treating my very first patient who draws Social Security."

Sophia's blue eyes lit up as her smile grew in amusement to match his. "Let me guess. Dalma Burgess."

"Yep." Wes chuckled.

"She okay?"

"She will be after I remove the fishing hook from her thumb. I'm waiting for Krista to numb it first."

Sophia wrinkled her nose. "Ouch. You better take good care of that sweet lady. Oh, and Agnes says Doc always gives her an extra sucker, so don't forget." Sophia produced two red, heart-shaped suckers from her drawer and stood up to hand them to him. "These are her favorites."

He tucked them into his lab coat pocket. "An extra sucker. Got it."

Sophia grabbed his arm before he made it into the hallway, and the subtle scent of peonies and citrus grabbed ahold of him too. "Then be sure to come back and let me know how it went." She squeezed his arm before letting go.

"Sure thing." With a smile stretching to full capacity, Wes hurried to the exam room to take care of the hook.

In no time, Wes had Dalma squared away and was back in Sophia's office, telling her all about how Dalma had taken it upon herself to pull the hook out of her thumb once it was numb. The little lady told him he just needed to clean it up and wrap it tightly—and the doctor did as the ninety-year-old patient had instructed. Sophia laughed at his retelling until tears pooled in her vivid teal eyes.

Giving her that moment of freedom from all the heaviness she continuously carried around felt Herculean and only fueled him to want to do it more. Wes thought he owed it to her after Sophia had shared the warmth of her laughter on their fake date. It had woken something in Wes that had remained dormant for so long it seemed lost forever. Each time she'd laughed in his presence since, it breathed a little more life into the withered part of his soul that was supposed to hold hope.

For the first time since the day his life died, Wes began to give the notion of living again some serious thought.

9

The continual drift of daily living pushed Sophia to move forward, and she did so without protest. Getting through the ebb and flow of each day on autopilot, she constructed a carefully placed smile and offered polite words. Behind them was a scared, beaten-down woman screaming at the top of her lungs, begging to be released from the hopeless circumstances she'd been thrown into that had left her lost and confused as to who she was supposed to be.

The Sophia she used to be would never have agreed to an inane deal such as fake dating. She had needed the job, so she chose to go along with Wes's request. But that choice, made in desperation, was beginning to resemble a pint of sour milk. It was only a small nuisance—until it spilled.

She was afraid it had spilled all over town. The rumor mill picked up on their first date, as well as them sitting together at church, and ran with it just as Wes had predicted. Folks were even talking about how sweet it was that Collin insisted on Wes walking him to children's church. Sophia considered the fake-dating job done, so when he'd tried scheduling another date night the following week, she'd brushed him off with excuses that were as flimsy as a wet tissue but somehow held for two more weeks.

If Sophia thought Wes was going to react with anger and demands, she was surprisingly mistaken. For some reason, he let her get by with it. Probably because begging for a date was beneath him. Instead of arguing, he quietly sulked, and she sure as day didn't know how to respond to that. She was used to raised voices and warning shoves. Not the silent treatment and the cold shoulder.

Even though Wes was annoyed with her, it didn't deter him from presenting her with a cooler bag each morning. And each morning when Sophia tried refusing the offering, Wes responded with carefully slung comments that even though calmly spoken still left a considerable sting.

"A good mother takes care of herself for the sake of her child."

"Collin needs you to be a good example."

"Neglecting your health isn't fair to your son."

And that's all it would take to have Sophia snatching the bag out of his hand and stomping off. They kept their distance from each other most of the time, and as another Friday afternoon rolled around, she had every intention of keeping it that way.

The plan was to swing by his office on the way out and do a drop-and-dash with next week's schedule, but one glimpse of Wes sidetracked her. She noticed his lab coat and tie had been removed and his caramel locks looked a bit disheveled. Running his hand through his hair toward the end of each day was a habit she picked up on. It reminded her of Collin. The little guy would twirl one of his curls around his finger when he was sleepy. But today Wes wore a look that didn't quite suit him. More haggard than simply tired from a day's work.

"Hey," Sophia said softly.

Wes glanced up from the file he was scribbling in. Behind his designer glasses, she could clearly see pain tightening the corners of his hazel eyes. "Hi. May I help you?" His voice was polite, but his tone sounded bone-tired.

"I think the better question is, can I help you?" Sophia edged closer to his desk.

Wes dropped the pen and leaned back in his chair while tracking her movement. "Is that the schedule?" he asked, disregarding her question.

She handed him the paper. "I e-mailed you a few record-keeping choices. The last on the list is the same system your practice used back in Alabama. I included it in case you want to stick with something familiar. I can set up an installation for the one you pick by next week and start sorting this filing system." She hoped that would help him in some small way.

"Great. I'll review them tonight and let you know. It'll be a big relief to get this filing system updated." He plucked a file from the cluttered paperwork on his desk, looking similar to hers, and lifted it in the air before dropping it. "I've not dealt with these things since my residency years."

Sophia placed her bag on a spare chair and sent her mother a quick text to let her know she would be late. She then grabbed another chair and slid it close to his desk.

"What are you doing?" Wes asked.

"We're going to see about finishing off some of this work so you can get home at a decent time." Sophia picked up a pen and swiped one of the files. "I pay attention, Dr. Sawyer, and I know you stay way too late each night."

"I have nothing to go home to, so . . ." His eyes immediately dropped to the desk.

Sophia's throat thickened as she watched him dive into another file to get away from the admission he'd just laid out there. Was that a clue as to what was bothering him?

They went through a few files before Sophia worked up enough nerve to speak. She didn't know if it would hurt him worse, but the only diversion to come to mind was to start talking about Collin. "So I tried Collin on broccoli last night."

Wes didn't look up but his pen stilled. "How'd it go?"

"The little guy made it vanish."

He lifted his head and finally met her gaze. "See. I told you he'd like it."

"I didn't say he liked it." She playfully rolled her eyes. "After supper we played with his LEGO blocks and I started getting a whiff of something. I went to change his diaper and guess what was tucked inside?"

The tension around Wes's eyes finally softened as he chuckled. "He's too smart for his own good."

Sophia snickered. "Tell me about it. At first glance, I thought something was wrong with him, but the only thing wrong was the little scoundrel filling his diaper with broccoli spears without me noticing." Feeling a little more settled, she filled the next hour with more talk about Collin as they steadily worked until the desk was cleared.

Sophia picked up her bag and settled the strap on her shoulder. "If there's nothing else, I'll see you Monday."

"Sunday. You're still sitting with me in church, remember? Or are you backing out of that part of our agreement as well?" There was tease in his voice instead of the normal pompousness.

"Sunday then." She crossed her arms but couldn't keep the smile from curling her lips upward. "For someone who's such a stickler on rules and proper etiquette, I'm surprised you find nothing wrong with deceiving people about us seeing each other."

Wes simply waved the accusation off as he grabbed his coat and briefcase. "We've shared a meal and we sit together at church. No deception has taken place. If the town chooses to take our time together and misconstrue it into a relationship, then so be it."

"You're very cut-and-dried on things, Dr. Sawyer." She raised an eyebrow.

He beckoned her to follow him out. "Less drama that way."

She tilted her head and released a laugh. "Yeah, because fake dating is drama-free." She waited for him to volley a snide remark in return. Instead, Wes stared at her as he locked the side door behind them. "What?"

Wes shook his head and began leading Sophia to her SUV. "That laugh of yours . . . it's an experience." He opened the driver's door and helped her inside before leaning down slightly. "Thank you for sharing it with me." Wes glanced over the roof and then lowered his eyes again. "I needed it today."

"Are you okay?" Sophia asked as she snapped the seat belt into place.

The careful smile he wore wobbled before completely slipping from his handsome face. He propped his forehead on the arm he had resting on the roof of her SUV and slowly drew in a breath. "Some days, it just hits me out of nowhere . . . Today was one of them."

Sophia reached to unlock the seat belt, but Wes placed his hand on her shoulder.

"It's getting late. You need to get home to Collin." Abruptly Wes closed the door and struck off toward his car.

From the time she'd spent with Wes, Sophia knew for certain he was genuinely a good man, but a lonely man who was in need of a firm support system. Sadly, she was only able to offer support riddled with weak spots. What little strength she had was all for Collin at the moment.

A muffled horn beeped and drew her attention.

Glancing in the rearview mirror, Sophia realized Wes was waiting for her to exit first. She waved at him even though her instinct told her to put the car in park and make him open up to her. But if she wasn't a willing participant in the opening up, then she certainly couldn't expect him to be either.

• • •

Saturday was bright and sunshiny. Thankfully a breeze kept the gnats at bay and the humidity from settling too thick around the seaside park where a dozen toddlers toddled around the play sets while their parents watched on.

"You could have called me, dear. I would have pitched in to make this more of a special event for our Collin," Ty's mother commented as she glared down her nose at the cheese doodles and juice boxes.

Sophia pushed the number 3 candle into the tractor-themed cake with a bit too much force, burying the bottom of it in buttercream. She had to discreetly pull it back out slightly, but there was no fixing it. Each time she tried, it leaned more to the left and got more green icing smeared on it. "It's fine, Helen. This is what Collin requested." Ever since they'd moved back and Collin had spent time on her family's small farm, the little guy had become obsessed with tractors.

"He's three, dear. He doesn't know what he wants." Ty's mother flicked the notion away as if it were a pesky fly. She'd flown in the night before from Atlanta and chosen to stay at a hotel instead of the offered guest room at Sophia's. She explained that Ty couldn't make it, but she'd brought his gifts for Collin. Collin began to fall to pieces when Sophia tried to explain this to him earlier in the morning.

"I no wan' toys. Jus' my daddy. Pease, Mommy." Collin cried and begged, but there was nothing Sophia could do about it.

Needless to say, Collin had one of the biggest meltdowns he'd had in quite a while. It took Lincoln Cole, of all people, to pull the little guy out of it when he showed up with his dad's German shepherd, after Sophia called Opal in a panic. Lincoln explained he was dog-sitting for his parents while they were on a cruise, and he needed Collin to help him walk the dog. And just like that, a burly man and a shaggy dog soothed him. Sophia had made a silent vow to never pinch Lincoln Cole again.

"Did you hear me, Sophia?" Mrs. Prescott asked in a cutting tone.

Blinking the dreadful morning away, Sophia regarded the woman who thought the world revolved around her NFL player son. "I'm sorry, Helen. What was that?"

"Could you please get on with the gifts? I have a plane to catch this afternoon." Mrs. Prescott fanned her face with her hand while dabbing a napkin along her neck. She was dressed in a white pantsuit and actually had the nerve to keep giving Sophia's shorts and sleeveless blouse once-overs as if she were the one who didn't know how to properly dress during the dog days of summer.

"Yes, ma'am. As soon as we sing and he blows out the candle." Sophia gave her a tight smile before hurrying off to gather the children.

Once the song was concluded and the candle blown out, Sophia handed Collin her gift first. The little guy beamed when he tore the paper and found the green plastic tractor under it.

"Yay! I pay now." Collin tried wiggling away, already making *put-put-put* noises like a tractor, but Sophia managed to wrangle him back to the mountain of gifts.

"You have more to open first, bub."

Collin was a good sport and opened the gifts from his little friends. He then opened box after box of outfits from Grandmother Prescott. Laughter moved through the parents when after catching a glimpse of clothing, Collin was quick to toss the boxes aside.

It was fun until Collin began opening the gifts from his daddy. The first gift annoyed Sophia, but by the time the little guy opened the last, she was livid.

"What three-year-old has any business with a cell phone?" Sophia asked later that day as she plopped down on the edge of the golf course with Opal and Josie settling underneath the shade tree beside her. They'd arrived to help her unload the ludicrous bounty of gifts at the condo but had stuck around to let her vent. She happily took them up on it.

"Apparently the child of an NFL superstar," Opal answered, not helping matters.

Sophia reached down and plucked at a few blades of grass. She watched August walk behind the toddler as he drove one of Ty's over-the-top gifts, a battery-powered tractor, across the number nine green, coming close to clipping the flag. "He's not big enough to be driving that thing."

"The box said ages three and up." Josie shrugged, and it was all Sophia could do not to shove her.

"And do you think he's old enough to have his very own iPad Air?"

Josie lifted her shoulder again. "At least Ty sent a protective case to go with it."

"I can't believe y'all are defending him!" Sophia tossed a handful of grass clippings, sending them raining down on her two friends like confetti.

"What's really bothering you?" Opal asked, brushing

the grass off her gauzy peasant top, her collection of bracelets clanging against one another.

"The man is trying to buy his son off. It's like he's saying, 'Sorry, Son, I can't make it, but please accept these ridiculously extravagant gifts and my mother as consolation prizes.' It makes me sick." Sophia brushed her hair behind her ear. "Collin doesn't need material things. He needs his daddy."

Josie reached over and patted Sophia on the leg. "I'm really sorry."

Sophia leaned against the tree and stretched her legs out in front of her. "That made me mad enough, but then Mrs. Prescott handed me an envelope from Ty before she left. He'd scribbled a letter about loving us and wanting to take care of us. Along with the letter was an obscene amount of cash that he instructed me not to deposit." She shook her head and huffed. "The man is clearly floating money around that he shouldn't. The gifts he gave Collin are well into the thousands. I just don't want to get caught up in his sweet talk and financial mess."

"What did you do?" Josie asked.

"I handed the envelope back to his mother and told her to return it to him. She wasn't happy about it, but she didn't want to cause a scene, so she took it and left. Thank goodness." Sophia looked heavenward and watched the late-afternoon sunbeams wiggle their way through the tree branches.

"I can't blame you there." Opal scooted beside her and leaned on the tree while moving a hand along her tummy. Sophia couldn't wait for Baby Cole to start showing as more than a tiny paunch.

The women moved their attention to the little guy on his tractor with a paint-splattered artist hot on his heels.

Sophia was tired of being the downer of the group,

so she redirected their conversation to a lighter note. "Josie, you and August know how to wear paint well." The couple came straight from teaching an art session at Palmetto Fine Arts Camp, and both were dressed in their usual outfits of tees and jeans that were speckled with paint. Sophia found that little quirk endearing.

Josie giggled. "August certainly does. Isn't he just something to look at?" The blonde tilted her head and openly admired her husband.

Sophia snickered. "You sound like a lovesick teenager mooning over her boyfriend. It's so sweet."

"It is," Opal agreed. "Speaking of boyfriends . . . I was disappointed to hear that your boyfriend wasn't at the party, Sophia." Leave it to Opal to spoil the lighter topic.

Sophia scoffed. "*Fake.* It's fake and you know it."

Opal scoffed right back. "Well, whatever you want to call him, I don't understand why Wes wasn't invited."

"Stop meddling," Sophia warned as she stood and brushed the back of her shorts. She walked away, wishing the same could be so easily done with the bothersome situations she found herself snared in at the moment.

Later that night, Ty called and only spoke briefly with Collin before having the little guy hand Sophia the phone. Ty tried talking Sophia into flying out to see him. Of course she declined, but he put up one heck of a fight. The man was just as good at manipulation as he was at rushing a football field. Sadly, it had taken her too long to figure out how to see through his deceitful tactics.

After a long night of tossing and turning, church the next day should have been a reprieve from all the stress. Instead, Sophia could barely keep a grip on the escalating sensation of coming unraveled as she sat on the pew beside Wes.

As they stood to sing the offertory hymn, Wes leaned close and whispered, "Are you okay?"

Sophia kept her eyes glued to the bleary hymnal in her hands and pretended to not hear him. For some reason, him asking her that in his smooth, sincere tone made her want to break. She wanted to scream and let loose a litany of complaints on how unfair life was treating her. To lash out until someone else felt the sting of her despondency.

After the usher passed by, Sophia's eyes fell to the aisle and she contemplated how freeing it would be to just fall out of her pew and let it all out in one momentous fit. She could picture it now, her limbs flailing about and the rage spewing from her mouth until someone showed up with a straitjacket.

With a great deal of effort, Sophia bottled up the lunacy of that idea and tucked it away with the distress that had conjured it in the first place. When the song concluded, she wedged her purse between them on the pew, using it as a boundary.

Wes gave the purse a thoughtful look and then did the same with her but said nothing. After that, his attention remained on the pastor for the remainder of the service.

As they left the sanctuary, Sophia's mom was quick to pounce on Wes before he made it too far.

"Wes, dear, would you like to join us for Sunday dinner? It's a special one for little Collin's birthday. I've made all of his favorites." Lucy grinned wide while looping her arm through Sophia's to keep her rooted in the invitation.

"Oh, I thought yesterday was the big celebration." Wes directed his remark to Sophia, stirring her guilt for not inviting him.

"That was for his little church friends. Besides, today is his actual birthday. We would love for you to celebrate with us," Lucy offered, adding an enthusiastic head nod while nudging Sophia, but it didn't encourage her to join in. She was barely holding on to her unsteady composure as it was. "Opal, Josie, and their hubbies will be there too."

The expression on Wes's face looked a lot like hurt at the mention of Sophia's friends being invited and not him. Sophia swallowed past the lump of guilt lodged in her throat and whispered, "Wes, would you like to join us?"

"I'd like that, but I left Collin's gift at my house." Wes rubbed the back of his neck and looked over at his fancy sports car.

"You could bring it by their place later on today." Lucy released her hold on her daughter and ordered, "Sophia, give Wes directions out to the farm," before dashing off.

"Are you sure about me joining your family for dinner?" Wes asked quietly once they were alone.

"Collin will be tickled for you to be there. I need to get him from his class." Sophia turned on her heel.

"Directions?" he called out before she got too far.

She swatted the air. "I'll text them to you shortly." Sophia was tempted to give him the wrong address but decided against it.

The meal was a bounty of Italian dishes that Sophia's mom prided herself on making from recipes her own grandmother had brought with her from Sicily. The woman's gravy, aka red sauce, was drool-worthy. Judging by Wes's exuberant appetite, he agreed. The man was going head-to-head with both Neanderthal Lincoln and Big-Boy August with shoveling it in, and Sophia was impressed that he was keeping pace.

At her mother's insistence, Sophia managed to eat a couple of meatballs and a chunk of fresh focaccia by the time Wes polished off his third plate. Collin followed his example and ate with gusto, too.

"Wes, I'd like to thank you for hiring our daughter," Sophia's dad said as dessert was served.

Mitcham Gaines was a country boy through and through who'd managed to snag himself an Italian beauty—his very words—while attending the state fair back in the seventies. He'd recalled the story for Sophia several times over the years about how he followed Lucy around booth after booth until she agreed to a date. It was a sweet tale, but Sophia had no faith in love stories anymore.

Lincoln took it upon himself to snort out a laugh. "Poor guy. We know the challenge in putting up with Sophia."

Opal swatted her husband's arm as Sophia stuck her tongue out at him. "Hush and eat your dessert."

Wes paused between bites of cheesecake. "Sophia's been an asset to Carolina Pediatrics. Hiring her was a wise decision."

A warmth spread inside her chest as Sophia stared at him, but Wes kept his focus on dessert. Whether he truly meant it or not, she was grateful he spoke so kindly about her in front of her parents.

"Collin, are you ready for your presents?" Sophia's mother asked, sending the little guy bouncing up and down in the booster seat that had recently replaced the high chair.

Lincoln and Opal gave him a giant collection of sand toys, promising the little guy a day at the beach the following week. And Sophia wasn't surprised when August and Josie presented him with an art easel and children's art supplies. They were more invested in her son than his own father, and that fact both comforted and hurt Sophia.

Papa and Grandma gave Collin a remote-control car, and the rest of the afternoon was spent on the porch watching the little guy crash it into every tree and bush in the front yard. Eventually he began twirling a curl around his finger, so Papa swooped him up and declared it time to watch the race on TV, which meant they reclined in his chair and dozed off before the first pit stop.

The porch swing creaked back and forth as Sophia sat beside Wes in silence. Her mom had stretched out on the couch, making the swing their only option. Sophia hinted that Wes could mosey on home like her friends did, but he didn't catch on—or pretended he didn't anyway.

Instead, he sat beside her while she listened to the gritty hum of the race drifting through the open windows. She surveyed the yard and regarded the gardenia bushes planted sporadically around it and beyond. Her parents planted a new bush to celebrate each wedding anniversary. A total of thirty-seven bushes thus far, and the perfume the yard emitted during certain times of the year was so alluring. It was such a beautiful testament to their love. One that Sophia both admired and envied.

"Do you need to talk about it?" Wes quietly asked after a while.

The first time he asked that, at his beach house, Sophia took it to mean that if it wasn't a needed conversation, he'd rather not have his time wasted on it. But in the last several weeks she'd come to know him a little better. Now she picked up on the sincerity of the question. He recognized that the issue bothering her was important, and that talking about it might be a need, not a want.

She sighed and fiddled with the lacy hem of her white sundress. "Do you ever feel like you're about to come out of your skin?" She watched him out of the corner of her eye, worried he'd find her crazy for asking, but was relieved when he nodded.

"All the time. It's why I took up running." Wes shifted to catch her gaze, jostling the swing before sending it back into a lazy rhythm. "I thought I could outrun whatever was causing it, but it's taken years to realize the exercise only tamps it down to a more manageable anxiety."

"So you're diagnosing it as anxiety and prescribing exercise to treat the symptoms?" She shoved his arm in tease, and unable to stop herself, she added, "Always playing doctor."

Wes leaned closer. "Now that you mention it . . . there are other, more imaginative techniques proven to reduce anxiety, but I'm too much of a gentleman to share those with you." Then he followed it with what else but a sultry wink.

Holy moly! The man knew how to flirt. *Really?*

Surprised by his comeback tease, Sophia sprang to her feet and knocked her elbow against the swing armrest in the process. "Ow!" She jumped around while cradling her elbow, hoping the flapping motion would ease the zing of pain racing all the way up to her shoulder.

"You hit it just right, didn't you?" Wes asked as he stood and rubbed in a spot that immediately eased the pain to a more tolerable level.

"Then why's it feel so wrong?" Sophia managed to say through her clenched teeth.

Wes grinned, and it made her heartbeat stutter.

"Are you kidding me?" She reached over and poked the charming dimple in his left cheek with her index finger. "Dimples . . . You're just too much."

The man's boy-next-door looks made her instantly wary. Ty could pull off the exact same innocuous facade when the situation warranted it. Tugging out of his grasp and looking anywhere but at his handsome face, she muttered, "I need to get Collin home."

Wes scrubbed a hand down his face. "I apologize, Sophia. I was kidding around, and what I said was in poor taste." He stood staring at his feet for a moment before turning away and descending the porch steps. "Please thank your parents for dinner," Wes said over his shoulder as he made haste to his car.

Sophia stood and watched the shiny black car ease down the long driveway, barely kicking up dust. She didn't understand why they had some elastic tether that kept bringing them a little closer only to snap back the progress. Shaking her head, she went inside to gather her baby and hopefully her dignity before heading home.

Later, as she finished giving Collin a bath, Sophia heard her phone chiming with a new message. The notion to ignore it became a moot point when her baby, being the sweet boy he was, grabbed it and brought it to her. She squinted at the name on the screen.

Wes was the last person she would have guessed, and asking to come over to deliver Collin's birthday gift was also a surprise. After skimming her outfit of damp tank top and yoga pants that were victims of Collin's splash fest, she sent him a one-word reply, **Okay**, and hurried to change. But before she made it to her room, there was a knock on the front door. Grumbling under her breath, Sophia did an about-face and went to open it.

"Good evening, Sophia." Wes was casually dressed in sweatpants and a T-shirt with three large Target bags in his grips. They were basically dressed the same, yet she felt frumpy and he looked anything but.

"Maybe you *are* a vampire," she mumbled quietly, wondering how long he had been waiting outside.

"What was that?" Wes's brows pinched as he cocked his ear in her direction.

"Nothing." Sophia moved back and gestured for him to come in. "Collin, you have company."

Collin ran down the hallway and yelled, "Hey, Wes!"

Wes raised an impressed eyebrow at Sophia. "Hello, Collin. I've brought your birthday gifts." He sat in the middle of the living room floor and waited for Collin to join him.

"I like gifs." Collin nodded his head and took the offered bag. Looking inside, he frowned and pulled out pack after pack of underwear. "I not wan' 'em." The little guy looked right disappointed.

Sophia gave Wes an exaggerated eye roll, knowing what that gift meant. She crossed her arms and leaned against the armrest of the couch as Wes tore open a pack.

"These are special superhero undies. Only brave boys can wear them. Aren't you brave?"

Collin shrugged but took the pair Wes held out to him and inspected them. "You got superhero undies, too?"

Wes glanced at Sophia and then angled away from her, but not before she caught a glimpse of the color rising in his cheeks. "I wear big-boy underwear," he answered. "Don't you want to try them on?"

Collin was out of the diaper in a flash and pushing his feet into the big-boy underwear. After he had them pulled on, he ran over to Sophia and did a little dance, shaking his tiny butt. "See me, Mommy?"

Sophia giggled. "I see you, bub." She glanced at Wes. "Where's the tiny toilet he'll need?"

"I don't believe in that method." Wes produced a toilet seat cover. "Just set this on top and place his stepstool in front of the toilet."

She smirked. "You've done a lot of potty training?"

"When parents come in and ask for advice, I provide them with proven techniques." He held the seat up. "My research has indicated this is an easier approach. Unless you think you'd enjoy cleaning out the tiny toilet instead of simply flushing the big one."

Well, when he put it that way . . . "We can try this way first. Any more advice, Dr. Sawyer?"

"As a matter of fact . . ." Wes pulled out a large tub of toy cars. "Collin, every day you don't wet your superheroes, Mommy will give you a car."

Collin's eyes rounded at the giant container. "I wan' 'em!"

"They're all yours. Just don't wet the superhero. Or poop on him for that matter."

Wes went as far as setting the toilet up and going over how to use it with Collin. The little guy sat there a short while and then stood in front of it like a "big" boy, but nothing happened.

He tired of trying and went to play in his room. Sophia thought Wes would head on out but wasn't sure if she was pleased or disappointed when he took a seat on the couch and patted the cushion next to him.

"Mind if we have a chat before I go?"

Hesitant, Sophia walked over and sat down beside him.

"You're sad a lot of the time," Wes commented while looking her straight in the eye. "I don't like it, and so earlier I thought teasing you a little would lighten your mood." He shifted and placed his arm on top of the couch behind her. "I'm not good at that, obviously. I just . . . I wanted to make you laugh again. Instead, I offended you. Please know that wasn't my intention."

Floored by his sincerity, the only thing Sophia could do was sit there and nod like a bobblehead.

"When my wife was sad or upset about something," he began barely over a whisper, "the only thing I had to do was tease her and it always seemed to make her feel better. I had no business trying that with you."

His admission hit Sophia low in her belly, finding it

endearing that his wife's happiness took such precedence in his life. And then he went and tried to do the same with her and she ruined it by cold-shouldering him for it.

Clearing her throat, Sophia said, "No, I'm sorry. You did nothing wrong. It's on me and my personal issues." She wondered if she would ever be able to participate in a healthy relationship, or if the toxic relationship with Ty had poisoned any hope of it happening.

"Okay." Wes nodded and then scanned the room. He seemed ready to move on to another topic, but Sophia knew she needed to reassure him that it most certainly was one of those "it's not you; it's me" situations.

She briefly placed her hand on top of his. "Thank you for trying to make me feel better. That was very considerate of you, and it actually worked until I went and made it awkward."

One side of his mouth kicked up, producing that darn dimple. "I did?"

Sophia snickered. "Yes, you did with your unruly mouth." She lowered her voice and said, "That's so unbecoming of you, Doctor."

"Your husky voice is uniquely appealing," he admitted out of nowhere, flooring her again. She never knew what to expect to come from his lips anymore.

She wrinkled her nose. "I sound like I have a permanent cold."

"I like it." A blush warmed his cheeks as he removed his arm from behind her and stood, clearly trying to avoid round two of awkward moments for the day. His attention moved to the door as if he were planning to make an escape. Before he moved, a squeal came from Collin's room.

The little guy came racing down the hallway and into the living room while waving his underwear in the air like a flag. "I not wet 'em!"

"That's great!" Wes squatted down and helped Collin slide his underwear back on.

"I get a caw now?"

Wes chuckled and ruffled her excited son's curls. "Sure. . . . Wait. . . . Did you peepee?"

Collin bobbed his head exuberantly.

"Where?" Wes asked slowly.

Collin took off toward to his room with Sophia and Wes on his heels. He pointed to the tiny garbage can in the corner.

Wes moved over and peered inside before giving her a sidelong glance. "At least he didn't go on the floor."

The hilarity of the moment hit her and sent Sophia into a fit of laughter. She laughed until her sides hurt and her face was damp with tears. Wes watched her in awe for a few beats before joining in.

When she regained her composure, she pointed at the offensive problem. "You found it, you clean it."

Surprisingly, Wes scooped up the can and walked out of the room without protest. As he passed by her, he taunted, "That's progress, miss, whether you want to admit it or not. He didn't *wet 'em.*" The last part was mimicked in a toddler voice, cracking Sophia up all over again.

After the can was washed out with bleach and Wes went over how to use the real potty once more, he opened the giant container and handed Collin a car. He then produced a book from one of his bags about a super kid learning to go to the potty and read it to Collin while they all sat on the couch. It was a silly rhyming book and Wes kept erupting into boyish giggles while trying to read it straight-faced.

In the midst of the giggle-reading, Collin grabbed Wes's face with both hands and mushed until Wes had fish lips. "'Top laughin', Wes. I not know what you say."

Needless to say, it took a long time for both Collin and Sophia to settle down later that night after Wes left. The ache in her jaw from grinning gave her a reprieve from the ache in her heart, and for that she was thankful for the silliest night she and her son had enjoyed in quite a while.

Weston Sawyer, unbeknownst to him, had given Collin the best birthday gift of all, and it had nothing to do with the contents of those three shopping bags.

No, it had everything to do with the time spent making memories that were filled with laughter and grins. Not tears and grimaces.

10

Sunset Cove was beginning to feel like more trouble than it was worth. As Wes stared down at one of the local thorns in his side, he had to wrestle with his manners to keep them front and foremost. Said thorn had shown up under the guise of delivering baked goods several long minutes ago with a sidekick in tow. His eyes flicked to Dalma and took in the blue three-piece suit she was wearing with a pair of camouflage rain boots. Blinking several times, he refocused on what Bertie was yammering on about.

"They said—" Bertie began with her eyes squinted.

"And who are *they?*" he interrupted.

Bertie overlooked his sarcastic question as she shoved the platter of cookies into his hand. "That girl is in need of some help. They said she's gone and caught anorexia." She tsked and patted the side of her fluffy gray hairdo. It was freshly teased and had a purplish tint it didn't have the last time she visited to deliver brownies and gossip on some other person he'd never heard of before.

"Miss Bertie, I can assure you, anorexia isn't something you catch. I can also assure you that Sophia isn't anorexic. It's clearly been *noted* by you time and time again that she's gone through a few trials lately—but you know what? It's neither of our business to be discussing her personal life." Wes hoped his aloofness mixed with professionalism was enough to get the nosy women off his porch.

Dalma reached over and swiped a cookie off the plate.

Bertie tsked. "Dalma Jean, those are for Dr. Sawyer."

Dalma tilted her head to the side and openly checked Wes out as she chewed. "He's fit as a fiddle. Ain't no way he's going to eat these. Plus, he's so sweet on our Sophia Grace that I bet there's no room for any more sugar." She gave him a knowing wink.

Wes was about to dispute her comment, but then he remembered Sunset Cove was under the illusion that he was sweet on Sophia. He also knew deep down it wasn't entirely an illusion any longer.

"Heard you took her out to dinner a couple weeks ago?" Bertie peered up at him as she caught Dalma's hand going in for another cookie.

"Yes, ma'am. And I can confirm the fact that Sophia ate." Not much, but Bertie didn't have to know that. He recalled a flyer that was in today's newspaper and said without thinking, "Actually, we're taking a cooking class together this Friday night at the rec center."

"So you two *are* an item?" Bertie smirked.

"An item is singular. There are two of us." Wes offered that nonsense with a wink of his own as he slid Dalma another cookie and took a step inside. "Thank you for the cookies. I'll be sure to share them with Sophia."

The old bird gave him a sly look. "You do that, sugar. See you *soon.*"

"Yes, ma'am." He closed the door before she started up again. Walking to the kitchen, he placed the cookies on the counter and glared at them for all the things they stood for. He drummed his fingers against the cool marble and contemplated how to talk Sophia into going on another date with him. She'd remained firm on no more fake dates, and the phone numbers had picked right back up again. No matter how clear and up-front he was with each woman, it only seemed to be taken as a challenge.

Of course, Sophia thought that was the funniest thing. It wasn't.

"What do I have to barter with?" Wes mumbled to himself, looking around the kitchen. "Nothing. I got nothing." Suddenly yesterday's incident came to mind, so he unplugged his cell phone where it was charging by the coffeepot.

Two rings in, that lovely voice answered with a terse "What?"

"Hello to you too, Sophia. I need your help."

"How?"

Wes fished the flyer out of the recycling bin. "Remember yesterday, when you and Collin came over?" They'd been next door at the Coles', but Collin had spotted Wes on the back deck and all but had a fit until Sophia brought him over to visit.

"Yes," she answered hesitantly.

"And after our walk on the beach, I hosed Collin down and cleaned the stink off him? You remember that, right?"

"I remember, Wes. Get to the point already. Good grief. It's like talking to Opal." Sophia let out a growl that sent a grin to his face. He wouldn't admit it to her, but that feistiness was attractive.

"You said if I cleaned him up, you'd owe me a huge favor, so I need to collect on that Friday night at . . ." He scanned the flyer. "Seven."

She grumbled something underneath her breath before relenting. "Fine. What should I wear?"

That was almost too easy, but then he recalled the

awful mess and stench, so perhaps she knew not to argue for once.

"One of those pretty dresses like you wore on our one and only date will be fine," Wes answered with a hint of condescension to help his cause. Jeans and a blouse were probably fine too, but he liked those flowy dresses on her. He was about to thank her, but the little spitfire hung up on him. Chuckling, he placed the phone on the counter and headed out to get in an evening run.

At least Sophia had finally agreed to another date. He didn't know why she was being so stubborn about it. Ever since Collin's birthday, the three of them had shared meals in private or just hung out together. But she'd refused each time he proposed another date. It made no sense to him and certainly wasn't helping the mission of repelling unwanted advances from several women.

"Women," Wes mumbled while setting out down the back deck steps. The sky was painting itself in rich pink and orange, so he focused on just taking in God's wonderment and leaving the trivial mess of Sunset Cove for a spell.

●　●　●

By the time Friday arrived, Wes was ready to leave Sunset Cove altogether. He huffed loudly as his passenger let out another round of giggles.

"It's not funny." He shook his head and glared at the road.

"It'll be funny to you once you get over it." Sophia giggled again and had enough nerve to poke him in the side.

"I'm driving here," Wes snapped.

"You're stopped at a red light, silly." Sophia exhaled,

obviously trying to tamp down the laughter. "You need to lighten up or tonight is going to be our last date."

"You didn't have a stranger break into your house."

"In all fairness, she was making you a surprise supper." Sophia snickered, sounding like she was trying to hold it in, but then a roar of laughter followed.

"How would you have liked finding a stranger cooking in your kitchen?" He white-knuckled the steering wheel and refrained from hitting the gas too hard when the light turned green. "I came down after my shower in only a towel."

She sniffled and dabbed at the corners of her eyes. "I'm sorry, Wes. *Seriously* sorry that I didn't get there in time to get a video." She barely finished the tease before bellowing out another laugh.

Wes shook his head and worked on taking several calming breaths. If it hadn't been for Sophia fetching Lincoln to help out, Wes would have had to call the law to get the deranged woman to leave. "I should have just locked the door and not worried about you having to sit on the porch until I was ready. Yes, that's the last time I'm considerate like that."

"At least I got there before she took her little robe off." Sophia playfully popped his arm.

Opal had volunteered to babysit Collin, so it made sense at the time to meet at Wes's house. He was just glad Sophia had dropped the little boy off before coming over. No way would he have wanted the image of that half-dressed woman branded in Collin's memory.

"I need to pack up and disappear in the middle of the night," Wes muttered as he pulled up to the rec center. He noticed Miss Giggles had finally dried it up. "What?"

Her face was all puckered up. "Don't you dare think

about pulling a disappearing act. My son would be heart-broken, and he's had enough of that."

"I'm not going anywhere . . ." He hated that his snide comment had dampened her mood, even if it was at his expense, so he reached over and tickled her side. "You do see why it's imperative that you hold up to your side of the deal with these dates?"

"I suppose so." A small smile eased over her sassy lips. "But it's not my fault you're so devilishly handsome and a doctor to boot. Honey, you're prime real estate."

"Too late to try flattery, ma'am." His eyes coasted over the brunette beauty, appreciating how the coral dress warmed her creamy skin, and he wondered if she didn't understand how much of a catch she would be. He noticed other guys turning to get a better look at her when she walked by, but clearly she didn't notice.

Sophia wiggled her fingers toward him in a prissy fashion. "There hasn't been such handsomeness around these parts since Channing Tatum came through a few years ago while filming a movie."

Wes tore his gaze off her and glanced down at his outfit—dark jeans, a pressed white button-down, and a light-gray sports jacket. Seeing nothing that warranted all the attention he'd been receiving, he slid his eyes to his snickering passenger. "Let's go get this over with."

"I promise to be the best fake date ever." She fluttered her long eyelashes, acting silly. The woman was too cute for her own good at times—a trait she'd clearly passed on to her son.

"See that you do." Wes tipped his head and exited the car. After opening Sophia's door and helping her out, he braved wrapping her arm into the crook of his as they walked inside.

Both of them all but froze at the door when they

spotted the group of women taking up three of the six cooking stations.

Sophia sucked her teeth beside him and whispered, "What is the Knitting Club doing at a date-night cooking class?"

"I guess it's open to anyone." Wes uprooted his feet and led Sophia to the only available station, which happened to put them front and center. Each station consisted of a stainless steel prep table and a four-burner stovetop. Ingredients and cooking tools were already placed on the tables in an orderly fashion.

"I saw the flyer for this in the paper," Sophia said quietly, "and it specifically said *for couples* and something about a romantic menu." She groaned. "It's going to be one long night."

Wes glanced over his right shoulder and caught Bertie staring. The sly old lady winked, but he pretended not to see her and turned back to Sophia. He twirled two fingers, beckoning her to turn around so he could help tie her apron. Leaning close to her ear, he whispered, "I may have accidently bragged to Bertie that we would be here." Sophia stiffened. "I didn't think they would show up."

She turned and placed her hands on her hips. "Well, we're sure to be the main topic of town gossip for a week or two, so at least we can give these dates a break after tonight."

Oh, she thought she had the upper hand again.

"We've only been on two, including tonight. Obviously it's merely been enough to present a challenge to some insistent ladies, so you can go ahead and count on us upping the ante for a while." Wes pulled his glasses out of the breast pocket of his jacket before shrugging out of it and placing it on the chair at their station.

"It was one overzealous woman. I think you're safe

now." Sophia gave him an exaggerated eye roll—something else Collin had inherited from her.

"Oh yeah?" He slid the glasses on and picked up the menu. "The lady who keeps giving out the milk for free was brazen enough to offer me a sample just yesterday. Yes, Sophia, I'm totally safe." He read over the instructions but glanced up when she made no comment. "What?"

Sophia blinked, looking a bit dazed. "Those glasses are just too much." She shook her head and snatched the card out of his hand. She seemed engrossed with the selections, so he took a moment to tie on his apron and scan the room.

Several sighs and groans came from the tables to their right. His eyes swept over and found most of the old ladies fanning themselves and grinning at him. Oh, boy, was it going to be a long night.

Sophia let out a hushed snort. "You're making the geriatric section swoon, Dr. Sawyer."

Shaking his head, he directed his focus on his fake date. "Please . . . Did you call them the Knitting Club earlier?"

"Yes, but that's just the front they use for the gossip ring they're actually running."

He chuckled and ran his hand through his hair as he stole a quick glance at one of the women. "What's up with the one glaring at us? She looks familiar."

Sophia tilted her head and peeped around his shoulder. "Ugh. That's Bertie's sister Ethel. She's the postmaster."

"*Oh*, now I remember. That will be my last trip to the post office, I can promise you that." Wes picked up a garlic press and inspected it. "And who's the orange-headed lady?"

They both took another peek that way and found most of the old ladies huddled like they were formulating a game plan.

"That's Trudy."

"She dropped off an entire pot of catfish stew at the office last week. Best I ever had." Wes chanced a smile in Trudy's direction, and she returned it with a wide grin and wave. Her vivid orange hair was such a bright contrast to her dark-mocha skin. Tipping his head, he turned back to the table. He'd learned quickly not to give too much attention, or it would be misinterpreted as an invite.

"Oh yes. That stew has won several cooking contests, but it's not worth her snooping around. She's like the private eye of the group."

A twinge struck him in the stomach. Apparently none of the town's grannies were safe.

Luckily, the chef stepped behind the counter up front. "Hello. My name is Jake and I'll be your instructor for this evening. Tonight's menu will begin with a starter of puff pastry bites stuffed with Brie."

He was a shrewd-looking man who meant business. Good. Wes was counting on him keeping the group in line.

"The main course will be a seared duck breast in a red wine sauce. It will be served with a medley of sautéed veggies. And lastly, we will prepare a fruit tartlet for dessert." Jake wasted no time and set into instructing the group on how to put the Brie bites together.

After the starter course, Wes began having such a good time cooking with Sophia that he completely tuned out the peanut gallery's whispered chatter. He watched her sauté the vegetables with precision. "You're really good at this, Sophia."

She sprinkled fresh thyme over the sizzling green beans and tomatoes. "My mother was raised in a kitchen and she raised me the same. I have so many great memories with her either elbow-deep in dough or working her vegetable garden. Always side by side." She glanced up at Wes, a tenderness pulling her lips into a smile.

"Sounds like we had similar childhoods." Wes reached over her shoulder and plucked a green bean from the pan, taking a bite and then feeding Sophia the other half. "My brother was always my dad's shadow and I was my mom's. While they spent most of their time tending to my dad's family-owned plantation where they host hunts, I helped Momma with her flower garden and cooking."

"Aww, I love it. A momma's boy." She winked while bumping her hip to his.

"Don't pick on me," Wes chided with his own wink as he took the tongs and plated the vegetables for her.

She giggled quietly. "No teasing here. I'm doing my best to make Collin a momma's boy. Although he's starting to stand me up any chance he gets if you're anywhere around." She bumped Wes's hip again before moving to gather the ingredients for the tartlet.

Wes had become so immersed in his conversation and time with Sophia he'd not even realized Jake was giving the next set of instructions. Refocusing on the chef, he started prepping the duck breast and continued to enjoy the fake date much more than he knew he should.

As the night continued on, Sophia was a good sport and played up teasing him and allowing him to feed her several bites of the dishes. For that Wes was thankful. Hopefully, it would help halt the anorexia rumors. Sophia didn't know it, but tonight's date was more for her benefit than his. . . . Well, after the surprise intruder, it was a little for his benefit as well.

As they finished up the main course, Wes noticed the Knitting Club had grown a bit rowdy. Snickering and catcalling at him when he walked over to the sink to wash his hands. Making brash comments and kissy sounds each time he and Sophia got too close.

Dalma even went as far as coming over to their table

and swiping one of the mini red wine bottles, claiming they needed extra sauce. "You sure are nice to look at," she commented while clutching the bottle to her chest and squinting up at him with glassy eyes.

"Uh . . . thank you."

"Oh no, honey. Thank you." Dalma wobbled a bit to the side and Wes reached to steady her. After openly staring for a few awkward beats, she finally shuffled back to her table.

By the time dessert was served, the old ladies were completely out of hand.

As Wes wiped a dollop of fresh whipped cream from the corner of Sophia's mouth, a chorus of whistles and catcalls erupted from the other side of the room.

"You go, girlie!" Bertie shouted, followed by more hoots and hollers.

"I think I have some cream on my lip, too," crooned the one they called Madge as she puckered her wrinkly lips.

Jake scowled at the group of hens, all rosy-faced and grinning wide, and shook his head. "Ladies, you were supposed to cook with the wine. Not drink it."

Their googly eyes wandered to one another and some seemed dumbfounded by the revelation. "Oops," Trudy said, sending the ole gals into a fit of snickers.

Sighing, Wes offered a pleading smile to the other two couples who were innocent bystanders to the night's she-nanigans. "Would you mind helping us get these women home safely? I can fit two or three in my car."

They divvied up the tipsy women between them and headed out. Wes and Sophia ended up with Dalma, Bertie, and Ethel. Bertie was even chattier than normal and Ethel, surprisingly enough, wouldn't stop singing. Little Dalma fell asleep, so her only contribution to the chaos on the ride home was a soft snore drowned out by the other two.

"This is one fancy-dancy car, Doctor," Bertie
commented.

"These leather seats are too dang slippery. What'd you
do, grease 'em?" Ethel complained on a hum. "Oooh,
look at the stars through the sunroof." She followed that
with a bluesy version of "Twinkle, Twinkle, Little Star."

"Sophia, child, you like to snatch up the rich boys,
don'tcha?" Bertie slurred, and when it became clear that
Sophia wasn't going to answer, she continued on rambling. "You have a good time, dear?"

"I did." Sophia patted her flat belly. "I ate too much,
though. Wes is an amazing cook . . ." She giggled. "Heck,
the man is simply amazing at everything, though."

Wes glanced over when Sophia's hand landed on his
where it was resting on the center console. "You sneak
some wine, too?" he whispered.

"No, silly." She winked before turning to look at the
wobbling heads he kept seeing in the rearview mirror.
"Do you girls know that other women in town are trying
to snatch my man?"

Wes knew Sophia was stirring the pot for his benefit, but his gut told him it would be at her expense. He
flipped his hand over and squeezed hers gently, but she
squeezed it back and continued. "What should I do?"

Ethel began singing a sloppy rendition of Mary
Wells's "My Guy" with Bertie singing backup. As they
belted out lines about *sticking like glue* and *no one was
going to tear her away from her guy*, Wes chanced a glance
at Sophia. She was staring out the window with her lips
set in a deep frown.

"Hush up, Ethel." Bertie leaned forward and said,
"Sophia Grace, you can't let any woman that comes sniffing around have your man like last time. It ain't dignified.

And it's right disgraceful for a Southern lady to carry on like that."

And there it was, just as Wes had predicted. It was time to shut them down. "Ladies—"

"First off," Ethel interrupted, "you need to put some meat on your bones. You're too scrawny to even stand up for yourself. Grow a backbone and let them floozies know Weston is your man!" Ethel was the orneriest woman Wes had ever encountered, but he liked how she put that last part.

"I'll tell ya what . . . us gals will send out a message to the local girls to back off." Bertie clucked her tongue and wobbled backward.

Wes let out a noisy breath. "Now the gossip ring sounds more like a front for the mob." Picturing the gray-haired—plus one orange-headed—mob grannies, he couldn't contain the snort of laughter.

"What was that, sugar?" Bertie questioned, grunting to right herself in the seat.

"We've gotten you home," Sophia interjected. She squeezed Wes's hand one last time before releasing it to help wrangle the sisters and Dalma out of the backseat.

The sisters had made mention that they were taking care of Dalma while her roommate was out of town. As Ethel slurred the information, she pointed two fingers toward her eyes and then tried aiming them back to Dalma, but she missed the mark when she stumbled. Wes didn't have much faith in Dalma being in good hands, but he had a feeling the little old lady did fairly well taking care of her own self. Even though she was less conventional than most. Wes made a mental note to swing by first thing in the morning to check on all three of the silly women.

Once they were back on the road and fairly winded from the effort it took to get the women inside safely, Sophia began chuckling in a hushed snicker until finally cackling out loud. It had been a tiresome night, but Wes would gladly relive it just to have her laughing like that.

"You're one interesting fellow, I have to hand it to you." Sophia shook her head.

"Well, I think we make a good team," Wes commented as he turned onto the beachfront road.

"The cooking part or the wrestling tipsy old ladies part?"

Wes chuckled. "Both and beyond. Even at work, I have to admit you run a tight ship. I like that about you."

They made it to the beach house within a few more minutes. That was one of the things Wes liked about Sunset Cove. Everything was under a ten-minute drive or even a walkable distance. He wasn't quite ready to end the evening, so he shut off the car and leaned back against the headrest. The ocean was just visible past the luminous sand dunes. It still amazed him how the beach glowed at night, even after witnessing it for a couple months now.

"I don't like how the town talks about you," Wes admitted on a sigh.

Sophia didn't answer right away. But when she did, it affected him in such a visceral way that he wanted to shield her and dare the world to mistreat her ever again.

"I'm not the doormat they've made me out to be. No one knows how I fought to fix my marriage. A lot went on behind closed doors, and that's where it'll remain. I had to learn the hard way that some things just are not fixable." Sophia sniffed and then whispered, "I feel like a failure who no one respects, nonetheless."

"You're not a failure and I respect you."

Sophia scoffed and reached for the door handle, but he stopped her.

"Your ex and his mistresses and these local women with loose morals are the ones who have failed and aren't respected. You can't allow them to steal your confidence in yourself." He reached over and gently grasped her chin to turn her face toward him. "You do realize it's their failures and not yours?"

Sophia averted her eyes, but Wes maneuvered himself around to where he could see her face. Those beautiful blue eyes were glassy and held too much sadness. It wasn't his place to do it, but his bones ached to banish the hurt from her and Collin's life.

"More important than what anyone else thinks, you have to respect yourself for Collin's sake."

Sophia tsked. "There you go again about my poor parenting skills."

"Are you kidding me, Sophia Grace?" Wes asked tersely. Tamping it down, he continued, "You and I both know you're an amazing mom. You've shown you're willing to do whatever is needed for the well-being of your son. . . . Shoot, you put your pride to the side and asked me for a job for his betterment." He took a deep breath and admitted something else. "I'm honored to call you my friend."

Sophia wiped underneath her eyes and gave him a fleeting glance. "You consider me your friend?"

"Absolutely. And I hope you feel the same about me."

She nodded. "Surprisingly, you have become a dear friend, Weston Sawyer. I appreciate you listening and how kind you've been to Collin."

"You two are the first new friends I've made in quite a long time . . ." Wes traced the stitching along the steering wheel with the tip of his finger, waiting for Sophia to open her door to end the night, but she made no move to do so. She was normally quicker to flee sensitive talks than he, but she seemed to be mulling over something, so he remained quiet and waited.

Sophia angled in her seat to face him but focused on her hands entwined on her lap. "Wes, may I ask you something personal?"

He considered her request, wondering if it was wiser to agree or to make a run for it. She was being brave enough to stay, so he would give it a go as well. His eyes locked on the door handle, but his lips moved to answer, "Yes."

"How do you cope with losing your wife and child? I've barely managed to overcome the demise of my marriage and career, but the tragedy you've endured . . . I can't even imagine."

The question hurt like a tender bruise taking another blow. He blinked the sting away from his eyes and cleared his throat to give an answer without divulging too many details. "I've had no choice, I suppose."

"It's not fair."

"No, it's not, but the Bible is clear on the fact that life is anything but fair. The story of Job is a good example of that."

"How can you be so understanding?" Sophia asked just above a whisper, her voice breaking.

"I wasn't at first . . ." He rolled his neck, one side popping in the process. "Throughout my career in Alabama, I witnessed the cruelest unfairness known to the world. A sick child dying in a parent's arms. I knew the possibility of unfairness could strike anyone at any time. It has no certain preference in victims, but nothing prepared me for what I faced in the aftermath." He took a jagged breath, feeling like he was inhaling burning shards of glass.

"I . . ." Sophia halted the words, obviously knowing there were none to soothe away the heartache.

He grasped the door handle, but before he could pull, a set of small yet strong arms wrapped around his neck. An exaggerated stretch of uncertainty passed before Wes gave in and embraced her back. The faint scent of peonies and citrus engulfed him, and before he could stop himself, he'd skimmed his nose along her neck to steal more of the appealing fragrance that had been teasing him from afar since she stormed into his life.

The hug lingered, and Wes was ashamed to admit he didn't want it to end. The feel of a woman's comforting embrace had become so foreign, having the sudden gift of it now was almost his undoing.

During his years at Regional, Wes did a fair share of research on the correlation between human touch and healing. The subject was quite debatable in the scientific realm, but his office was assembled of men and women who had a strong faith in God, so they all understood life went well beyond controlled aspects.

Plus, he'd witnessed firsthand what human touch could offer a cancer patient. Those patients who had constant contact with loved ones in forms of hugs, hand-holding, etc. thrived on hope and smiled even on the dark days. In contrast, those patients who were treated as though their cancer was contagious or as if they were too fragile to handle even the tiniest form of touch were often those who barely survived. Smiles and any flicker of happiness didn't exist.

Wes concluded, after years of observing patient after patient, that isolation could become its own form of cancer. It invaded any healthy cell of hope and killed off any faith that life could get better. In that moment, he realized isolation had not given him any reprieve from losing his

family. It only helped the grief and hurt to spread. Before
moving to Sunset Cove, he was pretty sure he was in the
last stages of it. He wondered if this tiny woman's touch
was going to help put him in remission.

Almost four years had passed since Claire had touched
him. It was an intimate act that he'd gotten so comfortable in that it was easy to take for granted. A caress, a
lingering hand on his back, a brush of her lips to his
cheek, his lips . . .

His body tensed and breathing grew into a labored
chore as the sensation of a tremor began building along
his shoulders. Sophia must have sensed it, because she
jumped back to her side of the car and looked as bewildered as he felt.

Neither could do anything but sit uncomfortably and
gape straight ahead until they collected their misplaced
composure.

"Wes . . ." She cleared her throat and peered at his
house, then back at him. "Do you . . . do you need me
to go inside and perform a safety sweep of the house for
rabid women?" Her sassy jab dissolved the pressure building in his chest, making breathing and living a little more
manageable.

"Would you?" he deadpanned, earning him a toothy
grin.

"It's probably wise. Who knows if some shameless
chick managed to scale the side of the house and crawl
through your bedroom window while we were gone." Her
eyes grew wide in mock indignation.

They chose to laugh off the uncomfortable tension
produced by the hug and Wes's looming meltdown, and
that was fine by him. He was beginning to appreciate
laughing as a more suitable alternative to crying.

Wes had spent the better part of the last four years

crying through the misery, yet it never cleansed the pain
of his loss. The grief wouldn't let go so easily and clung
to his soul like a stubborn stain, refusing to at least fade
until it was less noticeable. In all that time, he'd never
thought to hope for a path to lead him out of the shadow
of tragedy and into the light of living a healthy life.

His brother's words whispered from his memory. *"I
hope you give this fresh start a real chance. . . . You know it's
time. You deserve to be happy again."*

Happiness, in the form of a spunky brunette and silly
little boy, had shown up in the recent weeks, tempting
him to join in.

If only he could be courageous enough to accept that
it was time to move on.

11

Even though it had been a couple weeks since Agnes had graced Carolina Pediatrics with her presence, today had been set aside to give her a proper sendoff. Sophia was quite impressed that Wes had taken it upon himself to plan the entire party, even having it catered. He might not be a man quick to start a conversation, but he was on top of caring for others.

The employee kitchen was filled with the guests and a celebratory vibe, yet Sophia's phone and thoughts wouldn't allow her to join in. She continuously hit the Ignore button and would have turned it off altogether had it not been for the need to be available in case her mother called about Collin. No matter how many times she hit Ignore, Ty wouldn't give up.

Somehow the media had gotten wind of the IRS debacle, and Ty and his manager thought Sophia would happily agree to a few public appearances to help redirect the focus and maybe fuel a rumor of their reconciliation. He'd already called to try talking her into it and she had refused. His response was all sugar and love, but she should have known he wouldn't give up that easily.

After Agnes opened her gifts and said her last goodbyes, Sophia sent the rest of the staff out the door in Agnes's wake, assuring them she'd handle the cleanup. She dropped her shoes off in her office and was heading back to the kitchen when the phone began buzzing once again in her pocket. Knowing Wes hadn't left yet, she glanced over her shoulder to make sure she was alone in the hallway before answering.

"What do you want, Ty?" Sophia asked, and from there an excess of slurred curse words and vile accusations spilled from Ty's end of the phone.

"You vowed to be by my side. Good times or bad. I thought you were stronger than this, you little coward!" Ty spat the words out and followed it by calling her a more colorful name. Forget the sugar and love. This time it was all vinegar and hate.

"And you vowed to honor me. Not abuse me or cheat on me . . ." Her voice rose, so she tried quieting it down by releasing a cough before continuing. "You broke the vows first."

"You drove me to do those things!"

Sophia sputtered a haughty laugh. "Oh, wow. Who's being the coward now? You won't even take responsibility for what you did wrong." She blinked the sting from her eyes and swallowed the tears wanting their freedom. "And just so we're clear, you're the one who demanded control over our finances. It's after you took over that this mess happened, so don't you dare try blaming it on me!"

"How can you turn your back on me after all I've done for you?" Ty growled.

She rubbed her forehead and tried to tamp down the escalating rage building as quickly as a tornado. "I don't owe you anything. Have you forgotten we are no longer married?"

Instead of answering her, Ty continued to sling insults mixed with the guilt trip, so she hung up on him and hit Ignore as soon as the phone began ringing again.

Shaking her head, Sophia turned to go put the phone

in her office but bumped into Wes standing in the way. His hands, gently yet firmly, grasped her shoulders to steady her. When he kept them there and tilted his head slightly to search her eyes with his attentive ones, an entire conversation seemed to pass between them.

Are you all right?

No.

Will you be?

Hopefully.

"Do you need to talk about it?" Wes finally asked after they stood in silence for several long moments.

Sophia pressed her lips together to keep from unloading the weight of her worries. Even though they were forming a friendship constructed from a foundation of similar heartache, she didn't want to add to his burdens.

"I'll listen," Wes added, bending slightly to try recapturing her gaze, but she didn't allow it. "Letting it out can be good medicine."

Truthfully, Sophia was embarrassed by her predicament, which seemed cliché and shallow compared to what Wes had endured. Their pain might have had the same symptoms, but the cause couldn't have been more different.

"Good medicine would have been using some common sense to keep from getting to this point in the first place." Her muttered words finally had Wes's hands releasing her, so she bolted and left a lot unsaid in the hall.

•   •   •

Another celebration showed up two weeks later, and Sophia was actually going to be able to enjoy it. The mess with Ty had finally died down when some other celebrity figure was caught doing something deemed more scandalous than tax fraud.

Labor Day was considered the last hurrah for summer in the beach communities, and most tourists found their way back home after the long weekend, leaving Sunset Cove to settle down for a spell. The Sand Queens had always viewed the holiday weekend as their time to pay tribute to their summer achievements and make resolutions for the seasons ahead. The tradition went all the way back to their preteen years when the achievements had been easier and the resolutions simpler.

While others barbecued and lounged on the beach, the girls would sneak into Driftwood Diner and set up fancy finger foods and summer punch along the counter. For a splash of fun, purple Kool-Aid was always added to the punch, and flashy outfits were a requirement. Early on, the attire was plundered from their mothers' closets, and then later it was last year's prom or winter formal dresses. As the adult years knocked on their doors, the flashy dresses evolved to who could dress the tackiest. Opal won, hands down, most years. The girl could come up with a doozy of an outfit on a normal day, even more so when she put forth a little effort in the kooky department.

"This is going to be the best year to date," Josie mused while setting up the punch bowl. "We've never included guys in our fun. Makes me feel all grown-up."

Sophia placed a platter of crudités on the counter and gave Josie a dubious look. In wonky-patterned golf bloomers that looked more like shorts on her long legs and a silk blouse with a purple bowler hat on her head, she looked anything but grown-up. "We've matured greatly," Sophia said dryly while straightening the front of her psychedelic mod dress. She even lucked out and found a pair of pleather white boots and a platinum-blonde Afro wig.

"Honey, I'm here!" Opal sang out as she entered with

a tray. "Momma made us some of those pineapple cream cheese tea sandwiches. Aren't they just darling?" She held the tray out for their inspection, but both women scrutinized her outfit instead.

Sophia's hope of winning the tackiest trophy—which was a beauty queen trophy Opal purchased years ago from a consignment shop—plummeted at the sight of her. "Where on earth did you find that getup? You look like a Christmas leprechaun." Sophia waved a hand at Opal's ridiculous outfit—a green sequined top with a black bedazzled vest, metallic-gold Lycra pants, and red fur booties. Even the green-glittered headband nestled in the mess of red, blonde-tipped curls sparkled.

Opal set the platter down and shimmied. "You like it?"

"No, it's awful. You win," Josie grumbled. She redirected her attention to Sophia. "Wes is coming, right?"

"Yes, but only after I promised another public date." Sophia wrinkled her nose.

Opal settled on top of a stool and rubbed her small belly. "I've never seen two people so much alike. You're all posh and neat and too stubborn for your own good. What's so wrong with the dates that you have to give him such a hard time when he asks you out?"

"I'd rather we just hang out in private so there's no putting on a show for the town, but he insists we go out in public."

"I see nothing wrong with that. Couples can do both." Opal shrugged.

"But we are not a couple. Friends, yes. Couple, no." Sophia adjusted her wig that was as uncomfortable as the conversation.

August walked in from the kitchen entrance with his arms loaded down with bags of chips and a wholesale-size tub of dip. "Yo, ladies."

"What is that junk?" Sophia asked as she watched him shove the pretty platters aside to make room for the chips.

"Real snacks. I need more than dainty rabbit food." August opened a bag of chips, peeled the lid off the dip container, and dug in.

The girls watched him crunching away while the floral granny skirt he was wearing swayed as he moved his hips to the beat of the song playing over the sound system. He'd paired the gaudy skirt with a baseball jersey, and his black hair was hidden underneath a big floppy straw hat. On his feet were none other than combat boots splattered with paint.

"Cute skirt," Opal teased.

August jerked his chin in a manly manner. "Thought you would like it, but those gold pants are killer."

Heavy limping steps hit the deck outside and produced a giant wearing orange coveralls rolled up to just below his knees with a camouflage beanie on his head. He carried a tray of hot wings and a case of root beer, and that somehow added to his comical appearance.

"Linc, glad to see you managed to put on shoes," Sophia teased, eyeing his Converses—one navy and one white.

Other than a sardonic glance at her boots, Lincoln ignored Sophia and directed his path over to his wife. He bent down to give Opal a kiss before joining August in feasting on their junk food.

The girls were giving the two men a hard time when the door opened once more. Wes came to a halt and gave each one of them a curious once-over.

"Hey, why'd he get to dress normal?" Lincoln whined, using the back of his hand to wipe wing sauce from the corner of his lips.

"Neanderthal," Sophia muttered before turning her attention to the preppy man at the door.

Wes smoothed his tie and leveled Lincoln with a haughty look. "I'm wearing a plaid tie with my plaid shirt." He lifted the hem of his khaki linen pants and showed off the brown leather flip-flops. "This is not normal."

The girls snickered, and the guys glared with envy.

When it was made clear that the guys wouldn't be following the Sand Queens' traditions, the women banished them to the deck with their junk food and soda and commenced to enjoying their holiday rituals—snacking, dancing, and talking. There was certainly a lot to reflect on since the last Labor Day. One Sand Queen had married her ruggedly handsome prince, and the one who'd married the year before was celebrating a pregnancy. Josie and Opal were in the beginnings of a beautiful time in their lives, while Sophia tried not to be bitter about tripping into a difficult season in which her marriage and career ended in one excruciating fell swoop.

"How about you, honey? Tell us about your summer," Opal instructed before taking a sip of purple punch. The women were perched on stools at the counter, chatting and grazing on the snacks, but Sophia hadn't added much commentary.

"Collin is getting the hang of the potty training. Not too many accidents lately." She smiled, proud of her little boy and appreciative of Wes being so supportive in the matter. "Momma brings him by just before closing each day so he can get his Wes fix. I swear, the boy is all about some Weston Sawyer."

"I think Wes has been good for the both of you," Opal said pointedly but moved away from the statement fast enough that Sophia didn't have time to retort. "How about work?"

Sophia smiled again. "You know, it's been such a

pleasant surprise. Totally opposite of the fast-paced world of consulting high-maintenance clients, but I'm really enjoying the simpler work life. We're making good progress on converting the filing system to the new software, and I'm figuring out how to customize it to make everyone's life easier. It's very gratifying."

"I had no doubt you'd rock at running that place," Josie commented, using her napkin to wipe up a dollop of dip from the countertop. "You've never met a challenge you couldn't handle. I'm just so glad it's agreeing with you."

"Speaking of a challenge . . . I heard Miss Dalma made another visit to the doctor's office last week," Opal mentioned, and both Josie and Sophia groaned.

"That woman is like a wayward toddler." Josie snorted, shaking her head. She moved her plate to the side and propped up on her elbows. "What I don't get is how in the world she managed to get her arm stuck inside the crab trap."

"Well, if anything, Wes really does get a kick out of the challenge of tending to Miss Dalma's odd injuries. He's gone on and on about it. It's too cute." Sophia snickered, recalling how animatedly he'd spoken about it while they shared lunch that day.

"I thought Vanessa Sánchez moved in with Dalma," Opal commented.

"She did, but she still works part-time. The other Knitting Club members take turns sitting with Dalma during the day, but that's pretty much the blind leading the blind." Josie shook her head. "Most every afternoon August checks on her and she ends up roping him into doing something outlandish. Like last Thursday, when he arrived, Dalma had her small trolling boat wedged between the dock and the bank. Of course, August agreed to take care of it. By the time he got home, he was encrusted with inlet mud and had several oyster shell cuts."

Sophia wrinkled her nose. "I bet he stunk to high heavens too. Why didn't they just wait until high tide?"

"Because that was hours away and Miss Dalma's mind was set on getting it out right then and there. August knew if he didn't help, she would have tried to do it herself and probably broken her neck."

"True," Sophia agreed, thinking elderly minds did indeed work much the same as toddlers'.

While Sophia poured fresh cups of punch, Opal stretched out on the wood-plank floor. "Ugh . . . my thighs are getting thicker by the day." She slapped her gold-encased hips. "And look at these things. This is not my body!"

Sophia and Josie snickered, and then Sophia explained, "Honey, that's just the way it is. Your foundation has to be able to balance that big ball of a belly that's going to show up soon."

Opal raised her head and glared. "Was that supposed to make me feel better?"

"I bet Linc isn't complaining about all those new curves," Josie said on a giggle.

As though he had been summoned, Lincoln limped inside and picked up his pixie wife like she was made of glass. After giving her a soft kiss, he placed her on her feet. "No complaints here." He smirked while swaying Opal to the music. She grinned up at him, and it was easy to tell she was over her thickening thighs and hips. The woman was smitten.

Wes poked his head inside, and once he had Sophia's attention, ticked his head to the side, a silent request for her to join him.

She pulled the sweaty wig off and shook out her tangled hair while making her way to the screen door, where he remained. "Yes, sir?"

"May I take you home?"

"Sure." She turned back to the Sand Queens. "Josie, Wes said he'd take me home."

Josie swiveled around on the barstool and peered at them from underneath the brim of her bowler. "As long as you two behave and he has you home before curfew," she mocked in a motherly tone, which had no effect due to her silly outfit.

"We'll do our worst, *Mother*."

"Okay. Good night." Josie waggled her fingers and sent her stool swiveling back in the other direction as August took the seat beside her.

"Good night," Sophia repeated, following Wes out into the night. The air met her on a refreshing breeze, and she paused long enough to appreciate it. "You guys missed some great dancing," she mumbled, lifting her damp hair up so the breeze could cool her neck.

"I thought about asking the guys if we should join in, but Lincoln's leg is swollen, so I didn't think it was wise." Wes replaced Sophia's hands with his and held her hair away from her skin while combing through it. "It's a medical miracle that man still has his leg." He recapped the leg injury, using a lot of medical terminology that was over Sophia's head, but she didn't mind. Her focus was on the massaging motion of his fingertips along her scalp and neck. Wes could speak about any subject he wanted as long as his fingers continued delivering pure bliss.

Wes concluded the medical commentary and released her hair. Sophia reluctantly turned to head toward the parking lot, but he wrapped his hand around her wrist. "I walked here."

"You plan on giving me a piggyback ride home then?" She raised a skeptical eyebrow.

"The house is only a mile up the beach. I suppose I could carry you." Wes turned and bent down. It was tempting to shove him over, but she tamped that idea down along with the chuckle it tried to produce.

"Just let me take these boots off and I'll be able to manage the mile on my own two feet."

"Suit yourself." Wes straightened and helped to steady her as she worked the long zipper on the side of the boot.

Once she had both boots off and tossed into the back of Josie's truck, Sophia began trudging through the sand beside him. The beach was still lively with folks out and about, so they had to skirt bonfires and gatherings until reaching Wes's house.

"Do you mind if we sit out on the deck for a while?" he asked.

Sophia scanned the dark space that was barely illuminated by a few solar torches. "I guess not. Why?"

Wes unraveled his tie and unfastened the top button of his shirt. "For one, I've not spent much time with just you in the last week. I'd like to catch up. Plus, I found something for you. Give me a minute." He held a finger up and disappeared inside.

The outdoor sectional sofa had the best view of the giant Ferris wheel just south of Wes's house, so Sophia chose to sit there. Besides, the giant piece of furniture was downright comfy. Watching the brightly lit wheel slowly rotate, she heard the back door open and close. He sat close beside her and balanced a small gift box on her leg.

She picked it up and weighed it in the palm of her hand. "What's this?"

"An apology for my failed attempt at fake dating."

"It hasn't been a fail." She tried handing the box back, but he refused to take it.

"Clearly it has, but this is more than an apology."

She opened the box and found a delicate silver ring tucked inside. An anchor sat horizontally on top of the band. "It's lovely."

Wes took the ring out and slipped it on her left ring finger. "Even though marriage can be fickle, I wanted to give you a ring to remind you of an everlasting love." He tapped the top of the ring. "The anchor is a Christian symbol of hope. Each time you run your thumb along the back of this ring, you'll be reminded that no matter how many people break their promises, God never will."

Sophia moved the ring closer to a beam of light to get a better look at it, moving it one way and then the other, remembering the day Ty slipped a two-carat diamond on the same finger. Sure, she was blown away by the grandeur of the ring and the proposal, but it didn't hold a candle to the significance of this understated silver band.

Wes reached inside the box and pulled out a small card. "This came with the ring." He read, "'We have this hope as an anchor for the soul, firm and secure.' It comes from Hebrews 6:19."

"Wes . . . thank you." Sophia offered him a slight smile and touched the back of the band with her thumb, surprised that he'd picked up on her habit. His attentiveness said so much about him. Undoubtedly he had made one fine husband. "How long were you with Claire?"

He wiped his palms down the sides of his pants and released a heavy sigh. "We were college sweethearts. I went to a women's softball game my freshman year and was blown away by the agility of the pitcher." He smiled out into the night, seeming to wander deeper into his past. "I couldn't take my eyes off the blonde beauty. She owned that field. And by the end of the night, when Claire agreed to go grab an ice cream with me, she owned my heart."

Starting as college sweethearts seemed like an eternity compared to her mere four years with Ty. Knowing Wes had a better grasp on marriage than she'd ever had, Sophia asked, "What do you miss most about marriage?"

Wes blinked out of whatever memory had engrossed him and glanced at her thoughtfully before focusing on the glowing whitecaps of the ocean. "Sex."

Sophia sat straighter and popped his leg. "Wes!"

He shrugged, taking on the air of innocence. "You asked, and I'm just being honest. But it's more that I miss the intimacy of it. The closeness that was privately shared just between Claire and me. It was the two of us, but it felt like we were one, you know?"

Sophia did know. She and Ty had that for a brief time in their marriage, and it created the most precious gift of her life. She was blessed with Collin during the beautiful part of their time together. She would live the bad a thousand times over for his sake.

Wes cleared his throat, bringing her attention back to him. "It's been so lonely without Claire. I still miss her touch. Her comfort. Her steadfastness." He leaned back and spread an arm along the back of the couch, appearing weighed down by that loneliness. "What about you? Do you miss anything about your marriage?"

She thought it over until glimpses of happiness flickered past the painful memories. "Ty is an amazing man, until he's not. He can be the sweetest when the mood strikes him. One time he decided he wanted to make me a chocolate cake like my momma makes, because I was homesick. I had my doubts and voiced them." A quiet laugh released on an exhale. "That only spurred him

on. Said if he could handle a three-hundred-pound line-
man, then he could tackle a little ole cake. He thought
he could cut the sugar and balance it by adding more
cocoa powder."

"And?" Wes nudged her shoulder as he settled his arm
around her.

"It was awful. But Ty being the stubborn man that
he is, he was determined to eat it even when I refused.
Three bites in, he said, 'Okay, that's the worst cake I've
ever eaten.' We laughed it off, and the next day I received
a delivery from a fancy bakery in Charlotte. And *that* was
the best cake I've ever eaten." Sophia shook her head and
leaned into Wes's side. "As I said, Ty can be the best. I
just wish he could have thrown away his worst as easy as
he did that cake."

They grew silent for a while with Wes rubbing
warmth into her shoulder. Her thumb kept time by rubbing the back of the new ring.

"Tell me something else about Claire," she whispered.

His hand stopped moving, but a smile worked one
side of his lips up just enough that the dimple made its
presence known. It was dark, but Sophia could still see the
humor cast in his eyes. "She couldn't bake either."

They both snickered, but Wes's held an edge of
sadness.

"Claire was too free-spirited to measure her ingredients. Unfortunately, that didn't work in her favor when
it came to baking."

A loud boom sounded off in the distance, followed
by a fiery streak. A burst of glitter lit the sky near the
Ferris wheel. Their gaze moved to the sky and they quietly
watched the fireworks show.

"You and your friends have a strange way of celebrating Labor Day," Wes mused.

"Yeah, well, you guys were party poopers, so you missed hearing us recount the fun we had this summer and discussing upcoming plans."

"That sounds like a New Year's Eve tradition." Wes gave her an incredulous look.

"You've noticed by now we girls march to the beat of our own drums."

Wes tipped his head back and chuckled. "Yes, I have. What was your favorite summer memory?" Each time Wes talked, he drew her closer, but she had a feeling he didn't even realize he was doing it. The tingle heating her body sure noticed it, though. "It has to include me," he teased.

"Hmm . . . Probably finding you being chased around your kitchen by that crazy woman while she tried getting ahold of that towel you were wearing."

Wes growled while she laughed, but he pulled her closer until she was almost in his lap, effectively ending her laughter. Their breath mingled and their eyes locked. His flitted to her lips before closing. She stiffened, worried he was going to ruin the moment by trying to kiss her. But after what felt like a great deal of hesitance, Wes did the sweetest thing. Leaning forward, he rested his forehead against hers.

As Wes held her, Sophia realized they were sharing something pure and right. Even with her heart strumming at a considerable rate, there was no denying the fact that Weston Sawyer added a calm to her. Perhaps a better time for them both was on the horizon. Sophia didn't know what it could possibly be, but she could only hope it would be a more peaceful season than what they had both endured in the recent past.

12

October was the worst month of the year and it held the worst memories ever made. Not just one part of the month, but the entire thing. The beginning was supposed to be set aside for last-minute preparations, the middle a time of celebration, and the end a time to marvel in the wonderment of it. Regrettably, none of that came to be.

For the past three years, Wes had dealt with the vile time by hunkering down at his remote cabin in the mountains of Tennessee where no cell phone or Internet signal could find him. He longed to take off and go hide this year, but the responsibility of the new practice wouldn't allow him to up and disappear for an entire month, so he would have to cope the best way he knew how. Run. And when he had exhausted running, he'd run some more.

October 1 fell on Wednesday, thankfully a half day, and by the time he locked up, Wes was itching to run. As long as he kept in motion, grief couldn't catch up with him.

But if he ever got still . . .

I just need to outrun this. With that mantra on a steady repeat, he walked toward his car with purpose. Of course, his plan was interrupted by the ringing of his cell phone. He swiped a finger across the screen and said, "Hey."

"Hey, yourself," Seth answered in a whisper. "I need you to come get me." He sounded distracted.

Wes stopped walking and looked heavenward, but the

cloudless blue sky did nothing to settle him. "You better not be in jail again."

"No, man. I promise that was a onetime mistake. Just come get me."

Wes began moving again. "What's going on?"

"I met this chick at the airport. She said she'd give me a lift to your place, but she brought me to hers instead. Said she wanted to play doctor. . . . Dude, I'm feeling delicate. Hurry up."

Wes didn't know whether to laugh or lecture his brother, but then something occurred to him. "Why doctor?"

Seth snorted. "She thought I was good ole Dr. Weston Sawyer for some reason. What are you, Sunset Cove's most eligible bachelor or something?"

"Or something. I'm not a bachelor. I'm a widower." Wes cranked the car and debated just hanging up the phone and letting his brother lie in whatever dumb bed he'd made for himself.

"Whatever. Please pick me up and I'll never try pretending to be you again."

I've heard that before. "Text me the address. And you better clear up with that woman who you are by the time I get there." He didn't wait for a reply before ending the call and pulling out of the parking lot.

An hour later, the brothers arrived at the beach house, one chagrined and the other acting like he wasn't the cause of it.

"Wes—"

"We must never speak of it again." Wes sliced a hand through the air to stop the conversation before it got started. He dropped his briefcase by the door and headed into the kitchen.

"But—"

"Hello!" a sweet, raspy voice interrupted before Seth

could spit out another outlandish excuse. "The front door was left open, so . . ."

Both brothers turned, standing shoulder to shoulder, and found Sophia frozen in place, cradling a giant watermelon in her arms. Her eyes volleyed back and forth between them.

"She carried a watermelon," Seth blurted, thinking he was so cute. They both stared at the petite brunette in purple workout gear with her hair pulled back in a neat ponytail as she stared back. "I don't think she caught my movie reference."

"No . . . I did. Great movie. Just . . ." She blinked slowly and then squinted like she was trying to focus. "There are two of you?"

"I'm older and wiser," Wes admitted.

"Only by three minutes, and the jury's still out on you being wiser," Seth interjected.

"But you're identical."

"Yeah. And thank our heavenly stars Ma didn't give us dorky twin names that rhymed. Like Dan and Stan or Wayne and Shane." He tipped his invisible hat. "Nice to make your acquaintance, ma'am."

"Oh. My. Word." Sophia pointed to Seth and nearly lost her grip on the watermelon. "He's the country-hick version of your city slicker." She giggled freely, and if Wes wasn't so upset about the situation he had just encountered that one *must never speak of again*, he would have reveled in the beauty of it. "How did I not know this?"

Seth waved both hands toward her. "And how did I not know about you, darlin'?"

His brother was laying it on thick, so Wes popped him in the gut with the back of his hand. "Knock it off. . . . This is my office manager, Sophia. Sophia, my idiot brother, Seth."

"An office manager that delivers watermelons in cute running shorts?" Seth questioned but harrumphed when Wes delivered another warning smack to the gut.

Wes took the watermelon out of her arms. "Stop staring, Sophia. It's rude," he chided.

She twisted her lips and shook her head. "Humph. I guess this is what you would look like if you'd take that pretentious stick out of your backside and loosen up."

Seth chuckled. "I think I'm in love."

Wes disregarded both of them, walked around the kitchen island, and placed the watermelon in the sink.

Sophia answered his unspoken questions. "Daddy dropped off several by the condo. I thought I would bring you one and maybe ride along with you to pick up Collin."

Wes and Sophia had teamed up and gotten the little guy potty trained within a month's time. This month's challenge was to get him to stay all day at preschool. Last week was a bust, so Wes resorted to bribing him with a ride in his "race caw," as Collin liked to call the BMW, on Wednesdays. It was the only day his schedule would allow him to pick up Collin and he was already close to messing it up due to his reckless brother.

Wes hitched a thumb at his irritating brother. "My schedule is all off due to him." He studied his watch. "I was hoping to get in a run before I left, but that's out of the question now, I guess." He didn't have to turn around and look to know Seth was grinning like a schoolgirl eavesdropping on juicy gossip.

Sophia looked between the brothers again. "I don't want to impose on your time with your brother. I'll pick up Collin."

"No. I made a promise and I intend on keeping it." He loosened his tie and untucked his dress shirt. "I'm going to go change first." He rushed upstairs with his brother close behind him.

"Who is that and what's really going on here?" Seth asked as soon as he shut the bedroom door.

"I already told you." Wes stepped inside his walk-in closet and hurried out of his suit. "Plus . . ." He rolled his neck a few times before admitting, "We're fake dating."

"Why?" Seth shoved open the closet door and crossed his arms over his wrinkled tee.

Wes pulled on a perfectly pressed one, being mindful to pick a different color than the one his twin wore. "To help keep unwanted advances at bay. She's just coming out of a disastrous marriage and you already know why I don't want to date, so we're pretending to date so everyone else will leave us alone."

"How long have y'all been dating?" Seth leaned against the doorframe.

"Fake dating," Wes emphasized. "A couple of months."

"A couple months? Is that necessary?"

Wes cut him the sharpest look he could produce. *"Clearly.* Today is a perfect example of why I need the front of a fake girlfriend."

Seth raised both palms and took a step back. "Man, I said I was sorry. How was I supposed to know she'd—?"

"Not another word about it." Wes jabbed a finger into Seth's chest before moving to the back of the closet for a pair of jeans. He pulled them on and shoved his feet into a pair of Chucks.

"Since when do you wear Converse?" Seth stared at the shoes like they were offensive, even though he was wearing a scuffed-up pair himself.

Wes studied their shoes, how much they were alike yet so very different. He really didn't want to answer but did anyway. "I took Collin shoe shopping. He wanted us to have matching shoes." He thought Seth would laugh and taunt him about it, but his brother did neither. Just stood there with a concerned expression on his face.

"Collin is Sophia's kid?"

"Yes." Wes went to move past him, but Seth latched on to his arm.

The brothers' matching hazel eyes locked for a split second before he shifted his focus to his tidy room, with the color scheme of soft beiges and grays. Nothing like the room he'd shared with his wife back in Alabama. Claire loved any shade of blue and had decorated their entire stately colonial to suit her tastes. He didn't mind it as long as she was happy, but here in the new house Wes simply couldn't bear any blue resemblance of the life that was no more. When Lincoln Cole had asked for his preferences, Wes said anything but blue.

"How old is Collin?" Seth asked, still holding Wes's arm, trying to reel him back into a conversation he wanted no part in.

Wes looked anywhere but at his brother, already knowing what he was thinking. "Three."

"Weston," Seth said on a long drawl that was just above a whisper. So much sorrow was peppered in his name, but Wes stiffened his backbone to it and refused to give in to the emotional war starting to rage within him.

Wes yanked free. "It's not like that."

"You gonna get still so we can talk about this?" Seth's eyes filled with tears, and it was starting to unravel Wes's carefully constructed composure. That's how it had always been: when one hurt, the other hurt worse.

"If I stop, it'll catch up with me. I just can't face it right yet." He shoved his wallet and keys into his pockets and hurried downstairs before Seth could set in on a lecture.

Sophia stood at the kitchen island with a butcher

knife in her hand, slicing the watermelon. She glanced up at him. "You want me to ride with you?"

Wes contemplated whether it was safe for her to be left alone with his brother. Seth knew all of his history, while Sophia knew only the parts he'd shared. Not wanting to chance it, he nodded. "Seth, we'll be back in soon. Don't burn the place down while I'm gone."

"I'll do my best not to," Seth replied, but his tone had no tease. He eyed Sophia too seriously and then Wes. Luckily, she was finishing up the watermelon and didn't catch it.

Wes shook his head at his brother, warning him to let it go.

Seth shook his head back, clearly not willing to.

"Not now," Wes said to him quietly before addressing the tiny brunette looking way too comfortable in his kitchen. "I promised Collin I would be early, so we need to go, Sophia."

"I'm off the clock, Mr. Bossy Pants. Hold your horses," she sassed but washed her hands and obeyed anyway. It was one of her quirks that he secretly enjoyed. Sassy yet submissive.

Wes heard Seth cough out a laugh and mutter, "You have some more explaining to do."

Trying to shrug off his brother's accusations, Wes stormed out the front door to hold up his end of the promise. There wasn't much he could control at the moment, but picking up that little boy he could do. God willing.

They picked up Collin and returned to the beach house, and Collin had a similar reaction to seeing Seth as his mother had.

After staring for a while, Collin nodded his head and declared, "I like Sef. He can pay caws, too." The little guy unearthed a bevy of toy cars from his backpack and the three guys set out driving a course around the living room.

All the while, the boy talked Seth's ears off. Collin questioned Seth about his underwear, whether it had superheroes like his and Wes's did. Actually, Wes's didn't, but for some reason Collin believed it did. He further questioned Seth about whether he liked to sit or stand when he peeped. Seth cackled at all the little guy's blunt inquiries, but Collin remained serious and that only added fuel to Seth's laughing fire.

"I'm in love with this kid, too." Seth held his side while trying to rein in his laughter after Collin told him about Wes hosing him down outside when he accidentally pooped his pants.

"I not do dat again." Collin shook his head with his eyes rounded.

Sophia put together a pasta bake while Collin entertained them. After they shared the meal and took a walk on the beach, the two of them called it a night and headed out.

Wes cleaned the kitchen, enjoying the sounds of the ocean filtering in through the open windows, while Seth showered. He thought back over the last month, trying to see it from Seth's perspective, but only felt a sense of accomplishment over it. Sophia had finally relented and gone out on a few more dates with him, but they no longer felt forced. And more times than not, on the weekends she and Collin ended up over at his house after visiting next door.

He felt a great bit of pride over the fact that Sophia's appetite had been restored and that Collin giggled more than he frowned. He'd prayed for them and then put legs to his prayers and had witnessed the mother and son come to life right before his very eyes. It was the first time in years he'd been hopeful about anything.

In that instant, the memory of how he'd almost ruined it pinched the back of his neck. Rotating his shoulders a few times, he reassured himself for the hundredth time that he had stopped himself just before kissing Sophia that night on his deck. He blamed it on all of the talk about Claire. He blamed it on his loneliness. He blamed it on a lot of things since then, but the truth of the matter . . . he liked having her in his arms. Liked having her company. He simply liked her, and he had no idea what to do with all that liking.

A barstool scraped against the floor from behind him. "So are you ready to talk about it?"

Wes rinsed a glass and set it in the dish rack. "Don't know what you're referring to." He fished the plug out of the sink and watched the sudsy water drain out, not wanting to face the concern he knew he would find in Seth's eyes.

"They seem right at home here. It certainly didn't look *fake* to me."

Wes steeled himself and turned around. Crossing his arms, he leaned against the counter and met his brother's stare. Seth had his cheek propped in the palm of his hand, his wet hair flopping onto his creased forehead.

"The dating part is fake. The platonic friendship is real." Wes sighed. "I thought you'd be happy about that. You're the one who wanted me to get a life."

"You're right. I've pushed you to do just that for a few years now, but what I've seen today . . . man, I gotta be straight with you, I'm worried. It's like you've clung to them like a pretend family."

"It's not that. I promise."

"But you see where my concerns are coming from, right? You went from recluse to playing house overnight."

"You've not been here. It didn't happen overnight.

And I have enough sense to know Sophia and Collin aren't mine. *Mine* were taken from me four years ago *today*."

Seth straightened and shook his head. "I know. I hate this for you and . . . just please don't get hurt."

"I'm trying . . ." As predicted, Wes got still and the anniversary of losing his world caught up with him. All the hurt he'd been pushing down bubbled up and sent a stream of hot tears trickling down his cheeks.

As Wes's shoulders began to shake and the flood of grief engulfed him, he barely noticed Seth making his way around the island. His brother embraced him in a hug that was firm and filled with compassion. It was the strength needed to support him from falling apart. Wes gave in to the grief as his legs buckled and sent both of them to the floor.

And just like that, Wes was reliving the nightmare— one that would never remove its talons from his soul, no matter how many years passed. . . .

"I'm fat and miserable and my gut is almost too big to fit behind this steering wheel," Claire's voice whined through the speakers of Wes's car. Her little rant made him want to laugh, but after eight months of dealing with his pregnant wife he knew better.

Instead, he grinned at himself in the rearview mirror.
She's so dang cute.
Yeah, and you're one lucky son of a gun.
I know.

He moved his attention back to the road as the traffic light turned green. "Perhaps it's time you get your sweet behind still somewhere then." His grin widened to epic proportions, knowing she wouldn't take too kindly to his tease.

"I'm too busy for such mess as sitting still, and you better watch it, buddy."

Claire was one of those resilient beauties who only grew still when sleeping. Her athletic build was perfect for her two passions, horseback riding and softball. The bounty of ribbons and trophies from high school and college proved she was quite talented at both. Nowadays she had moved on to coaching, but that kept her just as busy.

"Would you forgive me if I promised to be your personal chauffeur and be at your beck and call?" Wes glanced over his shoulder before changing lanes. Rush hour was upon him and the traffic was thickening.

"How on earth would you be able to pull that off?" Claire asked. He could hear her changing radio stations.

"Leave the radio alone and focus on the road, dear." He laughed when she mumbled a tart reply, and then gave her his news. "As of today, I'm officially on paternity leave." He rolled to a stop at another light, noticing heavy clouds moving in.

Claire squealed. "Really?"

Wes chuckled. "Really. It's time you and I slow down and focus on preparing for Luke to make his debut."

"I can't wait," Claire said softly.

Warmth settled in his chest as he pictured the beautiful smile he heard in her voice. She had glowed with health and happiness in the last several months. They both looked forward to her being in that condition on a regular basis until their four extra bedrooms were filled with children.

"Oh!" She sounded startled.

"What?" He began to panic but settled down when she let out a giggle.

"Your son just kicked the tater out of me."

"That's my boy." Pride flooded him. He was so in awe over Claire growing them such a strong boy. The doctor was estimating him to be at least a nine-pounder at birth.

"Ugh, it's starting to rain cats and dogs," Claire said. He heard the sound of heavy rain followed by the whirl of windshield wipers coming to life on her end of the phone.

"Are you almost home?" Wes asked. He knew she'd spent the afternoon at the horse stable giving a riding lesson. It was only a fifteen-minute drive from their home out in the country.

"Yes."

"Good. Once you get there, take a nice relaxing bath and I'll be home shortly to rub your feet." Sadly, he had at least another thirty minutes left of his forty-five-minute commute.

She moaned. "Hmm, I'm such a lucky girl. Hurry up!"

Wes chuckled again. "We should hang up and concentrate on driving. I love you."

"Okay, you sweet, sexy man." Claire's flirting drove him crazy in only the best way and he couldn't wait to get home to her. "I love—"

You should have followed her last spoken word. Not the scream.

And certainly not the metallic explosion.

13

Something wasn't right. Sophia knew it, but she didn't know what was wrong. It began nagging her during supper at Wes's last night when she caught the twins—and hello, twins! That still blew her mind. Anyway, she caught them having one of those silent conversations. One that looked like Seth was leading it while Wes was trying to shut it down.

The niggling followed her into work early Thursday morning. Distracted, she stopped in her office long enough to grab the day's revised schedule and a few messages before shoving Wes's door open.

She screamed, and the papers went flying.

"Ain't you a sight for sore eyes!" Doc Nelson cackled out and slapped the desk, amused at having nearly given her a heart attack.

Clutching her chest, Sophia worked on steadying her breathing. "I'm so sorry, sir. I thought Wes—Dr. Sawyer would be in." She regathered her composure and then the scattered papers.

"It's okay, young lady. I should have had Agnes call you, but it was before the chickens got up this morning that I found out I'd be filling in here for the rest of the week." Doc offered a sad smile before squinting at the computer screen. "Is this schedule accurate for today?"

Sophia walked over to the desk and handed him the

papers. "No, sir. I had to revise it yesterday at the last minute." She waited for Doc to fill her in on what was going on with Wes, but he studied the paper instead. "Umm . . . is Dr. Sawyer ill?"

Doc didn't answer right away, and she was about to decide he wasn't going to at all when he let out a long sigh. "Wes ain't feeling his best, so I told him to take the next two days off."

"Oh. I hate to hear that. . . . Well, if you need anything, I'll be in my office." She pulled on a smile, but it refused to reach her eyes.

With no other choice, Sophia brushed off as best she could the notion of skipping out to go check on Wes and got to work. All the while, her thoughts looped around and tried gathering some detail or clue she'd missed that would set her mind at ease.

By the time five o'clock showed up, she'd made no headway. She arranged for her mother to pick up Collin and drove straight over to the beach house to figure it out. She knocked on the door, and after several long minutes, it opened.

She gasped. "Oh, Wes . . . you look just awful." Disheveled hair, scruff on his chin, dark shadows underneath his eyes. She'd never seen him in such a state.

His brow puckered. "I do?" Even his voice was a bit hoarse.

Sophia was really beginning to worry now. "I think you should go back to bed." She encouraged him to go inside, but he remained standing on the threshold in a wrinkled pair of night pants and a holey Alabama T-shirt. "Is there anything I can do for you?"

Wes glanced around the porch, running a hand through his hair. Then he leaned close to her ear. "It would make me feel better if you'd snuggle up with me in bed."

Stunned, Sophia yanked back and gawked at him. "Wes—"

"You can be my teddy bear." He reached for her after delivering a salacious wink.

That's when understanding dawned through the haze of shock. She slapped his hand away with enough force it left hers stinging. "Seth Sawyer, you scoundrel! That wasn't nice."

He chuckled. "Sorry. You stepped into that one, sweetheart. I couldn't help myself."

"You do look a little rough, though." She scanned his face again and found fatigue.

Seth's smile faded and sadness crinkled the corners of his eyes. "We had a long night."

"Is Wes okay?" She tried to look past him, but Seth stepped outside and closed the door, blocking her notion of just going inside and finding out for herself.

He rubbed the back of his neck and walked past her. "October is a bad month for him."

Sophia followed him to the edge of the porch. "What do you mean by that?"

Seth eased onto the porch steps, so she smoothed her skirt and sat beside him. Once she was settled, he said, "Yesterday was the fourth anniversary of losing his wife and son. They were killed instantly when a dump truck ran through a crossroads and T-boned her car. And if that isn't bad enough, his son, Luke, was supposed to be born that month." He sat quietly, resting his face against the palms of his hands.

"Poor Wes . . ." Sophia glanced around the yard. Her gaze stopped on the newly planted palm shrub, reminding her of the day she accidently killed his other one with her SUV and how Wes had helped to pull her out of a dark place that day. She wished she knew how to do the same for him. She'd banish October from the calendar if it were possible.

Seth let out a deep sigh and dropped his hands to look at her sideways. "I don't know what kind of delusional game the two of you are playing together with this fake dating, but you gotta see the danger in it."

"How?" Sure, she'd had her doubts in the beginning, but forming a friendship with Wes had been so organic and one of the easiest things she'd ever experienced. He'd been true to his word of not putting up with drama or being unnecessarily complicated.

"You realize your son is about the same age Luke would have been?" Seth asked, drawing her out of those pleasant thoughts.

Prickles raced along Sophia's skin. "I've not thought about it . . ."

"Yeah, well, you should. What happens when this little dating game plays out and you and your boy move on?" Seth hitched a thumb over his shoulder, concern pinching his brows. "What happens to my brother?"

"I don't—"

"I'll tell you what—he's going to fall apart all over again." Seth shook his head. "You didn't see Wes at the hospital holding his dead son." His head continued to move slowly from side to side. The memory was clearly still raw. "After . . . after it was confirmed that Luke didn't survive either, they put Wes in a private room with Claire and the baby. My brother held the baby in one arm and Claire in the other . . . I can't unsee that, so I know he can't." Seth scrubbed the tears away and sniffed before meeting Sophia's eyes. "Please . . . you can't hurt my brother."

A lump lodged in Sophia's throat as the details solidified into an image she couldn't fathom. She'd only thought about the possible impact of the dating ruse on Collin, not Wes. Once they ended it, she'd be there to help Collin move on, but her insides clenched with knowing that it would be Wes's ruin. "I don't intend to hurt him."

"You have to see this from where I'm sitting. Y'all hang out like a family."

"I do see it now. I assure you I'll be more mindful, but I honestly enjoy my friendship with Wes." Sophia tucked her hair behind her ear and gave Seth a soft smile. "He's pretty spectacular."

Seth returned the small smile. "If my brother has let you into his circle, then that can only mean you're pretty spectacular yourself. I just don't want him to use your son to fill the void of losing his."

"Do you think that's why Wes has gotten so attached to Collin?" Sophia asked, holding back tears.

Seth draped an arm over her shoulder. The gesture held a brotherly quality and felt comforting. "Sweetheart, your kid is obnoxiously adorable. Anyone would get attached. Heck, he had me at 'I pooped my pants.'" He joked but neither of them laughed.

"Wes hasn't talked much about losing Claire and Luke, but now that I know all of that, I promise to be more cautious."

"I thought he was going to mourn himself to death, to be honest with you. The hardest thing I ever witnessed. Most of that first year, Wes stayed rooted in the rocking chair in Luke's nursery. Basically, the only time he left that room was to run the five-mile trek through the woods to the cemetery to sit by their grave for hours at a time." Seth rubbed his forehead, looking even more haggard.

"If it's any consolation," Sophia said, "I've seen a big change in him over the last few months. Wes looked empty when he first arrived, but he's come to life. He goes out of his way for his patients and can give some old ladies in the community a run for their money in the spunk department." She laughed under her breath. "But he has such a cool and understated way of doing it that most of the time people are oblivious to it."

Seth chuckled, but his face remained in a grimace. "Yeah, the guy has dry humor down to an art form."

"He's doing okay," Sophia reiterated, placing her hand over one of Seth's clenched fists. The poor guy was riddled with worry for his brother. After a moment, she added, "I'd love to see him."

"Just give him a few days to get himself sorted." He rose to his feet and helped her do the same.

"Okay," she agreed hesitantly. "But please get in touch with me if there's anything I can do."

"Thanks, sweetheart." Seth gave Sophia a one-armed hug and waited for her to leave before moving back inside.

Resigned to giving Wes his space, Sophia decided it would give her some time to wrap her mind around the situation too. She arrived at her parents' farm as the night sky settled around it. The smell of hamburgers wafted through the air, so she walked around to the backyard, where she found her dad by the grill. He was dressed in his favorite faded jean overalls and red flannel shirt with a straw hat pushed low on his head, the ideal picture of a Southern farmer.

"Hey, Dad."

He flipped a few burgers and looked up through a steamy cloud of smoke. "Hey, darlin'. How was your day?"

"Okay. How was yours?" Sophia saw slices of cheese on the sideboard, so she busied herself with unwrapping them.

"Good. Got two cornfields harvested, and then the day got even better when my grandboy showed up to help me bale up the pine straw."

"Oh, I bet he loved that." Sophia finished unwrapping the cheese slices and handed them to him. "Is he inside with Momma?"

"Yep. I promised burgers if he'd take a bath." He began topping each patty with cheese. "Little stinker didn't want to take one."

"Your bacon cheeseburgers would talk a cat into taking a bath." She inhaled deeply and savored the succulent aroma of chopped bacon and ground beef. It had been her dad's special way of making burgers for as long as she could remember, so she decided to wait until after supper to have a talk with her mother. No need in spoiling anyone's appetite with the sad conversation that needed to be spoken. *It can hold,* she promised herself, while helping her dad load the burgers onto a platter.

After the burgers were devoured along with a mess of fresh home fries, Sophia's dad grabbed up a mason jar and took Collin outside to collect fireflies just as he used to do with her when she was a little girl.

Sophia stepped over to the kitchen sink, picked up a dish towel, and began drying dishes. "Momma, can I talk to you about Isabella?"

Her mother didn't answer right away, clearly taken aback by the request. It wasn't that the subject of Isabella was off-limits. It was just that they rarely ventured to talk about her. "Of course, honey." Lucy offered a weak smile while handing over a plate.

Sophia took the Blue Willow plate and slowly dried it. Her mother insisted on always using her fine china, no matter if the meal was prime rib roast or burgers. Sophia stacked it with the others and placed them in the cabinet. By then, she'd worked up some strength to delve into the difficult topic. "How do you bear the loss of a child?"

"You don't," Lucy answered in a small voice. She motioned for Sophia to follow her to the den.

"But—"

Lucy placed her hand on top of Sophia's. "Sweetheart, losing a child is a wound that refuses to heal. You and Collin and your father are like salve. You soothe it enough so that I can tolerate my loss, but the wound still remains unhealed. Even after all these years."

Sophia was only three and her sister, Isabella, five, when Isabella was diagnosed with leukemia. She made it two years before succumbing to the disease at the age of seven.

"What's brought this conversation on?"

Sophia blinked the tears away and glanced at her mother. "Wes lost his wife and unborn child in an accident four years ago this month. I'm trying to understand how to help him." She shrugged, feeling at a loss.

"I heard about that."

"How can I help him? What helps you?"

Her mother shook her head. "I think you're already doing what you can to help him. You and Collin seem to be a bright spot for him."

"And that worries me too. I don't want him to get attached to Collin."

"What's so wrong with that?"

"Because . . ." Sophia studied the portraits lining the mantel. *Family.* That was the story they told. "Wes isn't family. I don't want him settling into a false sense that he is and end up hurting him."

"Oh, honey. That is a tough spot." Lucy sighed. "Things are going so good with you and Wes, and honestly, I think it's the healthiest relationship you've formed since the Sand Queens."

Sophia arched an eyebrow as she stared at her mother.

"How's a false relationship healthy?" She'd been up-front with her parents from the start about the dating charade.

"I'm not talking about that part, but the true friendship part." Lucy resettled on the couch and crossed her legs. "What really happened?"

Sophia had already filled her parents in about the identical twin shock. There wasn't much she kept from them nowadays, since realizing the error of not confiding in them about Ty. "Seth and I had a long chat before I came over here. He pretty much warned me off. Said I'd just end up hurting Wes in the long run, and to tell you the truth, I worry I will too." She straightened the lapel of her navy suit jacket, ready to be home and in yoga pants. "I can't chance hurting Collin or him."

Lucy reached over and patted her knee. "You're scared, is all. Don't allow fear to be your driving force. Sure, take what Seth had to say into consideration and be careful. Maybe put some space between Wes and Collin. You know I love seeing my grandson, so please take advantage of that. But don't shut the door on you and Wes."

"I know . . . I just want to help him," Sophia whispered while her thumb rubbed the back of the anchor ring.

Her mother tapped a fingertip to the top of the ring, apparently catching her. "Seems that man has been your anchor in the last few months. Simply do the same for him."

Sophia gazed at the ring, remembering all the times it had reminded her that God was her anchor, just as Wes had wanted it to. But her mom was right. Somewhere along the line, Wes himself had also become an anchor for her. His attentiveness and persistence had aided in her regaining her appetite, potty training Collin, and cutting enough apron strings to allow him to go to preschool. She wasn't blind to the fact that most of the dates they'd been on had been for her benefit more than his.

Last week's date flickered through her mind, lifting the corners of her lips.

"What's that smile over?" Lucy nudged her leg.

Sophia bit her lip to suppress the smile. "Just thinking about Wes taking me to the Harvest Dance last week."

"Still can't get over the two of you making the paper."

"Well, the man certainly knows how to cut a rug." Sophia gave up and grinned even wider, reminiscing about how he dipped her and kissed the tip of her nose. It was playful, but the newspaper captured an image of it that looked much more than that. "He took me to the dance because the rumor mill said I was in hiding with bruises and a sprained wrist from Ty."

Sophia had taken Collin to see Ty in Columbia during his team's bye week. In all actuality, it had been one of the smoothest visits they'd had so far, except when it came time to leave. Collin fell to pieces, and not having any power to make that particular hurt any better for her baby, Sophia started crying as well. As they loaded up to begin the trek back home, Ty had reached into the car to give her a hug. Unfortunately, the paparazzi pictures that surfaced the following day made it look like his arm was in the process of punching her instead of embracing her.

Wes showed up at her door, demanding she put on her halter-top maxi dress to show off her bruise-free arms and shoulders and go out dancing with him. That date was all for her, even though Wes would never admit it.

"Well, the pictures definitely debunked that rumor. Baby, you were glowing at that dance."

"Yes, and that was Wes being my anchor. Now I need to figure out how to be his." Sophia stood. "Wish me luck."

"You don't need luck. You just need to pay attention to your intuition." Her mother winked before wrapping Sophia in a reassuring hug.

• • •

Sophia listened to her intuition, giving Wes the space Seth had advised, even allowing Saturday to skip by when Wes didn't answer her call. She figured if he needed her, he would have picked up. But by Sunday afternoon, she was about to come out of her skin. It wasn't a "want to" but a "need to." She needed to see him.

Sitting on Opal's deck in a floppy sun hat and oversize shades with the Sand Queens, a wave of déjà vu swept over her. She was even wearing black yoga pants and a black top. "We've already lived this scene not too long ago."

"Yes, but this time it's you who's trying to figure out a way into the vampire's lair." Opal tucked her lightweight cardigan around her, stretching the fabric over her baby bump.

Sophia reached over and smoothed her palm over the taut ball and spoke to it. "Little Cole, your momma is a Froot Loop. Just warning you."

Opal playfully shoved Sophia away. "No more than you are."

Josie straightened in the wicker chair where she was slouching. "Someone is in the kitchen."

All eyes darted that way.

"When are the cookies getting here?" Sophia asked as she watched the curtain over the sink flutter before the shadow disappeared. Her patience had worn so thin that she wasn't above storming over there and going toe to toe with Seth to get inside that house.

"Linc is on the way back with them now," Opal answered after checking her phone. She set it down on the table and kicked her feet into a vacant chair, the glitter of her bright-green toenail polish catching in the late-day sunshine.

Sophia crossed her arms and slumped in her chair. "Ugh. There won't be any left by the time that big oaf gets here."

"Momma made two batches for that very reason. One for Linc and one for *the plan*." Opal flicked her wrist dismissively, sending a tinkling sound ringing out from her bangle bracelets.

That brilliant plan was to draw the brothers out with a phone call promising fresh-baked cookies. And not just any cookies, but Opal's mother's award-winning loaded chocolate chip cookies. After Linc delivered the goods—one full container and one holding only crumbs—he disappeared inside, claiming that he needed to eat something salty to balance the cookies. Opal called and left a message, and in less than ten minutes, the guys took the bait.

The back door of Wes's beach house swung open and produced a man on a mission. The breeze played through his caramel locks as he bounded down the deck stairs two at a time.

"It's always a treat to see your handsome face, Wes," Opal commented as soon as he stood beside them on her deck. The large umbrella over the table shaded his face, but he seemed to be just fine. Sophia was relieved to see no trace of dark circles.

"You can look all you want, just so long as you hand over those cookies." He held his palm out and waggled his fingers impatiently until she placed the container in his hand.

"Wait a minute," Josie spoke up, something she rarely did. "You're not Wes."

Sophia had already figured that out, but it was fun seeing her friends make the same mistake she had on Thursday. She bit her lip to hold back the smile.

"Who are you and how'd you know that?" Seth quirked a thick eyebrow.

"For one, you're mouthy. Wes isn't. You also have a tiny mole on the top of your left cheek. Wes doesn't."

Seth touched a fingertip to the beauty mark. "Ain't you observant?"

Opal giggled. "That *ain't* definitely confirmed you're not our Wes." She hitched a thumb in Josie's direction as she stood up. "Josie's an artist. She's all about detail." She laced her arm around Seth's and beckoned him toward her door. "Sophia whipped up some of her homemade hot chocolate to go with the cookies. Let's go inside and have some."

Seth followed her in like a starved puppy, perfectly distracted—as was the plan.

Sophia snuck away and let herself in the back door at Wes's. The house was quiet and each of her tiptoed steps seemed to echo as she peeked inside every room on the first floor. When they all came up empty, she left her hat and sunglasses on the couch and moved upstairs. As soon as she hit the second-floor landing that opened into a quaint sitting area, movement out on the balcony caught her eye.

She walked over and quietly eased open the French doors. Wes made no indication he'd heard her except for scooting over in the canvas hammock to make room for her. She glanced at the rocking chair on the other end of the balcony, where it swayed beside a small table that held a lone coffee cup. After debating a long minute, she chose to accept his silent invitation and managed to settle beside him without tossing them both out of the hammock.

From the corner of her eye, Sophia inspected him as slyly as possible and let out a sigh of relief when she found him looking as perfect as ever in a pair of wrinkle-free lounge pants and a plain gray T-shirt. His bare feet were casually crossed at the ankles. No stubble on his chin and his hair was combed. The only thing amiss were the faint shadows underneath his hazel eyes, which were trained on her as she moved her attention up. She waited for him to call her out on staring.

It was impossible to keep space between them in the hammock, considering it was designed to cocoon, so she relaxed her stiff posture and rolled closer. He smelled of laundry detergent and soap, and she couldn't resist snuggling against his shoulder and reaching to entwine their hands. She felt his finger move over the band of her ring as she tried to conjure up some comforting words.

She finally settled on asking, "Can you describe the symptoms?"

"Oh, you know . . . the gamut of chest aches, swollen throat and eyes, insomnia . . ."

"I'm somewhat familiar with those symptoms." Sophia spoke in a serious tone, keeping her eyes fastened on their hands. If she looked up and connected with the grief she clearly heard in his voice, it would break her, and she wanted to be strong for him.

"Yeah? And what do you suggest for treatment?"

Sophia pulled her hand free so she could wrap her arm around his midsection. Holding him tightly while resting her ear over his heart, she replied, "I'm a poor excuse for a support system, but I truly want to be a better one for you."

Wes placed his arm around her to return the embrace, so securely that she almost rolled completely on top of him. "Sophia Grace, you sell yourself too short. You and Collin have been an antidote to many of my ailments."

"We have?"

"Yes. I don't know what all Seth said to you, but I have a pretty good guess. Just know I have a handle on things, okay?"

She propped her chin on his chest and finally met his eyes. Sure, sorrow mixed with the various hues of his hazel eyes, but there was also a hint of gratitude and affection. "Okay. I really wish there was more I could do . . ."

He combed his fingers through her hair, looking thoughtful, before asking, "Where's my cookies?"

The tightness eased in Sophia's chest at his lighter tone. "Those weren't for you." She dropped her head and snuggled a little closer, enjoying his warmth as it combated the growing chill in the fall air.

Wes dropped a foot to the floor and set the hammock on another sway. "No?"

"Nope. They were a decoy to distract Seth so I could sneak over here. It worked, but I'm afraid those cookies are probably long gone by now."

"You went to that much trouble for me?"

"Of course, and it was well worth it . . . You're worth it."

Wes's foot stilled as he put a finger underneath her chin to bring her gaze to meet his. "Thank you."

"I've missed you," Sophia confessed.

Crinkles formed at the corners of his eyes as he smiled. It was a sad smile, but a smile nonetheless. "I missed you too."

They might have only confessed to missing the other, but the wordless conversation they'd shared while holding each other said so much more.

A link woven from grief and heartache connected them. As the fibers tightened, a luminous strand of hope began binding them together. It both thrilled and scared Sophia. A verse from the Bible flickered through her mind as Wes rested his forehead against her temple and pulled her closer. *"Therefore what God has joined together, let no one separate."*

Was this what God meant by that? she wondered as tears began pricking behind her closed eyes. But before she got too caught up in the emotions whirling through her, she remembered Wes's declaration a while back. *"I'm still in love with my wife. The fact that she's dead doesn't change how I feel about her. I have no desire to give someone else my heart when it still belongs to Claire."*

There was no denying they shared something special, but clearly he was still grieving for his wife and child. Only time would tell if Wes could make room for Sophia and Collin in his heart.

14

Doc Nelson was a lunatic. Add Seth Sawyer into the mix of that lunacy, and the recipe was sure to produce a calamity of epic proportions. Oddly enough, the town trusted the two lunatics enough to let them loiter in the hallway of the police precinct instead of behind bars in a holding cell where they belonged.

Wes wasn't feeling as trusting as he stood there trying not to lose his cool while listening to them explain away their illegal shenanigans.

"That game warden had no right!" Seth grouched, having the audacity to be offended. "He's the one who acted like an idiot."

"Not from where I'm standing." Wes took a deep breath and stepped out of the way of a few officers as they walked by. This was definitely not the way he wanted to spend a long lunch break on a Friday.

"His corn bread ain't done in the middle. That's for sure." Doc tossed in his two cents and crossed his arms on a loud harrumph. "The nerve of that kid . . . arresting me after I used to treat him for those nasty ear infections."

Wes glared at the two soggy men sitting on the bench, looking like petulant children awaiting a spanking. If they weren't grown men, Wes might have been tempted to do just that. The puddles underneath their feet indicated they'd already paid some price for their crime.

"I cannot wrap my mind around the fact that you two thought it made sense to try to outswim a boat." Wes rubbed his temples.

"It made more sense than being sitting ducks on the water," Doc fired back, even though it didn't help his cause in Wes's opinion.

Wes raised a skeptical eyebrow. "Look, old man, I realize you're healthier than most eighteen-year-olds, but you need to realize you don't have to act as senseless as one."

Seth stood, his shoes squeaking against the tile floor. "Don't talk to my buddy like that."

Wes gave him a stern look, the one he'd been forced to give his twin in more instances than he cared to recall, effectively sending Seth back to a seated position. "It's not like either one of you can't afford a saltwater license. Or to go to the seafood market and simply purchase a mess of legal clams."

"It ain't about the money. It's about principle." Seth jabbed a finger in the air like a preacher would do when making a valid point. In his case, he wasn't even making any sense.

"And what principle would that be?" When his brother didn't answer, because it was obvious the two men just wanted to rebel against the saltwater laws and cause a ruckus, Wes left them dripping on the bench to find the game warden who had dredged them out of the inlet.

Fifteen minutes later, Wes signed the documents the game warden handed over. He was a burly man, tall with a bushy beard and matching eyebrows, and his name seemed to suit him. Bruce.

"Using M-80s to blow a hole in the mud, instead of digging for the clams, was a rather clever idea. If they'd had a license and hadn't made a run for it, I'd probably have let them off with just a warning." Bruce placed the credit card on the counter and clicked a few keys on the computer, and the printer spit out a receipt.

Wes handed over the pen and slid the papers across the counter. "I understand. Hopefully this will teach them a lesson." He put the credit card back in his wallet and then pulled his phone out to call August.

With Sophia dragging him to most gatherings with her friends, it meant Wes spent a good amount of time with August and Lincoln. A friendship was inevitable, even though those two couldn't have been more of Wes's opposite. They were outdoorsy types. Wes liked to run, but that was the extent of his outdoor adventures. They were big and burly. Wes knew he was only of average build and on the preppy side. God had divvied out a major helping of creativity to both the famous artist and the eclectic architectural engineer. Wes was all about medical breakthroughs and current studies. It definitely made for some interesting conversations.

August answered on the second ring. "Hey, man. What's up?"

"I've just sprung two hoodlums from jail. Do you think you could give them a lift home so I can get back to work?"

No way was Wes allowing them to make a soggy mess in his car, and he knew for a fact that August's truck was coated in mud at the moment. He'd shown up in it that morning to collect some sponsorship paperwork and Wes's donation for the Seashore Wishes mud run they were hosting at the Palmetto Fine Arts Camp. Seashore Wishes was a worthy foundation, aiding wounded war veterans in finding new careers. Lincoln was a wounded veteran himself. He'd told Wes about his struggles to overcome his leg injury and find a new path in life. Lincoln had formed the charity earlier in the year when he felt

God calling him to help others in similar situations. The entire town stepped up to support it, and Carolina Pediatrics was on board as well.

"No problem. I have to get Linc from Bless This Mess and then I'll be there."

"I'm not putting you out, am I?" Wes knew they were busy setting up for the run that night.

"Not at all. We heard what Doc and your brother did. Can't wait to razz the old man about it." August's deep chuckle echoed through the phone before he disconnected.

Shortly after, Wes squinted his eyes and waved as the muddy truck turned in to the station. The three men stood outside in the midday sun, where two of them were trying to dry out a bit. Linc and August waved back as the truck came to a halt beside them.

August hopped out and hurried to help Doc climb into the backseat of his King Cab. "Don't you know the saltwater fishing laws, sir?"

"Only enough to be dangerous," Doc fired back, sending the artist into a boisterous bout of laughter.

Wes shook August's hand. "Thanks for helping me out with them."

"No worries." August grinned.

"I think they have too much time on their hands. Is there anything they can help with at the camp to keep out of trouble for the rest of the day?"

"We can hear you," Seth commented, leaning out the open window.

Wes shot him a glare, thinking his brother's visit was wearing thin. He'd been here a little over a month now and didn't show any signs of leaving soon. Seth was like garlic bread—an enjoyable treat when freshly presented, but the lingering presence on the palate afterward . . . not so much.

"Your brother doesn't have a job?" August asked, shoving his hands into his front jean pockets. Wes noticed he was splattered with mud instead of the usual paint.

"It's one of those jobs where all Seth needs is a computer and Internet access. He's in the gaming and coding business." Wes said it with an air of aloofness, but he was right proud of his brother. Seth was a genius with an IQ of 133 but disguised himself as a back roads country boy.

August scratched the side of his neck and glanced at the two men in the back of the truck. "Since they're already filthy and clearly know their way around explosives, I could use their help finishing the obstacle course and setting up the fireworks."

"That sounds perfect." Wes looked for a fairly clean spot and clapped August on the shoulder. "Call me if they get unruly and I'll send Sophia over to straighten them out."

"Send her on now. I like that feisty chick," Seth smarted off.

Linc reached over and sent the window whirring up, mumbling something about it being wise to shut up while he was ahead.

They parted ways and Wes made it back to the office with only ten minutes to spare before the doors reopened after the lunch break. He made a beeline to Sophia's office and found her right where he'd left her almost an hour ago, behind the desk with those vivid blue eyes glued to the computer monitor.

He walked over and pulled her chair out until there was room for him to go to his knees and rest his head in her lap. "My brother is going to be the death of me," he mumbled, blindly searching for her hand and placing it on his head. She easily took the hint and began combing her fingers through his hair.

"How'd it go?"

Wes's eyes began rolling around as her nails scraped against his scalp. The massaging motion instantly dispersed the tension. "They're free for now, as long as they can stay out of trouble."

He knew it was selfish to always seek Sophia out for her soothing touch, but Wes was too drawn to the little spitfire, who had more comforting warmth than a thick quilt by a crackling fire. In the past few weeks, she had somehow managed to settle a deep hurt within him, and a peace had overtaken some of the shadows lingering in his soul.

"Did they get to keep the clams, at least?"

"I gave them to Bruce as a thank-you," he slurred, feeling sleepy all of a sudden.

"You better wake up." Her hand left his hair and popped him on the back. "I had to shuffle a few appointments from right before lunch to the afternoon."

Wes inhaled a deep whiff of her perfume as he rose to his feet. "You feel bad for me, right? Working all morning and then having to deal with that fiasco instead of eating lunch?"

"Of course I do. *Poor wittle Wes,*" Sophia answered in a patronizing tone, making him want to tickle her.

"Good. That means you're running with me tonight."

Her teasing expression morphed into all seriousness. "Nah-uh."

"Yes, you are."

"I can't run three miles in the mud. That's plain ridiculous." She glared.

"You run with me on the beach in the wet sand at least three days a week. It's more or less the same thing. Plus, it's for a worthy cause." He straightened his tie and then shrugged out of his jacket, knowing it was time to prepare for the afternoon appointments. After draping the coat over his arm, Wes snatched a protein bar from the snack drawer and shoved it into the pocket of his dress shirt. Thankfully, Sophia stocked healthier selections than what Agnes used to keep on hand.

"I'm not stupid. Mud runs are obstacle course runs where you have to wallow in the *mud*. Lincoln Cole designed the course, so I know it will be a whole heckuva lot different than wet sand."

"Run with me and I'll owe you one." Wes hurried to his office with Sophia following.

"You'll owe me at least two."

"Agreed." Wes hung the jacket and shrugged on his lab coat. The sounds of a door opening and closing indicated that the staff was filtering back in from their lunch break.

Sophia plucked the protein bar from his shirt pocket and unwrapped it before holding it up to his mouth. Wes leaned over and took a playfully big bite and winked. He couldn't help but smile when she rolled her eyes.

"Ugh. Put those darn dimples away and get to work," Sophia sassed, handing the bar over and sashaying out of his office with enough prissy spunk to draw forth a toothy grin. Today she wore a pair of leggings with a flowy blue top that Wes thought looked more like a dress. Whatever she wanted to call it, he thought she was downright lovely in it.

Wes tried to study the afternoon's revised schedule but couldn't rein in his thoughts about Sophia. Ever since she had snuck into his house back in October, she'd been sneaking into a special place in his heart. She'd been firmly by his side—whether it was working, running, church services, or an amicable date—and he liked her there. A lot.

Only thing he didn't like was that she was keeping
Collin away from him. The little boy had claimed his own
special spot in Wes's heart, and he couldn't help but miss
him. Sunday visits just weren't enough. Sure, he understood her hesitance after Seth's big mouth got in her ear,
but he wanted to prove to them he wasn't delusional
about their place in his life or his place in Collin's life. He
knew he wasn't Collin's father. That honor belonged to a
big idiot who was missing out on so many blessings by
putting himself before his son.

"Your first patient is waiting in the coral reef room,"
the nurse said as she knocked on his open door. "I'm
pretty sure you're looking at a sinus infection."

"Thanks, Krista. I'll be there in a minute." Wes
grabbed his stethoscope and headed that way, leaving the
worry of Sophia and Collin for later.

$$\bullet \quad \bullet \quad \bullet$$

The November night was cool and crisp. The mud was
icy and mushy. Sophia was frigid and prickly. And Wes
was over it all by the time they'd crossed the finish line
and received their sand-dollar-design finisher's medals. If
he'd cut her like the deadweight she was, Wes was fairly
certain he'd have finished in the top three.

"Never again," he muttered, wiping his cheek with
the back of his hand, knowing good and well it didn't
help. They were both covered in mud from head to toe.
Him, from maneuvering the obstacle course like they
were supposed to. Her, from being shoved into the last
mud puddle by Lincoln after he met up with them near
the end, where he was standing guard.

"You've shirked the whole dang thing, Miss Priss!"

Lincoln had yelled before giving Sophia a swift shove. The "puddle" was closer to the size of a small pond.

Sophia wrung the water out of her ponytail and huffed, bringing Wes's attention back to the present. "*Never again* is right." They were traipsing through the patch of woods that separated the obstacle course from the parking lot.

"It wouldn't have hurt you to do the obstacles."

Sophia stopped and hitched her hands onto her hips. "I ran the entire thing. No one said it was against the rules to go around the obstacles."

"You do realize you added at least two extra miles by doing that?" Wes mirrored her pose, feeling right exhausted. He had run the course as directed and then kept backtracking to find Sophia so she wouldn't get lost in the dark.

"We survived it, didn't we? Well, almost. That big oaf has it coming to him when he least expects it. I don't know why you'd even think I'd be into something such as this. I could have just made a donation and sat up on the bleachers at the finish line, with Opal and Josie and the other sane people. I'm not a mud kinda girl. . . ."

The full moon beamed through the tall trees, filtering ribbons of silver along her scowling face as she continued her rant. Even in such an angry state, Sophia was easily one of the most beautiful women he'd ever seen.

She reached out and jabbed him in the chest with a finger while fussing on and on about nonsense. Before she could retract her hand, he grabbed it and pulled her into his arms.

Wes's plan was to tell her to hush up already and release his hold on her, but when Sophia let out a gasp and melted into his embrace, that plan was all but forgotten.

His lips pressed against hers, effectively ending her rant and his long pent-up need to kiss her.

Wes had come to understand a lot about Sophia—and the life she had endured—as they'd grown closer during the past four months. It had been a loud life that seemed to be too aggressive and cumbersome. Many of their late-night talks involved her sharing the trials she'd withstood with Ty. She often expressed how exhausted it had left her. Wes was determined to be the opposite in their friendship, their working relationship, and in this kiss.

He presented it with no force, simply placing his lips against hers and holding the caress in a gentle manner. When Sophia didn't push him away or bite him, he brushed his lips from one corner of her mouth to the other and back again. Featherlight and slower than cool molasses.

The boisterous sounds of music and celebration beyond the trees seemed to fall away as his heart began pounding in his ears. It was scary yet invigorating. With shaking, gentle hands, Wes cupped her muddy face and deepened the kiss by a fraction. They were surrounded by a thick blanket of earthiness, yet her sweet floral scent was there, reminding him of how solid Sophia's support had become.

Wes thought the room had tilted the night he first heard the beautiful melody of Sophia's laughter, but that didn't come close to what he felt as she parted her lips to invite him closer. The entire forest tilted and spun until it turned his life completely upside down.

Dazed, they broke apart when a voice boomed over the camp's loudspeakers about something Wes was too boggled to catch. He stared at Sophia, trying to gauge her response to what he'd done. She looked as surprised as he was. Sure, it was something he'd pictured happening a time or two, but he never thought it would actually happen.

Whether to revel in the kiss or to feel guilty about it pushed and pulled against him as his eyes unfastened from her and looked around the shadowed space. He raked a hand through his damp hair and gathered several deep breaths.

"Sophia, I'm—"

"Don't you dare say you're sorry for kissing me." Sophia jabbed a finger right over his heart in the very same spot that felt both good and bad for what he had just done.

The feeling reminded him of a runner's high—exhilarating even though it took enduring a fair amount of pain to achieve it. He had spent the better part of the past month sorting through his feelings. Wes knew Sophia wasn't Claire. Not once had he tried to find his wife in the feisty brunette. But he'd be lying if he said he didn't sometimes catch himself picturing Luke through Collin, especially after Seth expressed his concerns about it.

As Wes watched Sophia ramble out another tirade with her arms flailing around, he knew in his heart that the concerns didn't hold a light to the visceral need to have them both in his life. This time when he pulled her back into his arms, the kiss was planned. Slow and tender, the caress was meant to convey just how enamored he'd become with her.

He knew he loved Sophia and Collin for who they were, not for what they could never be. He hadn't come to Sunset Cove with any hope of finding what he'd found. But here she was, standing before him in muddy clothes and enough sass to keep anyone on their toes. Wes knew—

A crackling sound whizzed through the air, followed

by a loud boom, and the sky came to life in bursts of color. The unexpectedness of the fireworks seemed to give him a little push.

Wes released Sophia from the kiss and blurted, "I didn't move here for this." He took a step back as the forest lit in hues of blue and red. "I didn't even like you when we first met." He shook his head, feeling overwhelmed and knowing his perfectly prepared speech was coming out all wrong.

Sophia looked as confused as she had every right to be. "Okay."

"No, it's not okay. I didn't *want* to want you, but—"

"Seriously?" Sophia growled and stormed off before he could finish.

"Wait! I'm saying it all wrong!" He hurried after her just as she set out into a sprint.

By the time he reached the parking lot, Sophia's SUV was pulling out. He ran to his car to follow her. The garbage bag he'd brought along to protect his seat from the mud crinkled underneath him as he got in and yanked the seat belt on, huffing and growling the entire time.

Colleagues and family members alike had always complimented Wes on how eloquent he was. Always clear and to the point. Surely he'd just debunked that in one fell swoop. He had to hold himself back from slapping a palm to his forehead. "Idiot!" he muttered, focusing on Sophia's SUV taillights.

As soon as she parked in front of her condo, she darted to her door, but he managed to catch her before she disappeared inside. He gently wrapped a hand around her upper arm.

"How dare you kiss me like that and then tell me you don't want to like me," she muttered through clenched teeth, snatching her arm out of his grip.

Wes placed his hand over hers where she was jamming the key into the lock. "Sophia, I don't *like*—"

"Momma needs to get home. Whatever you want to say can hold." She swatted his hand away and shoved the door open, but before she could slam it, Wes shouldered his way inside.

"No. This won't hold. I don't *like* you; I—" Before he could tell her he loved her, they both came to a halt in the dim living room.

Stretched out on the couch, watching TV while holding his son and looking right at home, was none other than Ty Prescott. He flashed them a megawatt smile before placing a finger to his lips in a hushing manner, giving the illusion of a perfect daddy. The little guy was snoring with his tiny arms latched around his dad's neck, as if even in sleep, he worried Ty would disappear again.

The image twisted Wes's gut. He hoped Sophia's stiffened shoulders indicated she was no more thrilled about Ty's presence than he was.

"What are you doing here? Where's Momma?" Sophia whispered.

"Hey, babe." Ty grinned again and winked at her. Wes had never wanted to punch someone so badly in all his life. "I sent her home."

"But what are you doing here?" Sophia moved closer and pointed at the boot on Ty's foot. "And what happened to your leg?"

"You didn't watch last night's game?" When she shook her head, Ty explained while rubbing Collin's back. "Made the game-winning touchdown only to be tackled at the back of the end zone. We got twisted up and I injured my Achilles tendon. I'm out for the rest of the season."

Wes wanted to tell Mr. Football to go recover somewhere else. That Ty wasn't welcome in their home, but he stopped himself when he realized this wasn't his home, nor was it his place to say anything.

"Who's this?" Ty asked, jerking his chin in Wes's direction with an attitude he had no right having.

"Oh, this is my boss, Dr. Weston Sawyer. I've told you about him." Sophia shifted her weight from one foot and back to the other. "We participated in a charity run tonight."

It bothered Wes that she didn't include the fact that he was her friend or her fake-yet-real boyfriend with whom she held hands on a fairly regular basis. Nor did she add that he was an amazing kisser. But Wes figured he deserved her omitting all of that after he'd just flubbed probably one of the most important moments of his life.

"Yeah, Lucy told me about it." Ty slowly sat up. "Babe, you want to put our son down?" He cradled the toddler close while placing a kiss against his messy curls.

It was the very same spot Wes had placed numerous kisses. Nauseated, he knew the deadbeat dad had more right to do it than he did, and there was nothing fair about that.

"Umm . . . let me change out of my muddy clothes first." Sophia hurried down the hall. As her bedroom door shut, the men's eyes locked.

"Thanks, man, for giving my wife a job while my lawyers work out our mess."

Wes caught Ty's use of the word *wife* but chose not to point out what they both already knew. He wouldn't say anything out of line while Collin was in Ty's arms.

Sophia was back in a flash, wearing black yoga pants and a long-sleeved black shirt. "Good night, Wes," she said dismissively before bending to pick up Collin and march toward his bedroom without one glimpse back.

Ty stood and stretched, giving Wes a chance to size

him up. The guy had at least six more inches in height than Wes and was broader through the shoulders. *Lincoln Cole could take him,* Wes thought, *but I'm not so sure I could.* The notion caught him by surprise because he'd never been a violent person. But something about Ty standing before him had his protective instincts on high alert. Perhaps some pride was mixed in there, too.

"Lucy filled me in on all you've been doing for *my* family. Heard you potty trained *my* boy and got him to stay at the preschool. Aren't you handy to have around?" Ty picked up the remote from the couch cushion and turned the TV off.

"Among other things," Wes replied dryly, knowing the docile conversation was heading toward a spitting contest and that just wasn't his style. Even though he was seething, he held on to an air of aloofness, determined not to give Ty the satisfaction of getting under his skin.

"Now that I have a few months off, I'll take it from here." Ty hobbled over to the door and opened it.

Wes remained where he was standing and glanced down the hall, knowing Sophia had no intention of reemerging any time soon. "Sophia is your ex-wife, so she's no longer your concern." He gave Ty a measured look.

Ty grinned like he thought what Wes said was cute. "I plan on winning my wife back." He made a lazy ushering motion at the open doorway.

Wes glanced down the hall again. He had the overwhelming desire to snatch Sophia and Collin and take them as far away from the wretched man as possible.

When Wes made no move to leave, Ty took a step over to him and whispered, "I'm good at getting what I want, and those two are all I want. I'm here to see that happen." He loomed over Wes, obviously going for intimidation. "They're *mine.*"

Wes stood taller and bowed out his chest. "You better not hurt them again, because I can promise you one thing . . . you won't get away with it unscathed this time."

Ty's smirk fell away, revealing a severe glower. "Who do you think you are?" The words came out in a hushed snarl and a manner that would have had most people backing away.

Wes didn't back down, even going so far as taking a step closer. "I'm a *real* man who knows it's never appropriate to hit a woman. A *real* man who knows how to stay faithful to his marriage vows and understands what a precious gift his wife and child are. One that would never put himself first instead of his family." His temper was about to get the best of him, so Wes leisurely walked out the door as if he didn't have a formidably fuming blockhead at his back.

Halfway down the outdoor steps, he turned around and glared at Ty. "If Sophia chooses to give you a second chance, I won't stand in the way. But you better think twice before mistreating her or Collin in any way. You *won't* get away with it again," he reiterated, leaving the threat to linger heavily in the air between them.

The only thing Wes could do at the moment was leave well enough alone and plead with God to protect Sophia and Collin. But despite praying all the way home, nothing about the night sat well with him.

By the time he stormed through the door at the beach house, Wes was close to coming undone. Seth walked out of his room in sweats, drying his hair with a towel.

"Get packed. Time to go home," Wes said, moving toward the stairs.

"Man, I told you I'm sorry about getting arrested again. Don't kick me out," Seth whined close behind him.

Wes shook his head as his hand gripped the iron

banister. It felt icy compared to his sweaty palm. He halted his ascent and turned to face his brother. "It has nothing to do with that. . . . We're both leaving. Sophia's ex is in town. It looks long-term."

"So? You just gonna run away? That's stupid." Seth slapped the towel against his thigh. "We both know you're in love with her. You gotta fight for what's yours."

Since Seth arrived last month, Wes had done a lot of talking and Seth had done a lot of listening.

"I'm not so sure I have any right to claim her." Wes held his hands out to show Seth how they were quivering with rage. "I need time to cool off. If I don't, you'll be bailing *me* out of jail for a change."

"You're right. You do need to calm down." Seth suddenly looked worried. Not a look he wore much.

Wes shoved his hands through his mud-crusted hair and paced in a tight circle. "It's taking every bit of my willpower not to grab the baseball bat and storm back over there to give that hotshot Ty Prescott a taste of his own medicine." Before Wes realized what he was doing, he was beating a path toward the closet where the bat was tucked, but Seth reached out and stopped him.

"Take a breath, man." Seth locked eyes with him through several stuttered breaths. "I think a weekend trip might do you good, but we're both coming back here Sunday to deal with this like men."

"I need to shower first. Be ready to drive." Wes shrugged off Seth's hand and took the stairs two at a time, hoping the six-hour drive to Alabama would give him enough time to cool off and give Sophia enough space to decide what course she wanted to take—without his interference.

15

As soon as she heard the front door closing, Sophia stepped out of Collin's bedroom to face whatever obstacle Ty planned to throw at her this round. She was stronger than she once was, but he was just as intimidating as ever.

"What are you doing here, Ty?" she asked while he locked the front door. When he turned and limped back to the couch, she noticed his cheeks were tinged red and a deep grimace shadowed his face.

Ty wiped the anger away with precision and resurrected an easy smile—the facade she knew all too well. "I figured with this free time on my hands while I recuperate, we could work on us."

Her heart squeezed before thudding harder in her chest. "There is no *us* anymore."

"Babe." Ty pointed to the cushion beside him, but she remained standing. "Please . . ." He tried his persuasive tone and followed it by tilting his head to the side and blinking with an innocence he executed flawlessly. There was no denying that the man knew how to glow with enough charm to light up a room.

Knowing better, Sophia held her ground. "I'll allow you to stay in the guest room just for tonight, but tomorrow you need to find another place to stay."

"Seriously?" He actually looked hurt.

"Yes. Ty . . ." She shook her head, feeling the mud dry-ing along her neck. "I'm in desperate need of a shower."

Ty stood. "Now you're talking, baby. I'll wash your back." He winked with a salacious grin.

"That wasn't an invitation." She shook her head again. "I'm exhausted. I can't do this tonight." She hurried to her bedroom and walked straight into the adjoining bathroom, being mindful to lock the door behind her.

Good thing she did, because not even a minute into her shower the door handle jiggled. Back in the day, Ty would sneak in and try to make her forget how nasty a person he truly was. She was naive back then and would quickly give in. But now, after several rounds of bruises and embarrassing headlines—not to mention signed divorce papers—she wouldn't be taken for a fool ever again.

She couldn't contain the smug grin when Ty let out a huff of frustration and finally gave up on the door open-ing at his whim like it used to. *Not again,* she told herself while scrubbing the mud out of her hair. *Never again.*

After the shower, Sophia texted her mom. **You leaving Collin with Ty. Not. Cool.** She powered the phone down to leave the rest of the argument for tomorrow and snuck into the hallway. All the lights were off and the guest room door was open. A faint glow indicated he was in there on his phone. She tiptoed into her son's room, gath-ered him up, and brought him back to her bed. Once she had the little sleeping bundle situated, she locked her bedroom door and climbed in beside him.

In the dark, Sophia listened to the comforting sounds of Collin snoring. She smiled, thinking he was an old man trapped in a toddler's body. As he let out a grunt and turned over, her thoughts drifted to the other important man in her life, and it sure wasn't that unwelcome guy down the hall.

Wes had floored her tonight with that kiss. It was so tender and pure. An intimate gift that didn't demand anything in return. It was everything a kiss should be, yet it was the first of its kind Sophia had ever experienced.

The doorknob jiggled, pulling her from the sweet idea of what could be. Even though the room was pitch-black, her eyes looked around. She pulled Collin closer and listened as either Ty's forehead or fist tapped against the door.

"I love you, babe . . . I love you." His words were muffled through the door before his limping gait moved away, allowing Sophia to release the breath trapped in her lungs.

Ty Prescott was a man of smooth words, but she had learned the hard way that they eventually came up empty. No actions backed them up to prove he loved her. The only thing proven had come from his fists, and at a hefty price.

Swallowing the threatening tears, she willed herself to keep the facts front and center. Ty was too charismatic for his own good. Paired with his handsome looks, it was a recipe for danger. If he planned to be around, it would be crucial for her to keep a level head, firmly rooted in reality, and ignore the fantasy he was a pro at presenting on a silver platter. It would be too easy to fall back into the old habit of listening to his pretty words and not paying attention to his actions.

With the weight of the situation pressing against her, Sophia didn't find sleep until hours later. She finally drifted off while trying to come up with a plan for handling both the situation with Ty and the unfinished conversation with Wes but woke up having found no answer to either one. The only thing to be found was the savory scent of bacon wafting around the room.

After taking care of bathroom duties for both herself and Collin, Sophia settled Collin on her hip and tried steadying herself to go meet whatever the Saturday held.

Walking into the kitchen, she found Ty standing at the stove in only a pair of low-slung track pants while frying eggs in a skillet. Except for the boot on his left foot, he was flawless.

Ty glanced over his broad shoulder, looking all rumpled and dreamy with his thick, brown hair disheveled in perfect disarray. "Good morning, my family." He grinned, squinting his brown eyes.

This isn't real. His sweetness is not real. He's no longer yours, Sophia reminded herself.

"Daddy!" Collin squealed, obviously not expecting to find him still here. He squirmed out of Sophia's arms and launched himself into Ty's.

Sophia took Ty's place at the stove while he tossed Collin in the air a few times before placing the giggling toddler on a chair and sitting next to him. She brought the eggs over and set them next to a plate of bacon and glasses of juice. She studied Ty with concern, knowing he was at his best but also knowing it wouldn't last. What stung about that the most was that her smiling boy would be the one hurt again when Ty's facade morphed into a darker form before he disappeared altogether.

With no appetite, Sophia pushed the eggs around her plate while watching Ty and Collin eat their breakfast with gusto, neither one of them noticing her. She watched as Collin fed his daddy a bite of egg and then Ty did the same to him in return. It was cute. It was what every breakfast should look like. But Sophia could count on one hand how many times it had actually occurred.

"What's our plan for the day?" Ty asked, reaching over to run the back of his hand along Sophia's cheek.

For Collin's sake, she didn't flinch from his touch but moved out of reach while feigning the excuse of needing to wipe up some spilled juice from the table. "Collin and

I are going to go pay Papa and Grandma a visit. *You* need to spend the day finding yourself a place to stay."

Ty's shoulders slumped as he turned his puppy-dog eyes on her. "Babe, I understand you need some time. I'll get my assistant on finding me a place, but you have to promise to give me a fair chance to prove myself." He reached over and combed his fingers through Collin's messy curls. "For the sake of our son."

It was his go-to guilt-trip line, and in the past Sophia was quick to bend for the sake of their son, but Ty was always the only one to benefit from it. What Ty seemed not to understand was that she wouldn't be bending in his favor ever again.

Sophia chose not to comment, letting him think he'd won the argument, and began gathering the dishes. While she cleaned the kitchen, Ty disappeared into the guest room and didn't reemerge until she'd finished loading the dishwasher.

She sensed his formidable presence behind her just before his lips touched the shell of her ear. "No one's perfect, Sophia. We all fall sometimes. Please give me a chance to stand tall again."

Sophia knew she didn't owe Ty that nor should she become so emotional over his words, but tears clogged her throat all the same. "I want you to stand tall for Collin," she whispered, taking a side step to get away from him. He had added a T-shirt to go with the track pants and a shoe on his good foot, so she figured it was best to push him on out the door while he was standing. Blinking several times, she offered a smile in Collin's direction where he was sorting through a pile of toy cars on the living room rug. "Okay, bub, it's time to get dressed."

Collin gathered a car into each of his fists and scurried down the hall.

Sophia turned to Ty. "Hurry up before he comes back out."

"Why?" Ty scratched the dark-auburn scruff on his cheek.

"It's easier this way." She picked up a few toys and tossed them into the basket.

"On who?"

"You, clearly, because no matter what, that little boy will fall apart as soon as you're gone."

Ty huffed. "It doesn't have to be this way."

Sophia added a toy tractor to the lot before facing Ty. "Oh? So you'll never leave him again for training camp or games? Or ad campaigns in California?" The last part of her remark had him wincing. Good, it was a painful memory for her as well.

Ty went to retrieve his duffel back from the guest room without another word, then gathered his wallet and keys from the coffee table, admitting defeat this round. "I'd like to see you tonight. Maybe take you out to dinner."

"We already have plans for tonight." Sophia and Collin normally spent their Saturdays at Opal's house, and at some point in the evening she would sneak over and spend some time with Wes.

"What kind of plans?"

"Really, Ty?" She narrowed her eyes at him.

"You're right. Sorry. I'll see you soon." He left with the least amount of theatrics ever.

It gave Sophia a sliver of confidence that perhaps she could stand strong this time and not give in to the intimidating man. She made her way into the bedroom to turn her phone back on, cringing when she found several missed calls from her mother. She tapped on the missed call notification to return the call.

Her mother answered right away and rushed into

an apology. "Honey, your granddaddy fell at the nursing home and we needed to go to him last night. That's
the only reason why I left Collin with Ty. You know I
wouldn't leave him if I didn't think he was safe. It was
close to ten, so I knew you would be home soon. I tried
to call you as soon as I could—"

"It's okay. Is Granddaddy okay?" Ugh. Now Sophia
felt like a heel for sending that terse text. The old man
was entering his eighty-sixth year, and it had pained
Sophia's parents to place him in a home two years ago
when Alzheimer's overtook his mind and body.

"He's bruised up, but luckily no broken bones."
Her mother sighed heavily. "Please forgive me for leaving Collin. Ty was going on and on about the counseling sessions, and he sounded so genuine about making
changes—"

"I understand, Momma. I'm sorry I got upset." Sophia
sat on the edge of the bed as Collin wandered in wearing
a pair of track pants that resembled Ty's along with one
of his daddy's team-logo shirts. It made her chest burn,
knowing he was going to be crushed to find Ty gone.
"Are you still at the nursing home?" she asked her mother.

"Yes. I don't want to leave him." She sniffled.

"Collin and I are bringing y'all breakfast. Tell
Granddaddy donuts are on the way."

Her mother let out a watery laugh as Collin bounced
up and down and sang out, "I love donuts!"

●   ●   ●

Sunday morning showed up right along with a beam-
ing Ty. He offered to drive them to church, and when
Collin answered yes for the both of them, Sophia had
no choice but to go along with her son's decision. They

looked picture-perfect walking into church together, but
Sophia knew it was only a front. Her insides pinched
with unease. Wes should have been sitting beside her during worship services instead of Ty with his arm wrapped
around her possessively.

As the pastor spoke, the Sunday of Collin's birthday
with Wes by her side in this same pew flickered through
her thoughts. She had pictured herself falling out of the
pew and letting out all her distress in one momentous
fit with limbs flailing and rage spewing from her mouth
until someone showed up with a straitjacket. Sophia still
wanted to have a conniption, but now she wanted to
scream at the top of her lungs that the man sitting beside
her wasn't the right one! That Weston Sawyer was, wherever he might be!

Sophia continuously gazed around the congregation,
expecting Wes to magically appear. He never did, and by
the end of the service, she wondered if he had really ever
been there in the first place.

Sunday dinner at her parents' house was everything a
Sunday dinner should be. A Southern spread consisting of
country-fried steak and gravy, mashed potatoes, and butter beans, with peach cobbler served for dessert. The only
thing wrong was Ty sitting in Wes's place at the table. It
was the first Sunday in a long time that was spent without
his quiet strength by her side and that didn't feel right. Ty
in his place was even more wrong.

Monday morning, Sophia was relieved when she
spotted Wes's sports car parked in the back lot at work.
But her relief was short-lived. In the office, she found him
closed off and more aloof than ever.

She stood by his desk, trying to capture his distracted
attention. "We missed you at church yesterday. Momma
even made your favorite for Sunday dinner. Lucky for

you, I made you a plate for today's lunch." She held up the plastic wrap–covered dish, but Wes kept his eyes focused on his computer screen. His glasses caught the glare of it, making it impossible for Sophia to get a read on him.

"Seth and I spent the weekend in Alabama," he mumbled, still refusing to look at her.

"Why? Is everything okay?"

"Yes. I was just homesick." His answer was terse to the point that it had Sophia's palms sweating.

She placed the plate on his desk and wiped her hands against the front of her pencil skirt. The weekend had stolen her assurance, so she'd chosen to dress smartly to gather some courage. Clearly it hadn't worked. Without further comment, she left Wes to sulk. About what, exactly, she wasn't sure.

Each time she tried to address him throughout the remainder of the day, Wes would cut her off with "Not now, Ms. Prescott," so she knew it was bad. He hated her last name about as much as he hated the man who had given it to her and only used it when he was in a sour mood.

After work, Sophia made a phone call to Opal, filling her friend in on what was happening and then asking for her help with a little snooping task. She picked Collin up and drove straight over to the Cole house. They let themselves in and found Opal sitting on the couch with Lincoln beside her.

Collin toddled over and stood staring at Opal's belly. It was becoming quite rounded and Sophia thought it was also quite beautiful. "Ofal, you gettin' fat."

Before Sophia could reprimand him for being rude, Opal giggled and said, "It's all Linc's fault."

Collin narrowed his blue eyes at Lincoln. His little brow pinched. "You make Ofal fat?"

Lincoln looked rather smug, smoothing the side of his scruffy beard. "Sure did. I'm right proud of it, too."

Opal swatted his arm. "That's enough gloating. Why don't you show Collin the rocking horse in the nursery?"

Lincoln stood and offered his massive hand and Collin placed his tiny one in it as they walked off.

Opal turned to Sophia once the boys were out of sight. "Wes left through his back door about ten minutes ago."

"Was he in running gear?"

"No. Jeans and a tee. Should make it easier for you to find him."

"Okay. Thanks." Sophia slipped out through the deck door and kicked her gray suede pumps off before descending the deck stairs. Her toes welcomed the cold sand as the breeze ruffled her hair. Taking a fortifying breath, she soldiered past the sand dunes, peering left and then right. A sigh of relief tumbled out when she spotted Wes nestled between the two sand dunes in front of his deck. She trudged over and stood before him, but his eyes stayed focused on the ocean.

"Are you going to explain to me why you don't like me?" Sophia asked, deciding to open with a little sassing. She dug her toes deeper into the fluffy sand, waiting for him to banter back, but Wes remained mute. She tugged her pencil skirt up until she could bend and sit beside him, close enough to feel his warmth without touching.

"You have to know what I feel for you goes beyond *like*," Wes whispered, not taking his eyes off the waves crashing several feet away. A seagull swooped in and plucked at a piece of seaweed that had washed up on the shore before fussing about it and flying off.

Once the bird was gone, Sophia asked, "Then why are you shutting me out?"

"I'm not your family, so I have no rights." His confession was almost exactly the same sentiment she'd shared in worry with her mother a while back, but it hurt worse coming from him.

Hundreds of words wanted to be said, but each one stuck to her tongue. It wasn't her place to start promising Wes more than what they were, if she wasn't 100 percent sure she could deliver. She reached for his hand and whispered, "But you're my best friend."

He finally looked at her, tears swimming in his sad hazel eyes. "I want more than friendship. It's what I was trying, yet failing, to tell you Friday night."

Sophia had assumed as much. That kiss conveyed more than friendship. Dare she say love was written in the very action of it? "I know, but—"

"But it's complicated." A faint smile whispered along his lips, not even distinct enough to produce his dimples, while he gently removed her hand. "And we need to stay focused on doing what's best for Collin." He moved his fingers back and forth between them. "He doesn't deserve complicated."

As they stood and brushed off the sand, Sophia couldn't suppress the urge to wrap her arms around him. The embrace was one-sided and sadly awkward, feeling like they had regressed back to how they were in the beginning. When it became clear he wouldn't be returning the embrace, she let go and began walking away.

"Sophia . . ." His voice trailed off behind her, echoing an edge of contriteness.

She kept walking and threw her hand up. "Good night, Wes."

He was right. It was complicated. But he'd also proved he was too stubborn to overcome it to be with her. She wouldn't beg. And she wouldn't be made a fool of again.

16

Loneliness was something that had become a constant part of Wes's life over the last four years. He'd come to terms with it being that way—until Sophia Prescott marched her sassy self into his life and demanded he pay attention. Now that she was only on the outer edge of his daily life at the office, he was lonelier than ever.

Even at the moment, on a crowded pier, surrounded by locals shoving their way around to claim prime fishing real estate, Wes was lonely. From the briny smell of fish to the sharp wind, he could hear Sophia's rant on it as if she were there by his side. Man, he missed her quibbling. Around the office they were back to a reserved uncomfortableness as they'd been at the beginning of the summer. Here it was closing in on December, and the frigidness wasn't coming from Mother Nature.

Wes trained his eyes on the gray water below, where the last hints of daylight kept touching it with gold flickers. He was flanked by Doc and Seth on one side and August and Lincoln on the other. What they'd done earlier could be considered kidnapping, but he brushed off the aggravation of being snatched off the couch and tried to make the best of this guys' night out.

"Man, you can tell the spots are running with all these folks out this evening. Y'all best have brought your A game if we gonna catch any supper." Lincoln baited his double hook with a chunk of mullet, a shrimp, and topped it off with a bloodworm.

"You need all that?" Seth asked, lacing only a single worm onto his hook.

Lincoln motioned around at the large crowd. "There's too many meal choices, so you gotta entice the fish to come to your hook instead of the thousand others bobbing in the water."

Seth and Lincoln set into going a few rounds on which bait was the best, but Wes tuned them out and cast his line with a single shrimp on the end. As soon as it had settled in the water, it was snagged. Without any theatrics, he reeled in the fish and put it in the cooler. He proceeded to do this several more times before the other four men could finish prepping their hooks.

"Are you getting any nibbles, Doc?" Wes asked. He noticed the old man had lowered his hook into the water with no bait on the end. Looked like he could add *senile* to the Doc Nelson description.

"Not yet." Doc tipped his fishing hat, setting all the silvery lures pinned to it fluttering about. His cottony white hair danced around the brim.

"Wouldn't it be easier with some bait?" Wes began reeling in his line with another spot fish wiggling on the end. At least they'd have a feast shortly, if they kept biting like this. August's father-in-law had said if they showed up at his place with a mess of fish, he'd have a pot of rice and some of his famous slaw prepared, with a cast-iron skillet of grease and his secret dredging batter ready for the fish. Wes's stomach growled just thinking about it.

"Don't much feel like it tonight, kid. Figured I'd just grow me a sit, so we might have ourselves a chat."

Wes glanced at the other guys. They looked busy

focusing on their fishing poles, but he knew better. His stomach clenched and he suddenly didn't care so much about the upcoming fish feast. "I don't have anything to say."

"Good. That'll mean you can listen twice as much." Doc leaned back in his metal foldout chair and eyed Wes. "That fool Ty Prescott has a hole in his bag of marbles and has no business actin' like he's taking a shine to Sophia Grace again. Sure gets my goat that he's sittin' in your pew at church while you off hidin' from the world."

"I'm not hiding," Wes snapped, placing the fishing pole against the rail. "And I won't make her life complicated by participating in some cliché love triangle. That's tacky and not my style. Plus, I think Ty's in need of that pew more than I am."

"Thought you didn't have anything to say?" Doc raised a bushy white eyebrow. When Wes's lips remained pinched closed, he continued, "Sure, that boy needs to get a good dose of Jesus. But we're here to discuss another problem tonight. Sophia is right back to being sad all the time. And that's your fault."

Wes whipped his head around to retort, but August clasped his shoulder. "It's true. She's miserable. And I can tell you on good authority that she's only keeping peace with Ty for Collin's sake."

"And that's why I'm staying out of the picture. No matter how much I hate the guy, he will always be that little boy's daddy."

"*Father* perhaps, but he ain't cut out to be a *daddy*," Lincoln interjected, still working on catching his first fish. "He has his head too far up his own backside to notice his child."

"So you guys are here to gang up on me for what?

To make me feel even worse for Collin?" Wes started packing up his stuff in the small tackle box he'd brought along, figuring the mile walk home would do him good.

"No." Doc wrapped his hand around Wes's wrist. "We're here to come up with a plan that will work in your favor, as well as for Sophia and her boy. It's high time that cocky scoundrel figures out the sun don't come up just to hear him crow."

August snorted. "Yeah, whatever all that means." He pulled in a fish and dropped it in the rapidly filling cooler. "Me and Linc have been doing our part to make Ty sweat as much as possible when he comes around. He's not cut out for taking much, so he normally tucks tail without much effort on our part."

"What do you mean by making him sweat?" Wes absently cast out his fishing line and settled back in his chair. He suddenly felt more like following wherever the conversation was leading.

"Let's just say he tends to lose his appetite around us. For someone who likes to use his fists, he ain't got much tolerance when the pressure is turned on him."

"You're roughing him up? Why ain't y'all included me?" Seth whined while rebaiting his hook with another worm.

"Nah. Nothing that extreme." August shrugged.

"Not lately, anyhow," Lincoln added.

"There's just one thing missing, and that's you, Wes." August pointed at him. "We think from here on out, every time we have to be around the punk, you need to be there too. Time to make your presence known."

"Yes." Doc waggled a finger at him. "And you're going to start by gettin' your behind back to church."

The guys finished filling the cooler and stepped over to the stainless steel sinks at the end of the pier to clean the fish. By the time they'd finished, arrived at Jasper's, and devoured their weight in fish fried to golden-brown perfection, the guys had worked out a formidable plan. "Operation Ty Extraction" was what Lincoln called it. That was all fine and dandy with Wes, but life had other plans the guys knew nothing about.

17

There was a popular quote most locals knew around Sunset Cove and probably any other coastal town, saying beach life was different from life away from the shore. Time near the coast didn't move by the hour; it moved by the currents, planned by the tides, and followed the sun.

But Ty Prescott thought life moved when he said so. He was persistent, Sophia had to give him that. Tonight she'd finally caved and agreed to go out to eat with him. Just the two of them, he persuaded, saying they needed some time to talk. He drove her to the next town over to a great little sushi hot spot, and she decided to give it her best effort as well.

Admittedly, the food was excellent and the conversation not half-bad. She noticed Ty trying to be attentive, catching himself when he began one of his me-me-me monologues. He was right cute about it, cutting himself off and redirecting the focus to her, and Sophia found herself smiling at him more during that meal than she had in years. It gave her hope that they could form a respectful friendship that would make the years ahead of coparenting more tolerable.

"I'm thinking about looking for a piece of land inland," Ty shared before taking a sip of water. "I'd like you to help me pick out floor plans."

Sophia chewed the edamame thoughtfully, wondering how best to answer. "Lincoln Cole is an architectural engineer. I bet he'd be the one to talk to about that." She inwardly cringed at the same time Ty did so visibly, making her wonder if mentioning Lincoln had been her defensive reflex to keep Ty in his place. If it worked, then so be it.

"Why would you even bring that guy up? You know what, never mind . . ." Ty shook his head and filled his mouth with another piece of sushi as if to help keep his comments to himself. "This yellowtail is so fresh." He nestled a piece between his chopsticks and tried feeding it to her.

The gesture felt too intimate, so Sophia plucked the bite from between the chopsticks and popped it into her mouth. "Hmm . . . so good," she garbled out, making light of it.

Ty somehow pretended the two small hiccups hadn't just happened and moved on so easily that he even had Sophia questioning whether they had actually happened. And she could almost forget that the same hand that reached out to wipe the soy sauce from the corner of her mouth was the very same one that had split her lip. *Almost.* But she flinched, delivering another hiccup to the evening.

This time, Ty didn't ignore it. He jumped back, knowing where her reaction had come from. "Are you ever going to forgive me?" he whispered, looking down at his plate.

Sophia watched him draw circles with the chopsticks, stirring the soy sauce and wasabi together. After a while, she found her voice and answered, "I have forgiven you, but I'm going to need more than a few months to forget."

Ty slowly nodded before lifting his eyes to meet hers. They were glassy and swirling with remorse. She waited for him to apologize again, but that never happened.

After a few blinks and a forceful clearing of his throat, Ty
went about finishing his meal in silence.

Within the last several months, Sophia had come to
appreciate silence when Wes was around. He wasn't much
for wasting words. But sitting here with Ty in silence was
stifling. Nothing comfortable about it when it came from
her larger-than-life ex. She could almost hear the gears
whirling inside his brain and was worried about what they
might be formulating. The only time she'd seen him that
thoughtful and focused was on a football field.

Please don't be forming a play with me involved, she
silently begged.

Once they arrived back at the condo, Sophia was still
waiting for Ty's next move. Unfortunately, he didn't dis-
appoint. He helped her out of the SUV, and after closing
the door, he gently pressed her against it.

"Ty—"

"Shh . . . Just give me a chance, babe. Please." Ty's
words were a whispered plea. He leaned in, tucked a long
lock of hair behind her ear, his eyes coasting every inch
of her face. "No one compares to you . . ."

Sophia's heart lurched in her chest when Ty bent and
pressed his lips against hers. Memories of their kisses
skipped through her mind. Familiar and confident, ener-
getic and skilled, Ty's signature style. The very same style
that used to leave her breathless and swooning.

But not tonight.

Suddenly she was tired of being Sophia Prescott. The
woman who was trying to be everything to everyone and
never her true self. It was time to stop being Ty's puppet.

Ty's lips pleaded with her tightly locked ones to
open, but Sophia kept him out. She raised her hands and
pushed against his chest until he finally took the hint and
stepped back.

"Don't do that again," Sophia said evenly.

"Babe, it's time we fix this." Ty pouted his lips and tipped his head to the side, still pleading.

"There's nothing to fix." She was careful to make her tone resolute but not terse.

"But what about our son?" He tossed his only leverage into the argument, but Sophia was done allowing him to play their son against her.

"I will always love you to a certain degree, but . . ." She took a deep breath. "There's been too much damage to repair our relationship back to the original, but I want us to work on repairing it to a new way. For the *sake* of our son, I want us to form a healthy friendship."

"Don't close the door on it becoming more."

"Ty—"

He raised his palms. "Let's just leave it here." He backed away and rounded the front of the SUV to the driver's door. "Good night."

And just like that, Sophia was left in the parking lot watching as the taillights faded down the street. The man was tenacious to a fault, going whole hog when it was something he wanted. Too bad it wasn't going to work in his favor this time.

Sophia took in her surroundings for a few beats, listening to the chilly breeze rustling through the trees and the pond fountain tinkling on the water nearby. Smiling, she was right proud of herself for being strong enough to stand her ground. After releasing a fist pump, she turned her back on her toxic past and went inside.

•   •   •

Come morning, Sophia's smile was long gone. Releasing a pent-up growl, she yanked off the third dress, tossing it on top of the growing pile of clothes deemed uncomfortable. Nothing felt right. Either the fabric was too itchy or the cut was wrong. Surprisingly, the last one was a bit snug— evidence that her appetite had finally returned to normal.

A quick glance at the clock on the way to the closet made her insides spasm with panic. The window for making a clean getaway was rapidly closing. The palazzo pants and a frumpy blouse—which should have been as comfortable as a pair of pajamas but wasn't—would have to do.

It was then, in a rush to grab her purse and dash into Collin's room, that it hit her. The discomfort had nothing to do with the outfits. The day ahead was ill-fitting. She couldn't figure out exactly why, except that she knew Ty would be present in it.

"Let's go, bub." Sophia scooped Collin up from the mess of toys he was playing with, placed a kiss in the midst of his silky curls, and raced to beat the inevitable. "Shoot," she muttered to herself as she hurried down the outside steps. "Too late."

"My two favorite people!" Ty's voice boomed across the parking lot as he closed his car door and walked in their direction.

"Daddy!" Collin echoed his enthusiasm and began to squirm about in Sophia's arms.

Ty ate up the distance between them in only a few hobbling steps. The boot on his foot was barely noticeable underneath the tailored navy trousers. He plucked Collin out of her arms and tossed him in the air, eliciting a fit of giggles and squeals.

Even though a foreboding feeling kept tightening along her shoulders, Sophia couldn't help but smile at how happy her baby boy was with his daddy back in his life. Her eyes betrayed her by coasting the length of Ty. Dark navy and silver were his team's colors, but he always wore them like they were his very own, just as he was this morning in the custom-made navy suit and the narrow silver tie. With the sun emphasizing the coppery undertone of his brown hair and warming his already-bronze skin, the man wore his good looks like a boss. Problem was, he knew it.

"Like what you see, babe?" Ty produced a wink to go with his signature aw-shucks grin before carrying Collin over to the Range Rover and loading him up in a brand-new car seat he'd purchased since arriving in town. That should have clued her in on how serious he was, but she kept ignoring all those signs, hoping they would go away.

Sophia watched Ty work at buckling Collin in, recalling another time she'd ignored signs and how devastating that turned out. The moment her former PR firm signed the talented running back, Sophia was smitten. She couldn't—or didn't want to—see past all the excitement and passion of finally experiencing her first love. It was a whirlwind romance for sure, and the naive young woman found herself married and pregnant before they made it through Ty's first NFL season. And it was perfect for the first two years, before Sophia started to notice the minuscule cracks in Ty's perfection. Intuition told her to pay attention to those cracks, but she looked the other way, hoping she was wrong. It took two more years of looking the other way before the Prescotts' glass castle completely shattered.

"I'll follow you guys."

"Why, babe? It makes no sense to take two vehicles." Ty glanced over his shoulder, seeming to be struggling with the harness.

Sophia nudged him out of the way and readjusted the harness to the proper fit before latching it. She placed a kiss on Collin's cheek before turning away and closing the door. "Collin has a playdate after church. It'll be easier to drive separate," she defended, even if the playdate was much later in the day. She rounded the back of the vehicle to dodge any advance Ty might have thought about making.

Minutes later, she was driving behind him, trying to push the uncomfortable fit of the situation off her shoulders. Sadly, it only grew. It had become almost unbearable by the time she and Ty dropped Collin off at children's church and made their way into the sanctuary.

The two rows behind her usual pew were filled with familiar faces. Opal and Lincoln sat with Seth. Behind them sat Josie and August with his two brothers. And sitting in her pew, with room for only one more, were Jasper, Doc, Agnes, and Wes. Of course, the available spot was beside him.

Sure, they all attended the same church most every Sunday, but they were usually sprinkled throughout the sanctuary instead of huddled together. They were clearly forming some type of united front.

"Good morning, young lady," Agnes said, motioning for Sophia to have a seat beside Wes. He picked up his Bible and placed it in his lap, as though he had been holding her a place. He offered her a polite smile before sliding his glasses on and looking toward the front.

The prelude music was coming to a close and the pastor was heading toward the pulpit, so Sophia knew there wasn't time to find another place. She sat, putting some space between them, only to be pushed closer as Ty wedged himself in beside her. Everyone in the entire pew had to shift over to the left to make room. Even so, they ended up packed like sardines.

"Ty, you can sit with us," Opal whispered near Sophia's shoulder. "There's plenty of room."

"That's okay. I don't mind sitting close to this beautiful woman," Ty whispered back, his warm breath tickling the side of Sophia's neck as he gave her shoulder a lingering squeeze.

Yep. It's the day that's not fitting right. Not my baggy pants or itchy blouse . . .

She feigned a headache after the service, declining her parents' dinner invite. Ty seemed too consumed with his phone to really care one way or the other.

Once she had Collin loaded up, Ty announced, "I have a meeting this afternoon."

Sophia squelched the sigh of relief. "That's okay. I think I'll join Collin in a nap before his playdate."

Ty glanced at his phone and nodded absently. "I'll try to pop over later and check on you."

Sophia was about to climb in when Ty pulled her into his arms and went in for a kiss. She shoved out of his embrace and held up both palms. "Never again are you to take anything from me without my permission."

"Babe—"

"I mean it, Ty. You're not allowed to kiss me. That's way out of line." Her eyes slid just past Ty's shoulder and caught on Wes. His face was high in color and his hands were fisted by his sides. Wes ticked his head in Ty's direction, but Sophia gave her head a subtle shake to warn him off.

"But you're my—"

"I'm not your wife anymore. We both signed the papers that are proof of that." She pointed toward his vehicle. "You should get to your meeting."

"Yeah. You're right." The words were agreeable, but his sharp tone said otherwise. Thankfully, he left without further comment.

Sophia released a pensive sigh as she glanced to where Wes still stood. Too many eyes were watching, so she only offered him a brief wave before climbing into her SUV. On the drive home, she pushed all things Ty Prescott out of her mind while trying to dissect what had been going on at church with Wes and the crowd rallying around him. It was odd. But what was even more odd was her overwhelming desire to hold his hand during the service, even with Ty on the other side of her.

Sophia heated up a bowl of leftover chicken and dumplings for Collin. Once he was fed, they lay down for a nap. After the toddler settled down, Sophia snuggled beside him for a spell and simply cherished the peaceful moment with him. She managed to drift off for a while, but that uncomfortable feeling was still there when she awakened and even followed her and Collin all the way to the park, where they met Collin's preschool buddy Dawson and his mother, Laney.

"What a beautiful afternoon," Laney supplied while stretching out on the park bench beside Sophia.

"Hard to believe we're only weeks away from Christmas and here it is in the midseventies," Sophia commented, her eyes trained on Collin and Dawson as they climbed onto the merry-go-round. She was about to walk over and give it a spin for them when Dawson's older brother offered to do it. Sophia thought she recalled Laney saying he was eleven, but she couldn't remember the boy's name.

"Heard your husband is in town." Laney nudged Sophia's arm and it was all Sophia could do to not instantly form disdain for the woman.

"*Ex,*" she corrected without offering any further information. She looked back at Collin and jolted. "Your son is going too fast."

"Eric, slow down," Laney yelled, but the boy kept running like he didn't hear her. "Heard y'all been out together. Girl, he's so hot." The woman had the nerve to giggle, not paying attention to her kids.

Sophia had no patience for the woman's silly swooning, her focus centered on her son. "Please tell Eric to slow down again."

"They're fine—"

A twinge of anxiety hit Sophia's stomach as she sprang to her feet to put a stop to the boy's rapid spinning, but she wasn't fast enough. To her horror, she watched Collin's little eyes round in fear just as he lost his grip on the bar in his hands. Before she could reach the merry-go-round, her boy took flight and landed with a sickening thump against the ground.

"Collin!" She knelt beside him where he coiled into a ball and groaned, but didn't move him for fear something was broken. She noticed a thick root protruding from the ground. "Baby, where does it hurt?"

"Eberywhere." He clutched his middle and began to cry in a stilted manner, giving Sophia a frightening clue that he was having a hard time breathing.

She pulled her phone out, called 911 for an ambulance, and then dialed Ty. He didn't answer, so she rambled off a message before hanging up.

"Poor baby. We can take him in my van," Laney offered.

"No, I don't think we should move him." Sophia hit the next contact that she needed and he answered on the first ring. Once she heard his voice, her own sob released. "We're at the park. . . . Collin had a hard fall. . . . Think he fell on a big root. . . . He's clutching his middle. . . . An ambulance is on the way," she managed to tell Wes between sobs as she rubbed Collin's back. A car started up and the engine revved in a growl on the other end of the phone, so she knew he was on the way. Hanging up the phone, she focused on keeping Collin still and calm.

The next hour was a blur. The ambulance arrived, loading them up and depositing them at the ER. Wes was already there waiting and without any delay had Collin whisked to the back for tests.

Somehow, while Sophia waited in a private room, Opal and Josie showed up, Sophia's parents close behind them. Undoubtedly and thankfully, Wes had enough wits about him to make phone calls on her behalf. Opal took over trying to reach Ty. After several failed attempts, Sophia remembered. "Ty's in a meeting. He'll get the messages eventually."

After what seemed like hours, Wes eased into the room and knelt before Sophia. He spoke quietly, garnering everyone's undivided attention. "After examining Collin and then performing an ultrasound on his abdomen, I detected a tear in his spleen. I ordered a CT to confirm the diagnosis, which it did."

Sophia gasped and made to stand, but Wes grabbed her hands and moved closer into her space. Using his firm touch and a stern look, he commanded she focus on him. She trained her eyes on his, which were magnified by his glasses. "What's that mean?"

"I have a pediatric surgeon on the way."

Her bottom lip trembled and goose bumps stung her skin. "Surgery?" The word barely squeaked out.

"It can be done laparoscopically." Wes said each word slowly. "Collin . . . will . . . be . . . fine. I'm going to walk you back to give him a kiss, and then I need you to sign the papers for the surgery so we can get him prepped."

Sophia sputtered and choked. "I can't . . ."

Wes gently squeezed her hands and pulled her to her feet. "Yes, you can. You are going to hold yourself together. Collin needs you to do that for him. You need to reassure him he's okay and that you're okay."

She swayed in place, so Wes tucked her into his side and walked her through the double doors. An undulating haze had taken over her vision, and she leaned into him and allowed him to lead her through the hospital. Her insides crumpled when she saw her baby boy lying in a hospital bed, but she managed to keep her reaction from showing.

"Mommy," Collin murmured, tired but with hope.

The nurse who was sitting by his bed moved out of the way.

"Thank you," Sophia whispered as she passed by.

The nurse gave her a kind smile before slipping out the door.

Sophia walked over and cupped his tiny hand in hers. "Hey, bub. Wes says you have a boo-boo."

Collin pouted his bottom lip out. "Him say I gotta take another nap so they can fix it."

Her chest was heavy from a mix of worry and pride. Collin sounded so calm, albeit a little peeved, so she knew Wes had done a good job with soothing him. "Yeah. He told me."

"I'm going to hang out with him until he goes to sleep," Wes said, reassuring them both. For that, Sophia was grateful. "First, I need Mommy to sign a paper to give me and my buddy Abram permission to fix the boo-boo, but I'll be back soon. Can Mindy read you a book until I get back?"

"Okay. But pease huwee."

Wes pulled a small book with Lightning McQueen on the cover from his lab coat pocket and handed it to the nurse. "I will. Give Mommy a kiss."

Sophia took that as her cue, leaning down and placing her trembling lips against his tiny puckered ones. "I love you, bub."

"Wuv you," he said back, his eyes already investigating the small book in the nurse's hand. "Wes dwives a race caw."

Mindy's eyes rounded. "He does?"

Collin nodded and wrinkled his nose. "But him not go fast enough."

"Well, ain't that something. I bet they go fast in this book." The nurse cracked open the book and distracted Collin as Wes ushered Sophia out of the small pre-op room.

Another blur of time followed during which Sophia filled out the paperwork and was then led back to the surgical waiting area. Josie and Opal were good with being supportive friends, offering to get Sophia something to eat or drink. Even though she declined all offerings, a water bottle ended up in her hands and was already half-empty by the time she realized she'd been drinking it.

Wes reappeared, wearing a pair of blue scrubs, and took the seat beside her. He pulled the cap off his head and tucked it in a pocket before gathering her hand in his and entwining their fingers. "They've already started. It's a simple procedure . . ." As he spoke quietly, explaining each step of the surgery, his thumb drew a comforting circle along her wrist. Once he finished explaining the laparoscopic procedure, he filled her in on aftercare that included a night or two in the hospital for monitoring.

Eventually they lapsed into silence, but an entire conversation passed between them for the next long stretch of time. Her side of it was constant hysteria—fidgeting, sniffling, trembling. His side of it was a constant state of reassurance—warm strength, fingers working through her hair, a steady hand on her shoulder as he pulled her into his lap for a long hug. That was where she was when the door flew open.

"Where is he? Where's my son?" Ty jabbed a finger toward Wes. "And why aren't you helping him?"

Wes kept his arms circled around her, only lifting his head in Ty's direction. "I'm not a surgeon, but I brought one of the best pediatric surgeons in to perform the procedure." He moved his hand away, glanced at his watch, and then wrapped his arm back around Sophia. "Collin should be in recovery anytime now."

Sophia didn't know what caused it, but suddenly Wes's entire body went rigid. She looked up to see him glaring at Ty.

Wes stood and gently placed her in the chair. Through clenched teeth, he said to Ty, "I need a word with you in the hall. Now." His words were just over a whisper but held enough grit to make Ty actually follow him out.

After several minutes passed, Sophia was about to check on them, but Ty came back in before she could.

"They paged Wes and let him know Collin is in recovery. He went to find out when we can go back." Ty rubbed at his neck and chose to sit on the other side of the room.

"What's wrong?" she asked.

Ty shook his head and scrubbed a palm over his mouth. "Nothing, just . . . when this is over and Collin is home, I think it's best you quit your job and get back to taking care of him full-time."

"What?"

Everyone in the room suddenly filed out, giving them some privacy. Well, everyone but Lincoln. The giant man stood guard by the door, arms crossed over his broad chest while his eyes remained frozen in a scowl directed at Ty. Sophia gave Lincoln a subtle nod, thanking him, before turning her attention to a fidgeting Ty. She expected Ty to get up and sit with her, but he remained across the room. "I don't trust that doctor friend of yours, and I'd just as soon have you focus on our son. Our accounts are now freed up. That's what had me tied up this afternoon."

"Oh." Sophia really didn't care about that at the moment. She was too antsy with wanting to get to Collin.

"Yeah. I just have to pay some stupid fine, but all's good. You don't have to work any more."

The door opened, and the nurse, Mindy, stepped in and smiled. "Wes said to come get you, Sophia, to bring you back to Collin."

Ty stood. "I'm his father. What about me?"

Mindy directed her smile way up to him. "I'm sorry, sir. I can only allow one back into recovery and Collin is asking for Sophia. But we should have him in a room within the hour."

Sophia hurried by him and was actually surprised when Ty took a step out of her way instead of blocking it. He was avoiding her for some reason. Perhaps finding her in Wes's arms had disgusted him. If it did, then so be it. Her priority was Collin.

The nurse was true to her word, and within an hour, they were in a private hospital room. Awkwardness overtook the room as Ty hovered in a corner while Wes stepped into the role of caregiver. Sophia's family and friends only stayed briefly at Wes's advisement, promising to visit again tomorrow.

"I wan' my hewo undeweaw," Collin grouched when he finally realized his bottom was bare.

"You had an accident in the ones you were wearing, but don't worry. Uncle Seth is bringing you some," Wes assured him.

Sophia didn't know if he even realized he'd referred to his brother as Collin's uncle, but boy, did it sound really right.

"I gotta peepee," Collin whined after a few more minutes.

"Okay." Sophia stood by the bed and contemplated how to maneuver picking Collin up without jostling him or the IV.

"I wan' Daddy or Wes to take me. I a man, Mommy," Collin slurred, grogginess from the anesthesia still slowing him down.

Sophia turned to look at Ty, but he threw his hands up and looked distraught by the idea. "Whoa. I might hurt him."

Wes stepped over without hesitation and tucked the hospital gown more securely around Collin. "Collin isn't fragile. He's a *man*." He winked at Sophia, more for reassurance than tease, as he slowly picked Collin up and began pulling the IV pole behind them to the bathroom.

As soon as the door shut, Ty pushed off the wall. "My leg is killing me. I'm gonna head out."

"They've brought cots in so we can stay." She pointed to the two cots stacked by the opposite wall. Several stuffed animals lined the remaining space along the wall, with helium balloons tied to them.

"Babe." Ty tapped his chest. "This isn't fitting on a cot. I'll be back first thing in the morning. Give the little man a kiss for me and tell him I love him." With that, he disappeared quicker than a wisp of smoke in a brisk breeze.

Words . . . empty words, she thought. Ty was a pro at spewing them out but hardly ever put any action behind them. The sound of the toilet flushing, followed by the water running, drew her out of the dismal thoughts.

Wes walked back out with Collin cradled in his arms. He was the most rumpled she'd ever seen him, yet the strongest. She could barely swallow the appreciation wanting to spring forth at the sight. Her finger swept the back of her ring as she silently thanked God for sending Wes as an anchor in the midst of this storm.

As he went to set Collin on the bed, the little guy clung to him.

"Hole me, Wes. Pease."

Wes smiled. "Sure." He grabbed an extra blanket and tucked it around Collin before walking over to the recliner and settling into it. "Mommy, why don't you stretch out and keep Collin's bed warm for him." Another wink as he rolled the IV pole closer and out of the way.

She did as he said, turning on her side to watch the two sitting together. Wes squinted at the clock on the opposite wall just as she noticed him holding two fingers against Collin's wrist to check his pulse. It warmed her how gentle and attentive he was, both doctoring and babying her son at the same time.

Tears pricked her eyes as she observed the stealth exam Wes performed while quietly chatting with Collin. He gauged Collin's temperature by pressing his lips to her son's forehead, checked his feet and legs for any signs of swelling, she was guessing, and then gently checked the three small incisions. After that, he even managed to talk Collin into taking a few sips of water before he dozed off.

"Why's he sleeping so much?" Sophia whispered, propping the side of her head in her hand.

"It's normal for someone after they've been put to sleep to be groggy a day or two afterward. Plus, he's been through quite an ordeal. You, too, for that matter. Bet you're worn-out." Wes looked at her, his eyes filled with empathy.

"A little." She shrugged.

A quiet knock tapped against the door as a nurse tiptoed in. "I'm Annie, the night nurse. I hate to wake him, but I need to check his vitals." She quickly performed the task, leaving Collin right there in Wes's arms, as he filled her in on his own examination, confirming what Sophia had suspected he was doing.

"I'm staying through the night, so if you'll bring me a stethoscope, a thermometer, and dressing supplies, I'll take care of him."

The nurse's cheeks pinked. "I don't mind taking care of him, Dr. Sawyer. It's my job."

"One that I know you can perform beyond well," he answered in that soothing tone Sophia had heard him use with distraught patients and parents numerous times. "But these two have had a long, rough day. I'd like very little disturbance so they can get some rest. I will call the desk if I need you."

"If you're sure . . ."

"I am."

The nurse tapped something into the computer before slipping out the door. Moments later, she was back with the supplies he'd requested and a cup of coffee. "Please call if you need anything."

"Thank you, Annie." Wes offered her a polite smile before she left.

"I'm hungwy," Collin announced, sounding half-asleep.

Sophia sat up to go find something, but Wes held his hand up and beckoned her to stay put. "Seth is taking care of that. He should be here any minute."

As if summoned, Seth bustled through the door, out of breath. "Man, I hope I got everything." He dropped several bags onto the end of the bed, gave Sophia's foot a supportive squeeze, and headed over to kneel beside Wes's chair. "Hey there, feller. Heard you have a boo-boo." He ran his fingers through Collin's curls, something no one seemed to be able to resist doing.

"It's okay, Unca Sef. Wes and his fwiend fix it," Collin muttered, producing a delicate chuckle from each adult. He sounded so grown-up.

"Good to hear." Seth gave Wes a pointed look with an eyebrow hitched dramatically high.

Sophia knew they were having one of those twin conversations relayed through gestures instead of words when Wes narrowed his eyes and shrugged one shoulder. She left them to it and began rummaging through the bags. She tore open a new pack of underwear and tossed a Superman pair over to Wes.

"There should be peanut butter and bananas in one of those bags," Wes said while cautiously helping Collin into the underwear.

"There is. I got that healthy natural kind you said to get." Seth moved back to Sophia and handed her the bag.

"Collin needs protein and whole foods. It'll help him heal," Wes retorted.

"Yes, Doctor," Sophia said with hardly any tease. She pulled out the jar of peanut butter and smiled appreciatively. Seth had thought of everything—plates, plastic cutlery, juice boxes, and wet wipes. She quickly sliced a banana and smeared each piece with some of the peanut butter.

Collin managed two pieces and a slurp of juice. He made a face. "I not wan' anymore."

His appetite vanished quicker than it had shown up, leaving Sophia concerned. "He didn't eat much."

"It's normal," Wes reassured her as he popped a banana slice in his mouth and passed the plate as if it were a tray of hors d'oeuvres. Soon the plate was empty and Collin was back to yawning. "Seth, let's get the little man into his new pj's."

Sophia fished them out and tore the tags off before

handing them over to Seth. Both men worked together to get the loose-fit bottoms on, and then in a flash, Wes had the IV unfastened and the prick site taped up.

"Whoa, look at that." Seth pointed to the stitched spots on Collin's belly. "Ain't you cool."

"No. I sleepy," Collin answered on another yawn as he rubbed his eyes.

Wes fastened the last button of the nightshirt and settled Collin against the pillows. "Then I think we should say our bedtime prayers before Uncle Seth heads out. Okay?"

Collin nodded his head and Sophia nearly sobbed. Weston Sawyer was everything a daddy should be. It hurt deeply that Ty had never focused so much attention on their son's well-being and had never once prayed with him.

Once the prayer concluded and Seth promised to see them soon, Sophia pulled out a cot and was about to pull out the second one when Wes stopped her.

"I'm going to sit up and keep an eye on Collin." He dimmed the lights and sat in the chair.

"Then I'll sit up with you." A quick glance at the clock indicated that more of the day had gotten away from her than she thought. It was already well past midnight.

Wes shook his head and insisted she lie down. "It's important you try to get some rest. He's going to need you a lot more tomorrow."

She did as he said. She watched Wes as he studied the computer screen. Every so often, he would walk over and check on Collin. At one point, he moved to her side and pulled a cover over her shoulders before dropping a soft kiss to the top of her head. Exhaustion began sitting heavy on her, so with the assurance that her son was in good hands, Sophia allowed her eyes to close and her mind to rest.

18

Sometimes in life a man just had enough. He reached his limit and that was that. By Thursday afternoon, Weston Sawyer had reached his and was ready to call in reinforcements to help him out with it. He wondered if it would put him on the town's bad side if he took out restraining orders on a half-dozen or so grannies.

"And how do you know all this?" Wes placed his forearms on his desk and leaned forward, eyeing the orange-haired gossiper.

Trudy settled the giant container of catfish stew on the desk before taking a seat. "Bertie brought Ty some cookies to be hospitable, of course." She straightened her wig and shrugged innocently.

"Of course," Wes repeated dryly while watching Dalma plunder through his small office fridge. "Found anything worth having in there?"

The little lady turned with a handful of berries, using her hip to shut the door. "They ain't the freshest but will do. You want one?" She held her hand out as if they were hers to offer.

"You enjoy, but thanks." Wes sighed, returning his attention to Trudy. "Is Bertie sure? Or is she making assumptions?"

"Honey, the ole gal may have to wear glasses, but when you catch sight of a naked man that big, there

241

ain't no way of not seeing it. Bertie said he had enough decency to act ashamed."

Wes already knew Ty was stepping out on Sophia. The selfish idiot had shown up at the hospital reeking of the evidence—bubble gum–pink lipstick smeared on the corner of his mouth and smelling of cheap perfume. If Sophia had been in her right mind, she would have realized Ty's afternoon had been spent with a woman, not at some bogus meeting.

He had practically pushed Ty out of the room and down the hall, out of earshot. The entire time, a sickly sweet perfume whirled around them. Wes leaned in and gave him a sniff. "That's not Sophia's perfume you're wearing. And she wouldn't be caught dead wearing that tacky shade of pink on her lips."

Ty instantly used the back of his hand to wipe his mouth and had the nerve to look at the pink smear with confusion. "What?"

"It's on your neck as well." Wes pointed to the spot near Ty's ear. "Your child was being rushed into emergency surgery while you were busy tangled up with a woman who isn't the one you're claiming as yours." Wes snorted with enough disgust that the man's cheeks actually reddened. "Collin and Sophia both deserve better."

Ty seemed to be chewing on something and trying to figure out how to spit it out, but he didn't get the chance. Wes's pager went off and all focus was back on Collin. He left Ty in the hallway but called out a warning before making the turn. "Just don't get too close to her or she's going to smell that rank perfume on you."

"Yoo-hoo, sugar. Did you hear me?" Trudy snapped her fingers, pulling Wes away from the recollection of nearly punching Ty right there in the hospital hallway.

Clearing his throat and rolling his neck, Wes said, "I'm sorry. What was that?"

Trudy clucked her tongue, admonishing him for not listening, he supposed. "She even made sure it wasn't our Sophia Grace in there with him before she left. Said it was some bottle blonde." Trudy wrinkled her nose as if she had any room to judge proper hair color.

Wes knew he shouldn't feel relieved that it wasn't Sophia, but he did just the same. He knew Ty had spent the night at Sophia's place at least the first night he was back in town. She'd been withdrawn the past few days, and Wes wasn't sure if she was just recovering from what happened to Collin or if she was putting space between them so she could work things out with Ty. Truthfully, Wes was being cowardly by not sitting down for a talk to clarify all of it. He was also worried he wouldn't like what she clarified.

"Scooch over," Dalma said, tapping Wes on his shoulder.

His mind was a whirling mess, so he did as she instructed without question. Dalma visited him at least once a week, whether she needed his medical services or not, and pretty much made her tiny self at home. He slowly blinked and watched as she rifled around the top drawer of his desk and unearthed a red sucker. When she moved to the other side of the desk, he rolled the chair back in place.

"Well, ladies, I don't know what to tell you. Ty's a grown man."

"Then let me tell you something." Trudy scoffed. "Someone needs to teach that fool a lesson."

The lady carried on and on, but Wes tuned her out as he tried massaging away the headache working on him.

Rubbing circles at his temples with his fingertips, he muttered, "I'll see what I can do."

It was his first day back to work since Collin's surgery, but he was in no shape to work by the time he managed to get the two women to leave. Agnes, subbing for Sophia, had picked up on it and called in the nurse practitioner to handle the afternoon patients while he sat stewing in his office.

Ty deserved to get caught for what he was doing, but Sophia didn't deserve to get hurt by it. Snapping out of the angry haze the best he could, Wes picked up the phone to man up to what needed to be done.

● ● ●

After work, Wes drove straight to Bless This Mess and met up with August in the parking lot. August led him to the back entrance and they let themselves in. They found Lincoln at a worktable with a set of blueprints laid out before him.

Lincoln glanced at them. "What's up?"

August walked over to a Crock-Pot and gave it a curious look. "Whatcha cooking?"

Lincoln scribbled something on a notepad before answering, "Furniture knobs. Trying to remove the paint in an environmentally safe way. Gotta protect my wife and kid." Pride edged into his voice.

"Well, we got another mother and child that need our protecting," August said, turning a chair backward and straddling it.

Wes sat properly in another chair and the other two men turned their focus on him. "Not sure if y'all realized it, but when Ty showed up at the hospital on Sunday, he was wearing perfume and lipstick that didn't belong to Sophia." Angry heat started rising along his neck. He opened the top button of his dress shirt and loosened the suddenly too-tight tie.

"Son of a gun. Did she notice?" Lincoln asked. Wes shook his head. "I think we need to go cut his *assets*," Lincoln said real slowly.

That made absolutely no sense to Wes, nor did it to August either, it seemed, until the artist let out a loud chuckle after several beats of silence.

"I like how you think, Cole. That's exactly what we need to do. We'll cut his *assets* real good this time." August grinned wide, his features painted in mischief.

Wes snorted when understanding finally dawned on him, too. "If Sophia were here, she'd be rolling her eyes and questioning your maturity level."

August shrugged. "She ain't here, so we can handle this punk with as much immaturity as we want this time."

"*This time?* What do you mean by that?" Wes asked.

August folded his arms on top of the chair back. "Not everything made it to the gossips and headlines when Sophia came back here earlier this year covered in bruises and cuts after that trip to California. Ty flew in a few days later, and Linc and I were kind enough to pick him up from the airport. We drove out to a piece of my family's farmland where Linc 'laid hands' on Ty and carefully explained that he'd better never touch Sophia again out of anger."

Lincoln popped his neck and August glared out the window, both seeming to be reliving what transpired. They looked right scary doing it too. Wes decided then and there he never wanted to be on the receiving end of that type of meeting with these two brawny guys, but he sure was glad to have them on his side.

"Ty came by Sophia's condo yesterday while I was

there. Before I left, he pulled me to the side and swore
he's a changed man. But two of those Knitting Club ladies
showed up at my office today to share with me that nothing's changed."

Lincoln dropped the pen, and even though his jaw
was covered with a dark beard, Wes saw the muscle tick-
ing. "How so?"

Wes filled them in on what Trudy had told him while
she handed over yet another container of catfish stew.

"Where's the stew?" August asked.

"We'll worry about that later," Lincoln answered for
Wes as he stood and shoved his feet into a worn pair of
flip-flops. "Right now I think it's time to have a visit with
Mr. Football. I heard he's staying in one of those swanky
beach houses on Fortieth Avenue. Let's roll."

The guys loaded up in Lincoln's Jeep, and within ten
minutes he was parking behind a fancy Range Rover at
a newly built beach house. It was all glass and concrete,
nothing like the traditional houses a few avenues south.

Wes had heard that after Hurricane Lacy took several homes down to their foundations two years ago, a
developer swooped in and bought out the homeowners.
They came in with a sleek, modern style to catch the eye
of a richer buyer. The new didn't mesh tastefully with the
old, so locals had coined the avenue Frivolous Fortieth.
Seemed like the perfect address for Ty, in Wes's opinion.

It was clear that Lincoln Cole meant business and had
not even an ounce of apprehension when he let himself
in the front door without knocking. All three stood in a
bright-white foyer while Lincoln hollered, "Ty, we need
to have a word!"

Ty limped around the corner, wearing only a pair
of boxers and the boot on his foot, looking bewildered.
"What do *you* want?"

"I think you need a refresher on what we discussed last time." Lincoln took a step forward with Ty taking one back. Both men were of considerable size, but Lincoln still had Ty by a couple inches and twenty or thirty pounds.

"I've not laid a hand on my wife out of anger since then." Ty raised his palms while trying and failing to pull off an air of innocence.

"*Ex*-wife," August corrected, and Wes almost shook his hand in gratitude.

A half-naked woman came into view with her makeup smudged and blonde hair in tangles. She let out a yelp and dodged out of sight.

"It's not what it looks like," Ty said, taking a step to block August, who seemed interested in finding the hiding woman. "She's my physical therapist."

"Oh, so she's getting paid to have sex with you? I think that's called something else." August lifted a thick eyebrow as Lincoln pulled him back by the collar of his T-shirt.

"What are you doing here?" Ty snapped at Wes as if just realizing his presence, which was probably the case since the two giants had been standing in front of him.

"Wes is here to keep us in line. To make sure we don't tear you to shreds," Lincoln nearly growled through a tight jaw. "But I think that's exactly what you deserve."

Wes watched August walk over to a familiar-looking platter of cookies that sat on the entrance table. He lifted one from underneath the plastic wrap and took a bite. "This tastes like a Bertie Matthews cookie, so I'm gonna go ahead and assume she's filled you in about our buddy Wes and his relationship with Sophia. You know, the parts you've not already heard about." August swiped another cookie and hitched a thumb in Wes's direction. "This dude has every eligible woman in town chasing after him, but he respects his woman enough not to even glance in their direction. Even after you showed up to cause trouble."

If Wes were a more confident man, he'd give August a hug for that one. Instead, he stood a little taller and jutted out his chin, trying to look as intimidating as his two friends in this testosterone-infused confrontation.

"His woman?" Ty said in a condescending tone, crossing his arms over his bare chest.

"Yes. Sophia is his woman, and it's time you respect that," August answered, then yelled toward the bedroom the woman had disappeared into. "Hey, sweetheart, come here for a sec!"

"Wait," Ty began, but she was already shuffling down the hall. As soon as she peeped around the corner with a sheet held against her chest, August lifted his phone and snagged several photos. "Hey!" Ty lunged for August's phone but never got close as Linc reached out and clotheslined him, sending Ty flat on his back with a loud thud.

Wes watched August fiddling with his phone just as his own began to vibrate in his pocket, so he knew those images were now also in his possession.

"These photos will stay out of any media hands as long as we can have your word that you'll leave Sophia alone." August held the phone up to show off the photo. "Because you make it clear time and time again that you don't respect her enough to stay faithful. She deserves better than that. She deserves Wes."

Wes stepped forward and peered down at Ty where Linc had him pinned to the polished floor. A burst of adrenaline-fueled bravado pumped through his veins. "You focus on being the daddy that boy deserves. And if you can't do that properly, it's best you pack up and head on out of town. There are three of us here and at least another half dozen that won't be putting up with anything less than your best from now on." He stepped back while Lincoln released his hold on Ty, and followed him to the door. Wes turned at the last minute and added, "Just so you know, I'll be here for the both of them. No matter what."

August pocketed his phone and swiped the platter of cookies. When Wes gave him a pointed stare, he shrugged and said, "They're too good to go to waste on Mr. Football."

Ty didn't protest. It made Wes wonder if underneath all that bronzed muscle he was nothing more than a coward. Shaking his head, he left a lot unsaid, knowing the message had been received loud and clear.

They loaded back up and headed down Front Street. Wes noticed for the first time how cool and dreary the day had turned. He pulled his phone out and sent Sophia a message to check on Collin and see if they needed anything. She responded quickly saying all was good.

"Now that that's out of the way, we have two pieces of business on our agenda, boys. First is taking care of those cookies," Lincoln said. "And then finding some bowls for the catfish stew."

"I concur," August piped in from the backseat while smacking away on the cookies. Wes figured that first piece of business would probably be complete before they arrived at their destination.

"Can we add a third piece of business?" Wes asked as Lincoln parked behind Bless This Mess. No one made a move to exit the Jeep.

Lincoln gave Wes a questioning look as he set the emergency brake. "Seth got into more trouble?"

Wes waved a hand and shook his head. "No. Nothing like that. I need to figure out how to get back on the right track with Sophia."

"Now that Ty is sorted out, why can't y'all just go back to the way things were before he showed up?" August shoved the platter between Lincoln and Wes. It held only two cookies.

Wes had no appetite, so he let Lincoln have them both. "I wish it was that easy." He started telling them about what all went down after the mud run, but Lincoln cut him off.

"Wait. This needs to be told over stew." Lincoln pulled the keys out of the ignition and exited. Wes grabbed the container out of his car and followed the guys inside. Once they were set up at the table in the back room of the store, slurping stew from coffee cups, Lincoln told Wes to continue explaining.

Wes kept his eyes on the rich red broth in his cup while sharing about the kiss and their exchange of words where his tongue decided to malfunction.

August chewed thoughtfully, brows pinched. "Yeah, I'd say it's never a good idea to tell a woman you didn't like her at first and then follow that with telling her you don't want to want her."

"Especially one as feisty as Sophia." Lincoln worked on refilling his cup, splattering the stew everywhere. "I bet she pinched you good and hard for that."

Wes mopped up the table with several napkins. "No, but she sure looked like she wanted to."

Chuckling, August leaned back in his chair. "I can't believe you messed up your first kiss like that."

Lincoln huffed a laugh. "It's kinda how my first kiss with Opal went down. I think I said something about not wanting to like her and not being able to take it anymore." A slow smirk barely peeked from his dark beard. "Then I laid a kiss on her."

"Man, the two of you stink in the romance

department." August picked up a pen and started sketching an intricate design along the edge of an invoice, but Lincoln didn't seem to be bothered by it.

"How about you then? Did you *paint* Josie a kiss?" Lincoln asked with a heavy layer of sarcasm.

August glanced up from the paper, looking rather smug. "Nope. I'm so charming, my woman actually kissed me first."

Lincoln snorted. "You expect me to believe our sweet, shy Josie was the one who initiated your first kiss?"

"You better believe it." August dropped the pen and spread his arms out wide and shrugged. "I told you I'm charming like that."

"All right then . . . Go Jo-Jo," Lincoln commented, sounding proud.

August tipped his head in agreement. "I mean, it was me who pulled her outside to dance in the rain. I'm pretty sure that made me irresistible."

"No. You just lucked out." Lincoln jabbed a finger at August before rising to grab three bottles of water from a small fridge. He passed them out and plopped back into the chair.

Wes had sat there, quietly taking in the conversation, but spoke up when the two guys seemed finished with razzing each other. "So what do you think I should do?"

"Simple. You have to win her back over." Lincoln certainly made it sound simple, but Wes knew better.

"I know, but how do I make that happen?" Wes asked with skepticism.

"You gotta do some kind of romantic gesture in epic proportions. One so big that it will either have her swooning with hearts in her eyes or punching you in the face." August shrugged.

"That doesn't sound much like a plan to me. And

really, I'm not a romantic gesture kind of guy. I hate cli-chés." Wes sighed, slumping further in the chair while unraveling his tie.

"Ain't no guy crazy about romantic junk, but if you love that woman enough, you'd stomach it for her." Lincoln stood again and started toward the front of the store but added before getting out of sight, "I know I'd do stupid like a boss if it made my woman happy." For such a serious man, that was saying a lot, so maybe Wes could pull off stupid as well.

"Linc is on the money with this one," August added, going back to drawing on the invoice. "You know . . . Jo and I have been asked to revamp the winter dance this year. We have a pretty romantic idea for the theme. It could be the perfect place for you to pull off something."

Lincoln returned and settled back in the chair. "Romeo here is probably right. You know our girls like to get all dolled up, especially prissy Sophia."

August shared more about the dance theme, and by the time the container of catfish stew was demolished, they'd hatched out a perfectly stupid romantic idea. Wes just hoped Sophia didn't punch him for it.

Wes stared at his hands a few minutes, wondering how far he'd have to embarrass himself to pull that off. He eventually headed out so he could go check on Collin before it became too late. The long week and eventful evening had worn him out, so he made only a brief visit before going home.

By the weekend, headlines and photos showed Ty Prescott moving into a town house near his parents in Atlanta, Georgia. It left Wes dumbfounded how easily the man walked away from his child. He recalled Doc saying Ty was "all hat and no cattle." Apparently so, considering the way Ty cowered from Lincoln. Wes wasn't completely clear on what had gone down between those two on that piece of farmland, but evidently Lincoln had put the fear of God in the poor excuse for a man.

Wes himself hadn't left the hospital for two days straight until Collin was released. Holding that child in his arms, so vulnerable and precious, there was no way someone could have made him leave that room. A part of his heart spent most of that time snuggled in his lap while the other part lingered closely. It was the first time in four years he felt close to complete. A tender spot that would always hold Claire and Luke seemed to heal just a little more, and Wes knew he had to figure out how to hold on to the second chance God had presented him in the form of that sassy, sweet woman and her exceptional child.

Wes longed to love Sophia and Collin as God intended them to be loved. They could be happy together. He was determined to make it happen one way or another and prove to Sophia that she and Collin were worth it. Even if he had to make a fool of himself in the process.

19

If I keep ignoring it, maybe it'll go away. Thankfully, it had worked with Ty and he'd finally moved on. Sophia had used that mantra in many a situation, but the one before her at the moment wasn't having it.

"That's it, young lady. Time for you to get out of this house." Sophia's mother stood rooted beside the couch where Sophia was sitting with Collin in her arms.

"We went out just yesterday," Sophia rebuked without taking her eyes off the cartoon on TV.

"Collin's follow-up appointment doesn't count. Here." Lucy thrust a gift certificate in Sophia's line of sight. "Jill is expecting you by two for a hair and manicure appointment. You best not stand her up."

Sophia took the card and skimmed it. "Momma . . ."

"Don't 'Momma' me. Go. You've been hogging my grandson long enough." She held her arms out and Collin went to her immediately.

Apparently he was ready for a break from her, and that stung.

"Gamma, can we go outside too? I tired of in here." He pouted his lips out.

"Of course, sweet baby. Some fresh air will do us all some good. We are going to pack you a bag and go back to the farm, where you can help me and Papa decorate the outdoor Christmas tree," Lucy promised and Collin lit up like a Christmas tree.

"I don't know if that's a good idea." Sophia stared intently at her mother, fearing it was too soon for Collin to participate in such activities.

"Nonsense. Collin's stitches are gone and the doctor released him. It's time he gets back to the usual things. You need to do the same."

Her mother didn't wait for a reply, simply went about packing Collin up. She ignored each time Sophia second-guessed whether it was wise to for him to be outside just yet or whether she should leave his side.

"Take a long shower, shave your legs, and pamper yourself a little. Then put on something besides yoga pants and a hoodie for your hair appointment."

"But why?" Sophia whined.

Lucy used her mother card and said, "Because I said so. And call up the Sand Queens and have them meet you." After hugs and kisses, Lucy and Collin were out the door, leaving Sophia holding a gift certificate promising services she was much in need of but didn't know if she had the energy to withstand.

Sophia placed the card on the coffee table, plopped down on the couch, and was close to just tipping over and trying for a nap, but she really did miss her friends. With everything going on from Ty's exasperating advances to Collin's injury, keeping in touch with Josie and Opal had fallen to the wayside. She straightened while tugging her phone out of the hoodie pocket.

Luck would have it, Opal and Josie were free to meet up at the salon and both seemed excited to make Sophia's sudden time-out into a girls' day. But luck wouldn't be on their side when it came to avoiding the Knitting Club. Within ten minutes of the Sand Queens arriving, the old ladies began trickling in, looking for last-minute appointments.

"Miss Bertie, what do you need to get dolled up for at such short notice?" Jill asked after she instructed her receptionist to check the other stylists' books for any available openings.

"The winter dance at the community center is tonight and we plumb forgot about it," Bertie answered, clucking her tongue. "I think we're starting to get old. Letting things slip our minds like that . . ." Bertie shuffled over and took a seat near Sophia where she sat in Jill's chair. "Honey, are you going to the dance?"

Sophia remained still as the scissors neared to trim her ends. "No, ma'am."

"Well, that's too bad." Bertie clucked her tongue again, sounding like she wanted Sophia to ask her why, but Sophia was smart enough not to fall into that trap.

"You're here getting spiffed up. Might as well go," Dalma commented as she sat beside Opal. She reached her tiny hand over and began rubbing the beach ball–size belly.

Sophia regarded the warm glow of Opal's skin and the serene smile she gave Dalma as the little lady patiently waited for the baby to kick. Opal definitely wore pregnancy well. Something Sophia hadn't pulled off so gracefully herself. Long bouts of morning sickness and an aggravating case of acne plagued her close to all nine months, but she'd do it all over again for her boy. Collin was worth any misery.

"Ah, this little one has a strong kick!" Dalma hooted, but then she grew still again with her hand splayed on Opal's belly. A moment later, she startled and laughed. "Isn't it just the most miraculous feeling ever when your baby is in there moving around?"

"Yes, ma'am." Opal returned Dalma's awed expression. "I just cannot wait to meet her or him."

"You ain't doing that scan where you find out ahead of time?" Ethel grumbled, rummaging around in her bag. "Sure would make it easier on all of us before the baby shower."

Opal giggled as if Ethel were funny, even though all of Sunset Cove knew otherwise. "Linc and I love surprises. It'll be fun to wait." She smoothed her hand around the circumference of her belly.

Ethel balked. "That's what you call fun? Humph." She shook her head and rolled her eyes. "I think dancing is more like it. And summer punch. And cake. Cake is fun. Not letting us know if you're having a boy or a girl ain't fun." She shook her finger at Opal.

"Why, Ethel, I think you're just tetchy over the fact that no matter how much snooping y'all do, this is one secret you can't steal." Opal said this in her sweet, condescending tone, getting Ethel's goat.

Sophia barely held back the snort of laughter while settling in the chair and simply enjoying all of the chatter around her. She didn't mind the Knitting Club's company so much when they weren't up to something.

"I just love the winter dance," Josie commented, sounding all dreamy about it. "August and I were asked to tweak the theme this year."

"Oh, I bet it's spectacular then." Opal did her little happy clap. "Tell us about it."

Josie grinned wryly. "All I can tell you is that Sunset Cove is in for a blizzard tonight."

"Ah, come on," one of the other stylists whined.

"You'll have to go to find out. It's like nothing the dance has ever seen." Josie looked too smug about it. Normally she'd shy away from bragging, so it definitely intrigued Sophia to figure out what they'd pulled off for the dance. With the creative minds of those two artists combined, it would be epic for sure.

"Linc and I will be there with bells on." Opal giggled. She maneuvered off the love seat with much effort to stand and stretched her back.

"Please tell me the bells comment was just an expression," Sophia asked, and when Opal pulled a string of jingle bells from her oversize canvas bag, she went ahead and snorted in laughter.

Jill spun Sophia around, taking the time to add some good-smelling mousse before blasting the brown locks with the blow-dryer. By the time Sophia's hair was dried and the dryer switched off, the Knitting Club members were growing restless.

"When are you going back to work, dear?" Trudy asked, her bright-orange hair filled with curlers.

"Agnes is covering until after Christmas," Sophia answered, leaving it at that. She watched through the mirror as the old ladies exchanged looks.

"So you know what Wes has been up to lately?" Bertie asked hesitantly.

Sophia knew what he'd been up to, working and attentively checking on Collin. She also knew Wes had remained standoffish when it came to her, so she figured he was staying in whatever place Ty put him in at the hospital. Too much had gone on to straighten him out on it, and she hoped the chance to do so wasn't slipping through her fingers.

"Well, we think you should know that Wes has been spotted around town with a woman." Ethel blurted what the others seemed to be alluding to, her face all pinched in disgust.

Sophia's stomach dipped, but she chose not to

comment, hoping they'd said their piece and would shuffle along soon to bother someone else. That way she could dislodge the knot in her throat so she could breathe and then maybe follow that up with a good ole ugly cry.

Sadly, they weren't finished just yet. The women followed Sophia around the salon like an overbearing shadow, spilling details of the dates—one where he took the woman to Sunset Studio and Gallery and then out to eat.

"Well, I caught him at another cooking class," Trudy, Miss Private Eye herself, chimed in.

Sophia glanced at Opal and Josie where they stood by the nail polish display, but neither one of them would look at her, and that was all the confirmation she needed to know it was true. Wes had been by her and Collin's side nearly every waking hour. How he managed working in some dates was beyond her, but he had every right. She was sure news of her date with Ty had reached him just as it had that nosy mother at the park. The last weeks were such a mess, leaving too much unsorted.

"Heard he's bringing another woman to the dance tonight." Bertie sucked her teeth, not finding the idea any more pleasant than Sophia.

"I hope they have a good time," Sophia said in an even voice, actually meaning it to some extent. If ever a man existed who deserved to be peacefully happy, it was Weston Sawyer. He certainly didn't deserve to be mixed up in her chaos.

By the time her nails were trimmed and lacquered a shimmery red that Josie picked out for her, Sophia had reached her limit. The Sand Queens wasted no time hurrying out the salon and back to the condo. Sophia seethed while Opal and Josie looked guilty for some reason.

"It's not your fault he's dating," Sophia snapped at them, sounding like it was entirely her two friends' fault. "He *should* date!" She paced around the obstacle of toys in front of the couch where Josie and Opal were sitting. "He's done nothing wrong." A hiccuped sob pushed through her resolve.

"Oh, honey, I thought y'all were together before Ty came in to town. What happened?" Josie leaned forward and tried catching Sophia's wrist in passing.

Sophia skirted out of reach. "We sort of were; then he kissed me after the mud run and then we quarreled about it. . . . Then I found Ty in my house and then and then . . . and then everything fell to pieces!" She tossed her hands in the air and stomped her foot. When her foot came down on a toy truck, it sent both feet flying from underneath her. Crashing against a few more toys on the descent, her back collided with the floor in an audible thump.

Josie and Opal gasped and after a moment both were hovering over her.

"Are you okay?" Opal asked.

After regaining her breath, Sophia rasped, "Clearly I'm not." Nothing physically hurt per se, but she was quite bothered by whatever damp thing was stuck to her backside. She pushed a fire truck with its lights flashing and the siren blaring away from her ear and rolled to her side. "Please tell me what that is on my butt."

They answered with a fit of giggles.

"It looks like the remains of a banana." Josie snickered. "Or at least I hope that's what it is."

Sophia didn't have the energy to move, so she just lay there and enjoyed the fresh scent of her clean hair covering her face. "Someone want to be a peach and get it off for me?"

After some debate, Josie volunteered to remove the squished piece of banana. She even helped to pull Sophia to her feet. By the time Sophia changed into a clean pair of yoga pants, she'd calmed down enough to join them on the couch and share everything that had transpired in the last month.

"Wes has been through enough. He doesn't need my baggage bringing him down," Sophia concluded, staring at her glossy red nails until tears blurred her vision.

"Now that's just a bunch of hogwash." Opal grunted, wiggling to get comfortable beside her on the couch. "You and Wes are great together."

Sophia shrugged. "I think Wes and I are still friends, but I think the other part we were developing fell to pieces."

"We just need to put it all back together," Josie said, making it sound so easy.

"Honey, it's doubtful it'll all fit back together." Sophia gave her a sad smile.

"Ooh! I have an idea!" Opal chirped enthusiastically, sending both downcast faces of Josie and Sophia to look over at her.

"Your ideas always make me nervous," Sophia admitted.

"No worries." Opal shooed the concern with a flick of her wrist. "Answer me this: What's the one thing Wes has been after you about since the get-go and you have given him a hard time about it since then too?"

"The public dates," Sophia answered, wondering where this was headed.

Opal nudged Sophia's knee with hers. "Exactly, so why not give the poor guy what he's wanted and stop making it more complicated than what it is."

Sophia mulled over the idea, thinking it sounded pretty simple. When Ty showed up last month, it made her finally grasp how unhealthy their relationship was, even when fists were not involved. Relationships weren't supposed to be riddled with complications and stress to the point of causing anxiety and bouts of nausea. "How am I supposed to do that if Wes is dating someone else?"

"I heard he's miserable but doing it to give you space to decide how you feel," Josie said quietly, squeezing Sophia's arm.

"This is what I propose," Opal began in a stern tone. "You get dolled up, go to that dance, and stake your claim. Show Wes he's worth putting yourself out there for, and show the rest of this town that nothing and no one is going to keep the fiercely amazing Sophia Grace Prescott down!"

Sophia scoffed, not returning any of Opal's zeal. "Soon to be Sophia Grace *Gaines*. I filed the paperwork to change back to my maiden name."

"Good for you, but what about the dance?" Josie whispered. "We're all going, so you won't be in this alone."

Sophia shook her head. "I have nothing to wear, and I'm thinking about heading over and staying at the farm tonight with Collin."

Opal huffed. "Give that poor kid a break from you. Seriously, you're as close to a perfect mother as it gets, but all children need some space." She placed her gold-glittered fingers on top of Sophia's hand. "Honey, to be honest, you've been smothering him since the surgery."

Sophia glanced at Josie and she nodded timidly in agreement. "Fine. I'll stay home tonight."

"No, you're going to that dance. I think I have a dress that'll work." Opal scooted off the couch and went over to her tote where she'd left it on the dining table. "I'll have Linc bring it over."

A shiver of terror hit Sophia's shoulders. There was

no telling what Lincoln would show up with if Opal had picked it out. "No, no, no. That's okay."

"It's done." Opal sent another text. "He's on the way. Now we just need to look through your shoes . . ."

A few hours later, Sophia stood at the entrance to the community center. Even though the night was chilly, it wasn't close to cold enough to produce snow. Yet the small yard was glistening in a white blanket.

"Is it real snow?" Sophia asked, glancing at Josie, who looked like a live version of Elsa from *Frozen*, wearing a stunning ice-blue gown with her platinum-blonde hair styled in a loose braid.

"Yes, it's real machine-generated snow. Hurry up. We're already late." Josie walked with a determined stride, making it a chore for Sophia's shorter legs, underneath the poufy ball gown, to keep up.

Sophia was still baffled that Lincoln had shown up with the most sophisticated gown she'd ever laid eyes on. Layers upon layers of luxurious fabric fit like it was specially made just for her. The A-line princess gown would make the most romantic wedding dress if it weren't for the deep-red color.

"Slow down, Jo," Sophia mumbled as they practically jogged down the corridor. As soon as they entered the dance hall, Josie let go of her arm and almost caused Sophia to stumble. "Seriously?" She was about to grumble when the room caught her attention. "Wow."

"Right?" Josie beamed.

"Did y'all tear the old place down and rebuild?" Sophia asked while gaping at the sparkly room. Icicles dripped from the ceiling until meeting the white centerpieces on the all-white tables. She took in the white candles, white snowflakes, and spindly trees painted white with white twinkling lights.

"Nah. The old place is still here. Just hidden behind the winter forest." Josie giggled.

"It's exquisite, Jo. You and August are magicians," Sophia said softly as she continued to peruse the enchanting scene before her. The room was dusted in a frosty array of decor and she half expected to see her breath in a cloud as she huffed heavily. Everything was white and everyone was dressed in a mix of silver, icy blue, and white. Everyone but her. Red in a sea of white.

Sophia glanced to her left to complain to Josie about it, but her friend had conveniently disappeared. Embarrassed, she clutched each side of the dress skirt, lifting it slightly so she could perform her own disappearing act. Turning around on her silver stilettos, she bumped smack-dab into a solid chest.

"Whoa, gorgeous. Where's the fire?" Seth gave her a once-over, playing it up with a low growl. "Hmm . . . think I have the fire in my arms. Sweetheart, you're killing it in that dress."

"Uh. No, I look like a fool in this dress. I didn't get the memo about the color theme." She stepped out of his reach and straightened the skirt.

"Well, I, for one, am glad you didn't get the memo. You are just . . . hmm." He grunted again with a good bit of emphasis. "Don't touch anything in this icy room, 'cause you'll make it melt."

Sophia reached over and popped him in the stomach. "Knock it off." She huffed and looked around but wished she hadn't when her eyes landed on Wes. He wore a silvery-gray suit, looking handsome as ever. A woman with raven hair and wearing a white sequin dress was chatting him up. On another huff Sophia turned her focus back to Seth.

The salacious look on his face was gone and had

been replaced with a degree of seriousness. "How's Collin today?"

She smoothed her thumb against the anchor ring. "Apparently he's well enough to run away with his grandmother and leave me abandoned."

"Love that kid." Seth grinned.

"Where have you been the last few days?" Sophia asked Seth. He'd accompanied his brother on almost every visit to check on Collin. "I thought maybe you'd skipped town."

"No skipping town. I'm actually looking for a place of my own. You know of any vacant condos?"

"Umm . . . no." Sophia wasn't so sure she wanted Wes's twin brother for a neighbor.

"Will you let me know if one comes available?" Seth asked, looking like he was holding a secret within the depths of his greenish-gray eyes. It was the first time Sophia had noticed his irises held more green pigment than Wes's.

"Is that what's kept you so busy?" She looked away and found herself staring in Wes's direction again. Thankfully, his back was turned to her, so Wes didn't even know she was there, but she knew it wouldn't take long for him to spot her. The dress looked like a red beacon in a sea of white.

"Nah. My active dating life has kept me busy," Seth said, smugness slipping back into his tone.

His answer had her sneaking a quick look at him before she scanned the crowd. "Oh, well, good for you." Sophia pulled on a smile, although it was superficial. Seemed the Sawyer twins were growing in popularity with the ladies once again around Sunset Cove.

"Yep, went to an art gallery for the first time and even took a cooking class. *I've* had a lot of fun."

Sophia cut Seth a sideways glance, thinking through what he just divulged. It sounded prosaic enough, but he had added a weight to it. One that said, *Pay attention to me.* And then it clicked. It was Seth in the pictures and not Wes, but why did he admit to it?

She pointed at the woman with her hand on Wes's shoulder. "Wes has a pretty date for the evening."

Seth snorted. "Heck no. That woman has been circling him like a vulture over roadkill. He keeps trying to shake her, but she just keeps circling back. I think you need to go rescue him."

"Why's that?"

"Because he's gone to some really elaborately dumb efforts to get you here tonight. He purchased you a beauty certificate so you could get your hair and nails done. He sent those old ladies to fill your ears with nonsense about those dates he set up for me. But I must say, he sure does know how to pick out a dress. Paid a pretty penny if you want to know."

Sophia's mouth popped open on a gasp. "What? Why would he do all that?"

"Men do dumb stuff when they're in love." Seth shook his head and wrinkled his nose. "Shoot, I told him all he needed to do was just show up with a box of Whitman's Sampler and be straight up about being in love with you, but he said you deserved better than just chocolates."

"But those are really good chocolates," Sophia mumbled, her feet already moving toward Wes.

"That's what I said," Seth replied from behind her.

Sophia kept moving until she was a few steps away, hearing the woman saying something about really wanting to dance. Not about to let that happen, she laid her hand on Wes's shoulder. "Sorry I'm late, honey."

Wes turned away from the woman dismissively. He

took in a stuttered breath as his eyes coasted Sophia's body. He mouthed, *Wow*, as he wrapped her in his arms. "My very own Italian princess."

Sophia smoothed her fingertips along his silk tie. It and the pocket square were the same deep-red hue as her dress. "Why red?" Sophia couldn't help but ask as she settled into his arms, moving her fingers to link behind his neck.

"Because you are one exceptional woman who should be set apart." The corners of his lips curled, producing those dimples she loved so much. "Plus, after tonight I want it to be perfectly clear to the town of Sunset Cove whose arm you belong on."

Her eyebrows rose in tease. "Oh yeah?"

"Yes. It's mine." Wes presented his arm and she didn't even hesitate to wrap hers around it. He led her to the very center of the dance floor just as Sam Hunt's "I Met a Girl" began playing.

Sophia glanced over at the DJ station and found Lincoln giving Wes a not-so-subtle thumbs-up. Opal sat beside him chowing down on cake, lifting the fork in a wave. "What's up with that?"

"Lincoln and August helped me come up with a plan to woo you. They said it had to be over-the-top like the cliché twin switcheroo, so if you want to punch someone, it should be one of them. We even came up with a playlist to help my cause. I picked this one because of your beautiful laugh."

Awestruck, tingles raced along Sophia's bare shoulders. "I can't believe you did all this . . . even having the Knitting Club doing your bidding."

"They owed us that much. Finally put their meddling to good use." Wes smirked, mischief whirling around his hazel eyes.

"Tricking me is considered good use?"

"Just this once." He pulled her closer, and she melted into the embrace.

Sophia tipped her head, catching her favorite meddlers, Josie and Opal, staring her way with giant grins. "I should have known those stinkers were in on this." The dress fitting too well should have been a dead giveaway.

"You're not going to pinch them, are you?" Wes nuzzled her neck, sending the warmth much deeper than the surface of her skin. "They were helping my cause to win you over."

Sophia combed through his soft hair and angled slightly away to catch his gaze again. "It was never a competition you had to participate in, Wes. I've been yours ever since you sang with my son at church for no other reason but to make him happy." She gave him a spirited look, lips twisting as she winked an eye.

He tilted his head, chuckling deeply. "And you won me on our first date." A groan rumbled deep in his chest. "The moment you laughed, Sophia, I swear my world tilted and I really never want it to right again."

The warmth reached her eyes, sending tears to wash over her view of him. "Where were all these smooth words the night we were covered in mud?"

The smile wobbled into a half one. "You rattle me with all your sass sometimes. I wanted to say it all, all at once, so it came out wrong."

Wes led them in a slow dance, both falling into a trance in the middle of a winter wonderland. It reminded Sophia of a fairy tale her mother loved reading to her when she was a girl. Letting go of all the stress, she allowed herself to finally believe the fairy tale could come true.

As they made a languid circle, Sophia looked up and locked gazes with Wes. "You have these amazing gold flecks in your eyes . . . and they seem to wink out of the creamy mocha more prominently when you're overwhelmed. Like right now."

Wes blinked slowly, the edges of his alluring eyes softening. "I've always thought they looked like the color of sand. . . . But your eyes." He cupped the side of her face and angled closer. "God must have dipped some water straight from the Caribbean and used it to color in your eyes. Tranquil, peaceful . . . You're my ocean."

She sniffed back the tears. "You can't say that while we're in the middle of this dance floor."

"Why not? I want everyone to know how I feel about you." He dipped his head until his forehead touched hers. "We've kept our feelings hidden long enough. From the world and from ourselves."

The solemn gesture of their foreheads touching in silence said more than what they could articulate in words. Love was there. It didn't need to be placed in a word to bring it to life.

As they gently swayed to another song, Sophia placed her lips close to his ear and whispered the words anyway. "I love you."

Wes's hold on her tightened as he released a heavy sigh. "I really like the sound of that." He angled just enough to meet her eyes. "I love you, too."

The night moved along as song after song declared how Wes felt about her. As they danced, he would explain how. And when the song "Born to Be Yours" began filtering through the icy landscape, the subdued mood transformed into a more celebratory vibe. The rhythm had a more upbeat tempo, and when Wes's hip kept time with it, Sophia let go of her inhibitions and joined in. She tossed her hands in the air and boogied with a freedom she hadn't felt in years. August danced over with Josie and the guys jokingly showed off some pretty impressive dance moves.

Giggling, Sophia shouted over the music, "You've got skills, Dr. Sawyer!"

Wes winked before he spun her out and then twirled her back into his arms. By the time the song came to a close, his cheeks were high in color and his caramel hair a bit disheveled. Breathless, he asked, "Have I managed to woo you even a little?"

Sophia tsked. "A box of Whitman's would have been all the woo you needed. And you could have just asked me to the dance instead of sending the Knitting Club after me."

Wes twisted his lips and tilted his head. "That sounds too simple."

She smoothed a wavy lock of hair back into place where it had slipped onto his forehead. "I'm really attracted to simple living. And I'm really attracted to the man who introduced me to that concept."

"Hmm . . ." Wes tipped his head to the other side. "Does us slipping out of here sound simple enough?"

"Depends on what you want to do afterward." She combed her fingers through his hair.

Wes glanced behind her. "I think we start by stealing a kiss by that snowman outside. After that, our crazy group of friends want to go swimming."

That last part had Sophia's fingers stilling. "Huh?"

Wes chuckled. "They want to go out to the camp for a late-night pool party. It's heated, and August and his uncle thought it would be perfect irony to end the winter wonderland night at the lagoon they have hidden in the middle of the country."

Sophia giggled. "I've heard about it but haven't seen it yet."

"Yeah. Lincoln isn't able to dance much due to his leg, so it's really for him. Opal wanted to make sure he had a good time tonight." Wes looked over her shoulder again and nodded.

She looked too and saw the Coles and Bradfords waiting by the door along with Carter, his wife, Dominica, and Seth, who were all apparently ready to slip out too. She laced her fingers with his and began pulling him in their direction. "Come on. I think we're due a Sand Queens meeting."

Wes made good on his kissing suggestion and then some. Hours flew by while they spent time at the camp pool, frolicking about like a bunch of kids. In the wee hours of morning, Josie let the shriveled, famished group into Driftwood Diner and cooked them a breakfast feast. And by the time they ate their weight in shrimp gravy and biscuits, dawn had shown up and Sophia was exhausted yet fully wide-awake. They all pitched in and helped clean up before scattering to go home.

Wes pulled up at his house just as the sun began peeking from behind the ocean and led her inside.

"When I purchased this beach house, I had a vision for it past the remodel. It was supposed to be my place of solace where I could come in and hide alone. But it never felt right from day one." Wes turned to her once they reached the living room. "The first time you and Collin came over was the first time the house felt settled somehow. Like you two were the missing part of the renovation." He slowly kissed the edge of her mouth before taking a step back to meet her eyes. "Sea Glass Castle has been as much your beach house as it has been mine from the start. It's lonely when you and Collin aren't here." Wes walked over to the vase of sea glass on the mantel and took it in his hands, turning the container in different directions as the early morning light glanced off the frosted jewels. "So after I moved in here and Lincoln told me about the sea glass, I was intrigued and did a little research. Did you know these beauties were once broken fragments of bottles and such?"

Sophia nodded her head when he looked up. "Yes." She'd done her share of ocean preservation research over the years. She knew all about sea glass but allowed him to continue speaking in his soothing baritone, knowing he was headed somewhere with it.

"They roll around and tumble in the ocean for years, and the entire time the elements are reshaping them into something new and more appealing. It reminded me of a Bible verse from 2 Corinthians. 'We are pressed on every side by troubles, but we are not crushed. We are perplexed, but not driven to despair. We are hunted down, but never abandoned by God. We get knocked down, but we are not destroyed.'"

Sophia recalled the verse and began reciting it with him. When they finished, Wes looked up and shared a tender smile with her. "I committed that verse to memory this year, trying to keep the right perspective," she admitted.

"You certainly have lived it. I have too. Now that we're on this side of that, it's easy to see how we are much like this sea glass." Wes returned his focus to the vase. "We started out last summer in shards of our former selves, both going through a turbulent journey, but our time together has smoothed out the jaggedness and formed us into something quite appealing in my eyes." Wes reached inside the vase and pulled something out before placing it back on the mantel. He turned and held out a delicate ring with a silver band encrusted in diamonds. "So you see, Sea Glass Castle is going to not only stand as the name for our home, but also stand as our testimony."

Sophia gasped. "Wes!"

"I know you're just coming out of a bad marriage. I'm not saying we have to marry any time soon. I just want you to know that's where I want us heading when you're ready."

She held her hand out, admiring the anchor ring he had given her. "But I don't want to take this one off."

"You don't have to. I had this one custom made to fit together with it." Wes slipped the sparkling band onto her finger and slid it to where it fit perfectly with the anchor ring. "I hope you'll agree to someday be my wife."

"Yes. Wes, I want to be your wife," Sophia answered simply. "And not just 'someday,' but soon." She was done with complicated and ready to enter the more peaceful season she just knew God had planned for them.

EPILOGUE

Winter around the Grand Strand had the appealing quality of serenity. A quieter time. Less hustle and more calm. Or so that's what the locals claimed. This was Wes's second winter living in Sunset Cove and he'd yet to discover that calm for himself. There was always something going down that kept him on his toes. Despite that fact, his lips tipped up in a smile as he thought about the latest distraction. He shook his head, knowing one more patient needed his attention before he could allow his mind to completely snap out of doctor mode. He was about to head to the exam room when a hot mess of a woman came bursting through the door, groaning like an animal on its last leg.

"I'm dying," she moaned, shoulders sagging and lips pouting. "This is misery."

"Stop being so dramatic." Wes studied her closely, thinking she looked a little green and her top a bit frumpy, but other than that she was as beautiful as always.

Sophia shot him a scathing glare. "Easy for you to say. Eight and a half months of nausea and your kid has decided to take up tap dancing—" her eyes bugged out, going for more of that sassy drama—*"on my bladder."*

Wes rounded his desk and stalked over, not stopping until he had his wife cradled in his arms much like he did on their wedding night last winter. He skimmed her sweet neck with his nose and lips, recalling his sassy beauty walking down the church aisle in that red dress. It would always be one of the best moments of his life. It wasn't conventional, but he liked them doing it their own way. "Only a few more weeks. You carry her just a little while longer and then I'll take it from there. Indefinitely."

Sophia snuggled close and giggled when he nipped at her neck. "I think you'll have to fight Collin over her."

"Our boy is tough, but I think I can take him." Wes leaned back slightly so she could see the mean face he was making. By her throaty giggle, he'd obviously failed at pulling off looking like a bad boy.

"Honey, you're too polished to be menacing." She tapped the end of his nose as if she found him cute.

"Seriously, are you hanging in there?" He glanced at her feet, which were bare since she'd kicked her shoes off as soon as she was in his office. "Not much swelling today."

"Uh-oh. You're in doctor mode again." Sophia tsked.

"No, I'm in taking-care-of-my-wife mode. And if she's sweet to me, I'll make her an ice cream sundae when we get home later." He was a pro at making extravagant sundaes at that point considering it was her constant craving.

"You're too good to me." She sighed and ran her fingers through his hair.

"You deserve even better than my best, Mrs. Sawyer." Wes leaned toward her until his forehead rested against hers. It was their private way of saying, *I love you*.

And did he ever. Each morning waking up beside Sophia, Wes just knew he couldn't ever love her more than he did at that moment. But each night when they climbed back into bed together after tucking Collin in and praying with him, Wes found more space in his heart to love her and his family even more.

Unable to stop himself, he pressed his lips to his beautiful wife's and hoped he was conveying all his love to her.

A throat clearing by the door pulled their lips apart.

"Sorry to interrupt, Dr. Sawyer, but Everly Cole is waiting in the sea turtle room." The nurse giggled as she rushed off.

Wes dropped one last kiss to Sophia's lips. "Let's go see if Miss Cole will let us give her the vaccines this time."

"Probably not. That one is as hardheaded as her ornery daddy," Sophia mouthed off, but Wes knew she was only teasing. They were all crazy about the redheaded angel with a smile as sweet as her mother's and a stubborn streak as ironclad as her father's.

"How's Josie today?" Wes knelt before Sophia and slid her shoes back on her feet.

"Poor girl is as queasy as I am." Sophia wrinkled her nose.

"It's early in the first trimester. Hopefully she'll move past it soon." Wes glanced up before working the second shoe on. "An entirely new generation of Sand Queens. Can you believe it?"

"And/or Sand Kings," Sophia quipped.

Wes placed his hands on either side of Sophia's rounded abdomen and pressed his lips to the center. Suddenly her belly grew rock-hard. Jolting, his eyes collided with hers as she took a measured breath. A punctuated moment passed as the rigidness faded underneath his palms.

"Oh yeah. I forgot to tell you. I'm having contractions." She gave him an apologetic yet sly smile.

Wes shot to his feet. "Sophia Grace!"

"I probably should have led with that, huh?" She shrugged.

Instinctively, Wes was a man on a mission. He swiped his phone off the desk and then he swiped his wife off her feet, striding out of the office at a clipped pace. "My wife's having my baby!" His shouting drew the Coles out of the exam room and they began parading behind him while hooting and hollering their own sentiments.

"My wife's having my baby!" Wes bellowed repeatedly like a wild man all the way out the door and on to the hospital until Sophia actually did have his baby. Six hours later, Wes and Collin jointly held baby Isabella Luka Sawyer.

● ● ●

The Sand Queens had endured their fair share of storms. Some more severe than others, but each time they chose to rebuild a life and move forward, each one holding on to the hope of a greater life filled with love and peace that came even during the midst of storms. For they knew the sun was patiently waiting to shine again. Faithful and true, it always did.

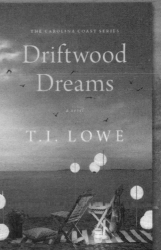

1

Weaving through a jungle of the most outlandish antiques he'd ever come across, Lincoln Cole was dumbfounded and intrigued all at once. Surrounded by unusually dressed pieces of furniture, he did a three-sixty and scratched at the scruff on his cheek. The scruff indicated he was more than a few days past needing a shave, but the rebellion that had taken root in him since the injury he sustained in Syria had overruled grooming protocol that morning. Waking up from the recurring nightmare often left him too raw to focus on such mundane things. At least he had managed a shower and a fresh change of clothes.

Whimsical feminine humming somehow found its way to him as he suppressed the limp wanting to reside in his left leg while hobbling another few steps forward. Although it was a sunny day in late September, his leg was telling him the pleasant weather wouldn't last for very long.

Nothing good ever lasts long . . .

Lincoln huffed in frustration over his own thoughts and stood semihidden in a section of old desks. He cast his gaze upward and blinked a few times. Various tables and chairs were suspended from the ceiling. A few had been converted into light fixtures, while the rest of them looked like they were being held hostage by thick cables.

"Good morning," a cheery voice came from behind him. "Welcome to Bless This Mess."

Keeping his focus on the ceiling, Lincoln spoke the first thing to flicker through his mind. "Is that even safe?" He pointed to the pieces of furniture that appeared to be floating above their heads.

"Oh yes. Code inspectors have deemed my mess safe."

The woman's teasing voice finally had Lincoln turning in her direction. Peering at him from the other side of a wooden hutch that had been transformed into a bath vanity was a sprite of a woman with the wildest head of golden-red curls he'd ever seen. The tips were lighter as if the sun had reached down and stolen the color. She closely resembled the mosaic fairy he'd seen on the outside of the building.

Clearing his throat, he offered a curt "Good."

A smile began to blossom across the lively woman's face as she smoothed some kind of flowy blouse with her petite hand, causing a gaudy collection of bracelets to clang against one another. Lincoln assessed her as he'd been trained to do in the military. He measured her no bigger than a minute and figured he could apprehend her with one hand tied behind his back, but he considered those big green eyes of hers and cataloged them as her secret weapon. They sparkled, but that wasn't what set off the warning bells. No, those eyes were watching him way too closely and had already seen way more than they should. Assessment complete, he began to slowly back away.

"I have the perfect piece for you." She held an index finger in the air, halting his attempted retreat. She skipped off in the opposite direction, sending the spirals of soft red-and-blonde hair into a dance. "I'm Opal, by the way," she said quickly over her shoulder.

She disappeared from sight, but he could hear the banging and clattering from his two o'clock, giving away her location. "I didn't come here for furniture."

"Oh, that's okay. This piece was meant for you, nonetheless, so I insist on you taking it." Her grunts came from the back and sounded like she was struggling with something.

Sighing, Lincoln looked heavenward at the craziness on the ceiling one last time before walking through the maze to find her. He stopped cold in his tracks when he found her sitting on a soldier's footlocker.

"I found this on a junking trip last year." Opal smoothed her tiny hand over the thick gray cushion that had been fitted on the top. It reminded Lincoln of a military-issue wool coat. "For some reason, I just knew it needed to be transformed into a bench seat. Possibly for an entry piece where someone can sit and remove or put on their shoes. Or maybe at the foot of a bed." She swung her feet back and forth, looking like a little kid. Flip-flops peeked from the edges of her fraying bell-bottom jeans each time her legs swayed forward.

Not letting himself get caught in the confusing inquiry of where she found such an odd pair of jeans, Lincoln crossed his arms and regarded the piece suspiciously. "Why'd you make it so tall?" His eyes dropped to the thick wooden spindles she'd used for the legs. They were painted a neutral gray to coordinate with the creamy beige used on the trunk. It was obvious she'd put a lot of thought into the piece, even restenciling the ID number along the front side in the same gray as the legs.

"I had a feeling the owner would need the extra leg

space. What are you, six-four?" She gave him a swift once-over.

Six-five. "Close enough."

She smirked like she had a secret. "If you're not here for furniture, then what are you here for?"

Lincoln moved his eyes away from the peculiar woman and swept them over the menagerie of furniture pieces while rubbing a hand through his long brown hair. Haircuts were another ritual he'd allowed to die several months ago, right along with his military career.

After giving her question some thought, Lincoln answered honestly, "I'm not sure." He turned and began moving through the rows as quick as his achy leg would carry him.

"You forgot your bench!" Opal called from behind him. "And you didn't even introduce yourself!"

Her petitions did nothing to slow his already-sluggish getaway. He didn't stop until he was piled back into his Jeep and heading down the beachfront road.

"Smooth, Cole. Real smooth." He groaned and released one tight-fisted pound against the steering wheel. Between the throb in his knee and the unsettling encounter with the store's owner, all he wanted to do was go back to his beach cottage and hide from the feeling that he didn't fit anywhere anymore. The doctors had done the best they could with his knee, putting enough hardware in his leg for him to be considered part cyborg, but no bolt or pin could put his destroyed life back together.

The promise he'd made to meet his buddy Carter for a late breakfast trumped the desire to hide. No matter how many vicissitudes had occurred in his life, Lincoln Cole still remained a man of his word. So instead of doing what his bones ached to do, Lincoln pulled up at Driftwood

Diner and made his way inside, where he found Carter was already perched on a stool at the counter.

"You eating without me?" Lincoln gave Carter a manly slap on the shoulder while inspecting an untouched plate of delicious-looking fare—biscuits and gravy, bacon, French toast, and eggs.

Carter stood and gave him a bear hug. Lincoln cringed at the contact. The Cole family was not an affectionate bunch. Handshakes from the men and hugs from the women that were so brief they could hardly constitute as hugs were what he was used to receiving. Carter and his family were the complete opposite, offering long embraces and draping arms over each other's shoulders without thought.

Carter finally released him and gestured for him to have a seat. "I was beginning to think you ditched me. Good to see you, man."

"Sorry. This bum knee won't let me get anything done fast. It's good to see you too." Lincoln stifled a grunt as he settled on the stool beside Carter. Moving in and unpacking the last few days had stiffened his leg considerably, making him feel more like a decrepit old geezer than the thirty-three-year-old he was. He pulled in a deep breath, stealing the enticing aroma of fried bacon and rich, robust coffee. "This place looks like it's ready to collapse, but it sure does smell good."

"The dilapidated shack is part of the charm, but wait until you taste the food." Carter waved over a tall blonde. "Josie, you think you could bring my buddy Lincoln one of your Hungry Sailor's Specials?"

"You got it." She offered Lincoln a welcoming smile. "What can I get you to drink?"

Lincoln motioned to Carter's cup. "Coffee would be great, please."

Once the waitress disappeared into the kitchen, Lincoln angled himself on the stool to keep a better eye on the perimeter of the dining area. The place was busy considering it was well past Labor Day, but most of the clientele looked to be made up of fishermen. The telltale signs of fishing bibs and hats gave them away. He noticed a few tables in the back corner occupied by young mothers chatting it up over coffee while their little ones either slept in their carriers or made a gaum in their high chairs.

"You settled in at the cottage all right?" Carter asked as he studied his plate, looking as starved as Lincoln but being polite enough to wait.

"Yeah. It's peaceful for sure." And peace was exactly what he was looking for.

The blonde waitress was back in a flash and placed several plates before him. The savory scents of breakfast meats and a sweet vanilla perfume wafting from a thick stack of French toast had him turning to face the counter.

"Wow." Lincoln picked up his fork and pointed it in the direction of one of Carter's plates. "Why didn't I get any biscuits and gravy?" he asked the waitress. "And is that shrimp in the gravy?"

"A batch of biscuits just came out the oven. I'll bring you out a serving in a minute. We use shrimp instead of sausage."

"It's genius," Carter commented.

Josie only added a timid smile as she placed a cup beside Lincoln's plate and filled it with aromatic coffee.

"Thank you, ma'am." Lincoln tipped his head before taking a sip. Still unable to shake off the bad night's sleep, it was exactly what he needed.

"You're welcome. I'll go grab you some biscuits and gravy." She backtracked to the kitchen.

Lincoln cut into the thick slices of toast and crammed a bite into his mouth. Before he could start chewing, Carter bowed his head and said grace, thanking God for the food and for Lincoln's safe return from overseas. Lincoln, feeling uneasy, waited to take another bite until his friend wrapped up the prayer.

He wasn't on good terms with God as of late. His gran and paps always said God wanted to answer his prayers and to see him prosper. Lincoln had wholeheartedly believed them until a rocket attack showed him just how naive he'd been.

Lincoln came from a long line of Marines. He was a Cole, and Coles were born to protect their country. His grandfather, great-uncle, uncle, and dad had all been career soldiers, and that was Lincoln's projected path. He'd managed almost two tours until an attack in Syria ended his plans, leaving him broken and uncertain of any future. The need for a little space to heal and overcome the shame of letting his family down was one of the reasons he finally accepted his friend August's advice to take a break from Beaufort, South Carolina, and headed up the coast to Sunset Cove.

"When's August going to grace us with his presence?" Lincoln asked between bites, trying to ignore his dismal thoughts.

Carter sopped up the creamy gravy with a chunk of biscuit and chuckled. "That one has been globe-trotting for so long, I think he sometimes forgets he's supposed to grace us with his appearance now and then."

August was Carter's nephew even though the two guys were fairly close in age and acted more like brothers. Lincoln had met them both at a summer ministry camp in Beaufort years ago when they were all teens, before Lincoln became a soldier and August a world-renowned artist. They had instantly clicked and had remained in touch over the years. August was the type of guy to draw others to him, so it was no surprise when Lincoln formed a close-knit bond with him similar to that he would later find with his military brothers. Carter was also a great friend, but he was now in love and that kept the sucker too preoccupied.

"He's back in the States now, though, right?" Lincoln shoved another bite of sweet toast in and followed it with a strip of bacon.

"Yeah. Wrapping up an inner-city art project in New York," Carter explained around a mouthful of food.

Lincoln chewed thoughtfully while musing over August. The guy was an artistic genius with a penchant for hair dye and piercings, and he could create art out of just about anything. Lincoln was right proud of how his friend had used that incredible talent to share with others through an international art ministry that introduced fine arts to the less fortunate. August had also found his place in the world of art. His paintings hung in galleries from California to New York. "He's really made a name for himself, hasn't he?"

Carter's face lit up with pride. "He sure has. He's gone and gotten famous on us."

Carter Bradford had made a name for himself in his own right. Until recently, he and his fiancée, Dominica, had been members of a praise and worship band that shared their talent at camps and conferences across the United States. Carter was the sound tech guy but knew his way around a piano and could pick about any song on a guitar. Dominica was the bass player. Lincoln didn't know what all was behind their early retirement, but he figured Carter would share it if he wanted to. And if not, Lincoln deduced it was none of his business.

Carter reached over and grabbed the carafe and refilled both their cups with coffee. "August told me he set you up with a job at Bless This Mess. When do you start?" He took another sip of coffee.

Lincoln stared down at his plate. "I'm not working there."

"Why not?" Carter groaned. "August promised Opal you would, and he doesn't make a habit of promising something he can't deliver. Was she upset?"

Lincoln's back tensed up, knowing good and well he'd just made his friend do something he himself wouldn't do. But then again, August had no business making promises on his behalf in the first place. "She had no reason to be upset. I didn't even tell her who I was, so she's fine. That woman doesn't seem to be one for getting upset, anyway." Lincoln shrugged and chomped down on another crispy strip of bacon.

Carter gave him a shrewd look while slowly chewing. "You're selling it a little too hard there, buddy."

"What?" Lincoln shook his head. "Am not." He wiped his mouth with his wadded-up napkin and took a sip of coffee. "Look, I'll have August call her up and explain that his friend changed his mind about the job. No harm, no foul."

"She really needs the help, Linc. Don't leave her hanging."

"She's weird. Why would August even suggest me putting up with her? She some kind of hippie or something?" Lincoln asked just as the waitress placed a piping hot plate full of biscuits and gravy before him.

He was about to dive in when he noticed she wasn't wearing that pleasant smile any longer. "I overheard you, and can I just say that Opal may be weird but she's a good weird. The wisest weird woman you'll ever meet. And I can guarantee you'd have a fun time working with her. No chance of boredom."

Lincoln shifted on the stool, aggravated and a little embarrassed. "I'm not looking for a good time." And he certainly didn't want to deal with Opal's intuitiveness, which he'd noticed even in their brief meeting. He grimaced.

"Clearly," the blonde muttered while walking off.

"Who does she think she is?" Lincoln glared at her retreating back.

"That's Josie. One of Opal's best friends. And you just got on her bad side. I'd leave a fat tip after how you just got caught talking about her friend—or find somewhere else to eat from now on." Carter waved a hand toward Lincoln. "And besides, look at you with all that long hair and your old Converses. *You* look like the hippie." He pushed an elbow into Lincoln's side and tsked. "Even got a rip in the knee of your jeans."

Lincoln suppressed the urge to tuck his shoulder-length hair behind his ear, knowing his friend would call him out on it. And he could razz Carter right back. With shaggy brown hair that the sun had faded quite a bit and wearing his own pair of tattered jeans with a surf logo T-shirt, Carter was a cross between country boy USA and SoCal surfer dude.

He let it go and muttered, "I'm not looking for complication, and that woman screams it."

Carter huffed a laugh. "It's just delivering furniture and helping Opal move stuff around. How's that complicated?"

The way she looked at me was complicated. Lincoln held that comment back and focused on enjoying every bite of breakfast just in case it was the last time he was allowed in. It was a mighty fine meal, so he hoped he wouldn't be banned from the premises.

"Your loss then." Carter shook his head, but after another bite of food, he changed the subject and filled Lincoln in on the fine arts camp he was going to open next summer. The conversation remained on that topic until their plates were clean. After settling the bill, and Lincoln placing a twenty in the tip jar while making sure Josie saw him do it, the guys headed outside.

It was quite a nice, sunny day on the beach with a subtle breeze, but the stunning ocean view wasn't the cause of Lincoln coming to a halt. No, it had everything to do with the redhead sitting on the hood of his Jeep. He eyed her with as much annoyance as possible before sliding his focus to the bench wedged in the back of his vehicle. He knew he should have put the top on.

Crossing his arms, he glared at her. "How'd you manage that?" His head ticked in the direction of the bench. "And just how did you know this was my Jeep?"

Opal didn't make a move to get down as he'd expected. Instead, she lifted her legs from the bumper and crisscrossed them, "Honey, this Southern drawl may come out a little slow, but I ain't. I also move faster than you and saw you climb into this beast before peeling out of my parking lot. How *rude*." Her dainty brows rose on that last word.

Lincoln ignored her reprimand and Carter's snort of laughter. "How'd your tiny self get that bench loaded up?"

She sent him a bored look. "I know how to work a dolly."

In his periphery, Lincoln caught Carter trying to slink away. His hand darted out and fisted in the back of his buddy's T-shirt. "Where do you think you're going?"

Carter yanked free. "Taking the high road. You got your ornery butt into this mess. Now figure out how to get out of it." He tipped his head at the young woman. "Opal."

"See ya later, Carter," she said in that breezy voice that was already raking Lincoln's nerves.

Lincoln watched in disbelief as Carter left him high and dry. He turned back to the peculiar woman, knowing he had no other choice unless he was going to physically remove her, and that wasn't an option. Clenching his fists, he waited for her next move.

DISCUSSION
QUESTIONS

1. *Sea Glass Castle* is not only the book's title but is also the name of Weston's beach house. How does the book's name relate to the main characters, Sophia and Weston?

2. Did you like Sophia when you first met her, whether in this book or one of the previous books? If not, how did you warm up to her?

3. Sophia certainly did not get a good first impression of Weston. Did you find this to be true for you as well? How might his circumstances have affected the way he came across to people when the story started?

4. Collin plays a significant role in this story: Sophia trying to take care of him, Weston easily settling into a fatherly role for him. Both adults had only good intentions for the little boy but didn't always get it right. How so?

5. The author enjoys infusing comic relief into her stories. Does any particular scene from this book come to mind?

6. Seth is the mischievous twin. Did he add another layer to the story or detract from it?

7. Even though Weston tried to start the next chapter of his life after losing his wife and child, how did he carry them into this new chapter?

8. Ty came back into town midway through the story, throwing a wrench into Sophia and Weston's blossoming relationship. How was his appearance the final period Sophia needed to firmly close that chapter of her life?

9. The turbulent journey of sea glass and the turbulent lives of both main characters come together at the end. How do they correlate?

10. *Sea Glass Castle* is the conclusion to the Sand Queens' stories. Does the series feel complete? Was the conclusion satisfying, or is there someone else's story that needs to be told?

SAND QUEENS'
SUMMER PUNCH

2 packets (0.16 ounce each) Kool-Aid unsweetened
   tropical punch powdered soft drink
1 46-ounce can 100 percent pineapple juice
1 12-ounce can pink lemonade concentrate, thawed
1 32-ounce bottle Simply Orange orange juice
1 liter ginger ale, chilled

Combine first four ingredients. Pour mixture into quart-size freezer bags, filling halfway. Seal each bag carefully and place in freezer until completely frozen. To prepare punch, chop frozen blocks of mixture and place in punch bowl. Pour ginger ale in and stir. Serve and be prepared to make more quickly! Yes, it will disappear. Just to be on the safe side, go ahead and double this recipe.

For special occasions, you can change up the recipe by using regular lemonade instead of pink lemonade and using a different flavor/color of Kool-Aid.

Note: I'd advise against allowing a member of the Knitting Club to prepare the punch. They have been known to switch the ginger ale for sparkling wine . . .

A NOTE FROM
THE AUTHOR

Each book in this series has been dedicated to my daughter, Lydia. And each dedication has come with purpose even if it wasn't obvious at the time.

In *Beach Haven*, I encouraged Lydia—and you (yes, you)—to *dare to be different*. I hope readers take away from Opal's story the fact that it's okay to be different. In my opinion, it's better! How boring this life would be if we all matched in personality and everything else. I personally want to be an Opal. To wear what I like, not what's trending. To write a story in my style, even if it doesn't fit into the box of what folks expect for my genre.

In *Driftwood Dreams*, I urged Lydia and you to *dare to dream*. Circumstances told Josie she couldn't, but sweet, encouraging August said she could. Finally the ole gal listened! I'm a great example of this, if I do say so myself. Had I not chased the dream of writing, listening to society whispering that a stay-at-home mom with very little college education could never be a successful author, what a poor role model I'd have become for my Lu. (I'm sticking my tongue out at critics as we speak.) Surround yourself with encouragers like August. I've had three specific blondes in my corner from the very start of this writing dream. They told me I could, and they wouldn't let me turn my back on the dream even when it seemed hopeless. Thank you, blondies. You know who you are.

When it came to *Sea Glass Castle*, I challenged Lydia and you to *dare to declare your own destiny*. I hope Sophia has shown you that you have the power to do whatever it is you're led to do. Do not allow someone else to tell you who to be or how to be. I love the saying "You do you." My hope is that Sophia showed us all that it's okay to *stop* being a people pleaser and to *stop* worrying about what others think of you. Who you are is between you and God and no one else. I guarantee you will never meet the expectations of others. Don't even bother. I encourage you to live up to God's expectations and your own, and no one else's. Sometimes those other fools are just too discombobulated about what their expectations are anyway . . .

SEA GLASS CASTLE
PLAYLIST

"Everything to Everyone"
by Everclear

"Waiting on Superman"
by Daughtry

"I Could Use a Love Song"
by Maren Morris

"Wonderful"
by Everclear

"Praying"
by Kesha

"I Have This Hope"
by Tenth Avenue North

"I Met a Girl"
by Sam Hunt

"Carolina"
by Parmalee

"Broken & Beautiful"
by Kelly Clarkson

"Born to Be Yours"
by Kygo & Imagine Dragons

ACKNOWLEDGMENTS

While completing this book series, I experienced my first traditionally published book launch with the rerelease of *Lulu's Café*. Wow, what an experience! So many folks went above and beyond to help me. There are too many to name, but I have to begin here with thanking them. The amazing marketing team at Tyndale House Publishers, Andrea Garcia and my publicist, Amanda Woods. And also Kaitlyn Bouchillon and my awesome *Lulu's Café* launch team. You spent an impressive amount of time and graciously dished out your enthusiasm for my "little book that could," and I look forward to partnering with you for this book series as well.

My Lowe family—Bernie, Nate, and Lydia. The card you gave me on the day *Lulu's Café* released is now displayed in my office as a humbling reminder that you three always have my back. It says in part, "You are, by every definition of the word, a success."

Yes, folks, that's my people. My family. My team. I know I'm blessed.

To my agent, Danielle Egan-Miller. I'm one happy girl to know you are the one navigating this epic publishing adventure. Thank you for keeping me on the right course.

Jan Stob, Karen Watson, and Kathy Olson, you ladies have been a joy to partner with, and I hope we will have many more opportunities to work together. You call me friend, and I feel the same way.

Jesus said he came so that I could live an abundant life. He didn't mean material abundance, but an abundance of love and peace in him and the loved ones he's blessed me with. I am grateful for my abundant life.

ABOUT THE AUTHOR

Tonya "T. I." Lowe is a native of coastal South Carolina. She attended Coastal Carolina University and the University of Tennessee at Chattanooga, where she majored in psychology but excelled in creative writing. Go figure. Writing was always a dream, and she finally took a leap of faith in 2014 and independently published her first novel, *Lulu's Café*, which quickly became a bestseller. Now the author of ten published novels with hundreds of thousands of copies sold, she knows she's just getting started and has many more stories to tell. A wife and mother who's active in her church community, she resides near Myrtle Beach, South Carolina, with her family.

Settle in for a cup of coffee and
some Southern hospitality in

OVER 100,000 SOLD

Lulu's Café

a novel

T. I. LOWE

Available in stores and online now

TYNDALE HOUSE PUBLISHERS IS CRAZY4FICTION!

Fiction that entertains and inspires

Get to know us! Become a member of the Crazy4Fiction community. Whether you read our blog, like us on Facebook, follow us on Twitter, or receive our e-newsletter, you're sure to get the latest news on the best in Christian fiction. You might even win something along the way!

JOIN IN THE FUN TODAY.

 www.crazy4fiction.com

 Crazy4Fiction

 @Crazy4Fiction

CP0021